BUCKNER'S MOVE

A James Buckner Novel

Christopher C. Gibbs

To order additional copies of this book, contact:
Xlibris
844-714-8691
www.Xlibris.com
Orders@Xlibris.com
826736

For Dan Corretorre

St. Louis

The city sits in the angle where the nation's two greatest rivers meet. It spreads west across a vast plain. It doesn't take much wet weather to threaten flooding.

*

Martha Jane Buckner, the only girl crime reporter on the *St. Louis Post-Dispatch*, stood in a doorway in the dark alley between Carr and Biddle streets. There were several doorways to choose from. This one smelled of urine. The others smelled much worse.

She had come up to St. Louis from the Lead Belt, Highland County. When her father's stroke ended his medical practice, the family was forced to move from the big house in Livingston, the county seat, to a much smaller one in Corinth. Martha Jane quickly tired of giving piano lessons to whining children and fled. Her brother came back from the war with a bum leg and now worked as Corinth's chief of police, sharing the small house with their parents. Then her father died and it was just her mother and her brother and she seldom visited.

As far as she was concerned, she had made the best move.

She glanced at her wristwatch. She shifted her weight. Her sodden shoes squished. The fashionable black wool cloche she wore over her fiercely bobbed hair dripped icy water down the back of her neck. Her wool coat, soaked through, weighed like lead armor. She pulled a pack of cigarettes from her pocket. One left. She tipped it out. Smoke this, she decided, and if Johnny Morris hasn't shown up by the time she finished it, go home and forget about it.

April had started cold. Several days of rain had given way to this murky night. The doorway she stood in offered no protection from the heavy mist that spread up from the river a scant few blocks to the east. The mist brought its own special cocktail of odors.

The whole spring had been like this, wet and sloppy, with flooding up and down the Mississippi and Missouri Rivers. The water was still two feet below flood here, but flooding had started upstream, and the water was expected to rise here soon. The *Post-Dispatch* Weather Bird predicted thunderstorms for later in the day.

As Martha Jane fumbled with matches, she heard footsteps coming down the alley from the Carr Street end. She slid the cigarette back into the pack and pack and matches into her pocket. She leaned carefully out of the doorway. Thick clouds blocked the full moon, and the only light in the alley spilled from a few windows on the floors above. She could just make out the tall, broad form of Lt. Johnny Morris. She stepped out to meet him.

"Marty?" came the soft, urgent inquiry. Morris reached under his coat.

"Yes! Who the hell else do you think it would be at this hour of the goddamned night in this kind of weather?"

"Happy to see you, too, Marty." Morris came closer. The two met in the middle of the alley. Morris loomed over her, taller, wider even than her brother, who was one of the few men she had to look up to. His raincoat glistened, and the rain plastered his thinning hair to his dead. His broad, fleshy face opened in a smile.

"What have you got for me, Johnny?"

"Straight to business. Okay. You sure you don't wanna go get a drink first? Warm you up? I know a place over on O'Fallon stays open late."

Marty Buckner was too tall, too raw-boned to be beautiful. Or even pretty, really. Her jaw was too wide and her nose was too big. And she wore her hair chopped off short like she'd got caught up in a thresher that wouldn't let her go.

But she had these eyes. They were dark hazel and they radiated an intelligence, and a challenge, that seemed to make men, some men, want to try to meet that challenge.

Some men, damned few, had actually proven able to accomplish that.

Johnny Morris was not one of those men.

"I'm not interested in becoming another notch on your bedpost, Johnny. I've been standing here forever. I'm freezing my tuchus, my new shoes are ruined, and I want to go home, where there's a bottle of pretty good rye waiting up for me. So come across. Tell me what's more important than some cop getting the occasional free lunch or fixing a parking ticket for another crooked pol."

"Jesus Christ, you're ripe."

"And you're Little Mary Sunshine. Come on, Johnny. Give."

"Right. Your loss." Morris reached into his coat again. He took out a slip of paper. "This is a helluva lot more than fixing parking tickets, and I got the list of names right here."

As she took the slip of paper from his hand, Johnny Morris lurched forward, slamming into her, carrying them both to the ground.

Falling, Martha Jane heard the boom of the shotgun going off, deafeningly loud in the narrow alley. Without knowing what had happened, she struggled to get out from under Morris's bulk.

He was no help at all, dead weight, or soon would be.

From the end of the alley came the sound, clear and sharp, of a gun breaking open, shells splashing to the ground. In an instant, the gun clicked shut and footsteps approached.

Nearing panic now, Martha Jane pulled herself free finally from underneath the late Johnny Morris, rolled over, and jumped to her feet. And then she ran, as fast as the muddy alley, her soaked shoes, and her wet coat allowed, down to the Biddle Street end of the alley.

As she turned east into Biddle she heard the gun of off again. Pellets shattered the windows of a darkened shop opposite the alley mouth.

Martha Jane did not stop running until she hit 11th Street, where she slowed to a fast walk, turning south, then down to Cole. West on Cole to 14th Street. When she got to 14th she stopped, ducked around the corner, and looked back. There were few people on the street, and none of them appeared to be carrying a shotgun. Not openly anyway. In this neighborhood, at this hour, that did not necessarily mean anything at all.

She decided against taking any more chances. She caught her breath and turned south on 14th, circling around, until she was at the entrance of the *Post-Dispatch* building on Olive.

The night man, huddled down into his uniform coat, grinned at her as he let her in.

"You been working late again, Miz Buckner?"

"No such of a thing, Charlie. Reporters work twenty-four hours a day."

"Not good for you, Missy. And bein' out in this weather, you gone catch your death."

"No kidding." Martha Jane kept moving into the big foyer. She shouted over her shoulder, "If a guy with a double-barrel shows up looking for me, you haven't seen me."

"Yes, Ma'am." Charlie laughed. Reporters. Always joking.

In the alley between Carr and Biddle Streets, a beat cop, responding cautiously to gunfire approached the body. Lights were going on in windows above. He reached down and turned the body onto its back.

"Holy Mary," he said, stepping back and crossing himself.

Then he blew his whistle and rapped his nightstick on the alley's muddy floor.

The piece of paper Johnny Morris had given Martha Jane lay next to the body. Mud blurred the faint ink scratchings and the water carried them away.

CORINTH, MISSOURI

Not long after his sister's meeting with Johnny Morris, James Bolivar Buckner descended the stairs to the basement of the Corinth, Missouri, town hall. He pushed through the doors into the police department, where Michael Mullen, the desk officer on the day shift stood arguing with Bill Newland, the night officer.

"I'm telling you, Bill, the experts are saying it's gonna keep right on going up. The paper said there has been a, lemme see, a 'distinctive revival of bullish activity.'" Mullen quoted, jabbing his finger into his palm to emphasize his point. "At worst it'll level off for a spell, let everybody catch their breath, then it'll start up again."

"I don't care," Newland replied. "I just ain't interested. I'll be keeping my money in Mr. Linderman's bank, if that's all right with you."

"You could cash in a couple of those war bonds you bought way back."

"No!" Newland barked. "Those're earning me interest and I ain't a-gonna touch 'em."

Officer Robert Carter came around the corner, yawning hugely. Like Newland, his shift was over. He dropped his report sheet detailing an uneventful night in Corinth's streets into the tray on the desk, and nodded to Buckner.

"What're they arguing about?"

"No idea," Buckner said. An electric percolator sat on the stove in the corner. Buckner got a cup from the shelf above and filled it with coffee. He sipped carefully, made a face, and turned to the still arguing men.

"I hate to interrupt, but could one of you financial wizards make us a fresh pot of coffee? This batch is thicker than mud and twice as tasty."

Mullen and Newland fell silent, staring at him for an instant, then

Mullen said, "Right. My job." He took Buckner's mug and the pot from the stove and headed upstairs.

"See you tonight," Newland said, glad to escape the boss's wrath.

He scooped up the magazine he had been reading.

"*Black Mask?*" Buckner read. The cover showed a grim man in an enormous cowboy hat clutching cards in one hand and a Colt .45 revolver in the other.

"Yep," Newland said. "'Six-Gun Showdown.' The Wild West the way it really was, right, Buck?"

"Couldn't say, Bill. All that was long before my time out there."

"Yeah, I guess things must've settled down by the time you were in the cavalry."

"I guess," Buckner said.

His father's stroke, and the family's sudden lack of revenue, gave him the excuse he needed to escape the suffocating boredom of college life at the state university. He fled and joined the army and served seven years on a series of Western posts, chasing gun-runners, Villistas, and renegade Apaches. It hadn't seemed particularly settled to him at the time. Patrolling the nation's porous southern border was hot, dusty, and occasionally very dangerous work.

Later, like thousands of Americans, he had gone to France with the Canadians in 1915, returning in 1917 with a wound that almost cost him a leg and left him with a permanent limp and occasional searing pain. The back of his leg was little more than a mass of raw scar tissue. He was able to see it if he used a hand mirror and twisted himself in a knot. He almost never did that.

Half the men in his unit had been immigrants born in England and the majority of the rest were first-generation Canadians, and they insisted on tea when they could get it. He had been served tea in the hospital in France where the doctors had stitched his leg back together, and in the hospital in Toronto where they taught him to walk again. His friend Judith Lee had preferred tea as well but, but he had never developed a taste for it. Judith Lee had moved on. He drank only coffee now.

Newland went through the doors and up the stairs.

Carter said good-bye as well and followed him out, passing Mulling returning with the percolator.

"I'll bring a fresh cup when it's ready," he said.

"Thanks." Buckner started down the hall, stopped, and turned back. "You're not buying stocks on margin, are you, Michael?"

"The Dow's up twenty percent since the first of the year, Buck." Mullen grinned. "Anyway, only a few. And it's practically a sure thing."

"All right."

"I figure I'll wait till next year, cash out, get a place of my own."

"Tired of living with your dad?"

"Sure. Who wouldn't be? Living at home at my age ... uh ...." Mullen trailed off into embarrassed silence. Buckner lived at home with his widowed mother. Deprived of a steady income, the family had been forced to move into the small house in Corinth. With his father long dead now and his sister off in St. Louis, he and his mother had the place to themselves. His mother devoted most of her time to good works, and his own schedule kept him out most of every day, so their paths crossed only at meals not.

"Well, Michael, I hope it works out for you." Buckner continued down the hall. Sometime later, Mullen brought a fresh cup of coffee, put it on Buckner's desk, and departed without a word. It was the first of several cups Buckner would drink through the day. And he needed it badly because today, to put a stop to Mullen's nagging, Buckner would devote his time and energies to the growing backlog of paperwork.

He acknowledged his failing. His predecessor, Baxter Bushyhead, part Cherokee and crooked to the bone, had run the department out of his hip pocket, and the only thing he kept records of was the payoffs the department collected from local businesses. Those records had been his downfall when Buckner got hold of them and brought them into the sunlight. Since taking over from the late Chief Bushyhead, Buckner had stopped the payoffs immediately. Just as quickly, he fired or forced out Bushyhead's thugs and began hiring new men. He hated paperwork, but he knew from his years in the army that it worked. In Michael Mullen he had found the man to oversee that paperwork. He had originally hired Mullen as a patrol officer, but when he discovered Mullen's gifts extended to shorthand and machine-gun-fast typing, combined with a deep need to bring order out of chaos, he made Mullen permanent booking officer and chief department clerk. And despite Mullen's dreams of becoming a tough cop like the ones in *Black Mask*, Buckner intended to keep him in those posts.

But there was only so much Mullen could do by himself, so one of his jobs, perhaps his most important job, was to make sure the chief of police stayed current with his paperwork.

"Buck, you are the only one that can sign off on all these things," Mullen regularly reminded him. "Without your signature, the town won't fund the department, and that means we can't get the equipment we need."

"And you won't get paid."

"And I won't get paid. Exactly."

And so Buckner filled his day reading reports, signing forms, writing letters, approving pay vouchers, stuffing envelopes. And, on the whole, he was not entirely unhappy with the work. He had been a police officer for ten years now, first as a deputy sheriff, then as chief of the town's tiny police department, and he appreciated the long spells when nobody was committing a crime. At least not out in public where it would demand his attention.

But he quit at five. He dumped a pile of completed work on Mullen's desk and without a word headed for home. Dinner was cold ham and reheated greens left over from the night before.

"Don't look at me like that," said Regina Long Buckner when her son raised an eyebrow. "I was at church all day and was simply too tired to cook tonight."

"Our church?" Buckner had eaten little and his mother's leftovers were reliably excellent.

"Of course our church." Mrs. Buckner spoke, as usual, assertively, not out of anger, though it might often sound like that to those who didn't know her well, but out of her absolute confidence in the correctness of her position. "Not that you ever darken the door"

"It's just that you help out at several around town."

"It was the Presbyterian Women's Mission Board."

"What remote corner of the world is getting help from the Board?" He finished off the last of the ham and began clearing the table.

"China. There's terrible fighting, people are starving."

"Isn't that pretty much an everyday matter over there?" Buckner put the dishes in the sink.

"I believe so. Which is why our work is so important."

"Can I leave the washing up for later?" Buckner asked. "Mullen had me on clerical duty all day."

"I suppose. Since I didn't cook dinner."

"Thanks. I'll get them later tonight." Buckner went to his room. He had furnished it to suit himself after returning from Canada. The floor and walls were bare. The only furniture were a chifferobe, a bed, and a side table with a lamp. A handful of books filled the small shelf under the lamp. One window looked out across the front porch onto the street, a second to the house next door. He kept the room dusted and swept and spotless.

He changed his shirt, put on a tie, and returned to the kitchen. "Don't wait up for me."

"I haven't waited up for you in twenty years," his mother scoffed. "I assume you are going over to drink at Elroy Dutton's place."

"Of course."

"There's a crime wave sweeping the country. President Hoover said so in a speech the other day. He said widespread violation of Prohibition has made people disrespect the law."

"I expect he's right about that. But it's a stupid law, so no wonder people don't respect it. Besides, when did you ever pay any attention to anything a Republican politician had to say?"

He grabbed his hat and coat from the front hall rack and was out the door before she could reply.

Elroy Dutton ran a saloon and gambling establishment, in open defiance of state and federal laws, just across the Iron Mountain Railroad tracks. This was where the black citizens of Corinth lived. And that's where Buckner did his drinking. He liked the whiskey Dutton bought from Neb Healey, southern Missouri's best manufacturer of moonshine. And he sincerely believed that the Great Experiment was doomed to failure. He made a point of violating it personally as often and as openly as seemed practical. And if President Hoover wanted to do something about it, he could come on down to Corinth and do it.

Elroy Dutton's place had no name, no sign over the door, had never needed one. A barber shop occupied the ground floor of the building Dutton owned. An elderly black man worked there. His name was Fleming Gaylord, and he could give you a haircut if that was what you wanted. But mostly he kept an eye on the door and a Remington pump-action 12-gauge close at hand if you looked like you wanted trouble instead.

Gaylord sat reading a book in the barber's chair. He merely glanced at Buckner, winked, and nodded him up the stairs. As far as he was concerned, having the chief of police in the place was a lot better than having a 12-gauge behind the door.

At the top of the stairs, a heavy door swung open on well-oiled hinges to reveal an enormous black man in a too-tight dinner jacket. He greeted Buckner with a worried frown.

"Evenin', Chief."

"Hello, Buster. The boss in?"

"Ah, well, no, sir, he ain't. Not this evenin'."

"No matter. I believe I see Dr. Peck over there," Buckner said, scanning the room quickly. "I suppose I'll just join him."

"Yes, sir." Buster closed the door.

A young man in a short white waiter's jacket and trim black trousers appeared and escorted Buckner to the table. From there, Elroy Dutton could usually be seen surveying his domain, invariably accompanied by an attractive young woman. Tonight, the only person seated there was Thomas Jefferson Peck, MD.

Peck wore his customary black worsted suit. His dead white hair, long over his frayed shirt collar, fell in a limp curl over his broad forehead. His pale skin looked gritty. His hands, with long, delicate fingers, did not tremble at all. As Buckner sat, Peck peered at him like a man trying to see through a fog. The fog was real and self-induced. Peck had escaped a society medical practice in St. Louis, in partnership with his father, in order to serve with the Second Division in France.

Nine months in an aid tent just behind the line of trenches on the Western Front, doing rough surgery on the shattered bodies of young Marines, had left Peck with a powerful thirst. Satisfying that thirst in a town where everybody knew him, and reported every indiscretion to his revered father—known as "Doctor Senior," as he was "Doctor Junior"—drove him to flight again. He got off the train at Corinth to go in search of alcohol. He found some, and by the time he got back, the train, actually several trains, had left without him. So he stayed. At least that was the explanation he usually gave when asked.

Now he treated a handful of patients and occasionally looked at dead bodies for the police department.

"Haven't seen you here in a while," Buckner said as he sat. "You doing your drinking at the Dew Drop Inn?"

"They don't call it that anymore," Peck said. His whiskey thickened voice was a wood rasp on oak.

"Right. It's The Corinthian. Is that why you're here instead? Because they changed the name and fancied the place up?"

"I come here for the music."

Buckner turned to the small bandstand against a side wall. A pair of doors flanked the bandstand, which held an upright piano and a drum kit and some chairs, but no musicians.

"They're on break," Peck explained. "But they promised when they come back they're gonna play Beethoven's Second Piano Quartet."

As he spoke four men came through one of the flanking doors, sat down, and began playing something jazzy, the stride piano taking the lead.

"Oh, well," Peck said. "I guess they decided to go with Willie "the Lion" Smith rather than Beethoven."

"He was a Buffalo Soldier, you know." Buckner said.

"Beethoven?"

"Willie "the Lion" Smith. Artillery gunner."

"Oh. Right."

The waiter arrived, put drinks on the table, and disappeared. Buckner watched the room. People sat quietly at tables, sipping drinks. A few couples moved around the dance floor. The music bounced along, led now by the clarinet. Everybody, black and white, seemed to be having a good time.

"Where's Dutton?" Buckner asked.

"Dunno. Hasn't been around at all."

"Is that why Buster looks so worried?"

"Do you ever take time off from being a policeman?"

"Sure. That's what I come here for. What I am doing right now, this very minute, as a matter of face."

"Well, then, let it go. He's obviously out entertaining one of his lady friends. Let's just sit and enjoy the music."

So Buckner let it go. But he had been a cop for a long time, and he was, he realized, just naturally suspicious. Watchful, he preferred to call it. It had been an essential skill, whether chasing Apaches in Arizona or watching for Boche trench raiders in France. And for a policeman it was practically a professional requirement, what they paid him for. So he didn't really care where Dutton was. And he didn't really care if Buster was worried about something. So he let it go.

He took out a cigar case, opened it, gave a cigar to Peck and took one himself. He lighted both. The two of them drank and smoked in silence, enjoying the bite of tobacco and whiskey. The cigars lasted almost an hour. As the band got up to take another break, Buckner stubbed his cigar out and got unsteadily to his feet. He and Peck together had consumed most of a bottle of Neb Healey's best.

"Watch yourself there, Chief," Peck said.

"I'm leaving," Buckner said. "Mullen's had me doing paperwork all day and promised me more of the same tomorrow."

"Then you're gonna need your sleep. That boy is one fierce taskmaster."

"Worse'n some sergeants I've had." Buckner sketched a salute. "G'night."

He made his way across the floor to where Buster stood. Only Buster did not open the door, just stood there looking worried.

"All right, Buster," Buckner said. "What is it? You've been moping around all night."

"I ain't posed to say," Buster whispered.

"Then maybe you ought to tell me, Buster."

"It's Mist' Elroy."

"Who isn't here tonight."

"Tha's what I'm sayin'."

Buster gestured and one of the waiters rushed over. Buster pointed at the door and started across the dance floor. Buckner followed as Buster led him through the other of the two doors that flanked the bandstand. It opened onto a short hall with two more doors. Buckner could hear soft voices and the clicking of a roulette wheel through one door. Buster opened the other and went through, Buckner right behind. He'd never been in Elroy Dutton's office before, but what he saw did not surprise him. It was unadorned and utilitarian. There was a desk and some chairs and a bookcase mostly empty except for a few boxes and files. There was a telephone on the desk, and a lamp, and nothing else. Buster was taking a piece of paper from one of the drawers. He glanced at it and gave it to Buckner. It was a Western Union half-sheet with a brief message: IN BIG TROUBLE COME NOW DON'T TELL BUCK STOP MARTY.

Buckner suddenly felt very sober.

"When did this come?"

"First thing this morning."

"When did he leave?"

"Right when he read that."

"Would he have someplace to stay in St. Louis?"

"Well, he gots that cousin lives up there, owns a furniture store."

"Address?"

"Somewhere around Washington." Buster shrugged. "Never been up there myself."

"Look in the desk."

Buckner insistence overrode Buster's reluctance. He opened his boss's desk drawer and took out a packet of letters held together by a rubber band.

"One of these." He handed the packet to Buckner.

Buckner thumbed through the letters, realizing as he did that Buster was probably close to illiterate.

"Gordon?" Buckner asked, holding up an envelope with a return address on it.

"That's the one. Joe Gordon."

"Thanks."

Buckner stuffed the envelope and the telegram in his pocket, returned the rest of the packet to Buster, and headed for the door. The waiter barely had time to get it open before Buckner was through it and down the stairs. His mother was still sitting at the kitchen table when he came in, a tiny glass half-full of sherry in front of her. Her participation in the nation-wide crime wave would last the rest of the hour it would take her to finish drinking it.

Buckner tossed the telegram on the table and said, "Do you know anything about this?" as he kept going to his room.

He stuffed a change of clothes into a bag. His mother called out "No."

He shut the bag and got out his old trench coat. As an enlisted man in the Canadian army, he hadn't been authorized to wear one—British officers only—but the colonel of artillery who played poker with him in the hospital in London had lost both legs at Mons. "Oh, well. I really could use something rather shorter anyway," he said when Buckner's club straight beat his three nines.

Buckner returned to the kitchen and shrugged into the coat.

"I have to stop by the department for some things. If I hurry, I can catch the late eastbound.

"All right. I'd appreciate it if you'd keep me informed."

"When and as I can." The front door slammed shut behind him.

Bill Newland didn't raise an eyebrow when Buckner came rushing in. The chief kept no regular hours, and was liable to appear right in the middle of a well-deserved nap. So Newland simply nodded and continued reading his magazine. On the cover of this issue was an angry, and evidently powerful, young woman in a daring low-cut red dress. She fired a Colt .45

automatic with one hand and cradled a Thompson submachine gun plus several pistols in the other arm.

Buckner went down the hall to his office, where he rummaged through his desk until he found his Chief of Police badge. He put that in a pocket. After a quick thought, he added his old Deputy Sheriff badge. He put his own heavy Colt 1911 and spare magazines into his bag. He unlocked his filing cabinet and pulled open a drawer marked "Evidence." From it he took a .38 revolver with an evidence tag still tied to the trigger guard, and an envelope fat with cash. He put both into the bag along with a handful of .38 rounds. As he went back down the hall, he heard the whistle of the approaching train.

"Going to St. Louis," he said as he pushed through the double doors. "Shotwell's in charge."

*

A few blocks away, a well-dressed, pleasant looking young man stood weaving slightly, looking about uncertainly. He did not know which way to go, and there was nobody around to ask. The widely separated streetlights showed him nothing helpful.

He looked both ways along the street. To his right an alley extended through to another street. He decided this might be a shortcut, and turned down the alley.

He went slowly, making his way carefully in the darkness. The whole place was dark. He decided folks in this town … what was the name of this town? … he had forgotten … went to bed damned early.

Half way down the alley he noticed it had started to rain again. Not hard, just a light dripping of water from an empty black sky. He turned up his collar against the rain and the chill that came with it.

A rest. That was what he needed. A rest. And a nip to warm him up. Then the final run to the train station.

He found just the spot, between some pallets and a loading dock, both sheltered from the drip.

The young man eased himself to the ground, his back against the wall. He found the bottle in his pocket with no effort at all and pulled the cork.

Lord but that stuff smelled bad. He drank it anyway. He emptied the bottle and carefully placed it on the ground by his side.

He felt sleepy. A quick glance at his wrist watch assured him he had a little while before the train was due in. Plenty of time. He closed his eyes and sighed contentedly.

He did not hear the whistle as the eastbound pulled to a stop barely a hundred yards from where he slept.

*

Corinth was a regular stop on the Iron Mountain Line. There was some talk of the Missouri Pacific System, which owned the Iron Mountain, reducing the town to the status of a whistle stop. But that decision had not yet been made, and the engine sat chuffing as Buckner hurried across the platform and swung onto one of the passenger cars. The train pulled out, jolting him into his seat. The conductor who came through recognized him.

"Where you headed at this hour, Chief?"

"St. Louis." Buckner handed him money from the envelope.

"Place'll be closed down time we get in."

"I'm not going shopping."

"Never figured you were, Chief." He handed Buckner his punched ticket and moved on.

Buckner entered the ticket price in his notebook. He sank down into the trench coat's warmth, tipped his hat over his eyes, and fell asleep immediately. The whiskey he had consumed earlier took over and he didn't wake up until the train pulled into Union Station. When it did, he had a splitting headache. His pocket watch told him it was just after seven.

There was a Harvey House in the station, and it was open for breakfast. English immigrant Fred Harvey had built a string of restaurants across the Southwest, staffing them with pretty young women, whom he then dressed like nuns in severe white and black specifically designed to negate their femininity. It was not entirely successful, however, because he regularly lost employees to customers who apparently could see beyond, or beneath those heavily starched dresses, black opaque stockings, and blunt black shoes and proposed marriage.

Perhaps it was the regulation white ribbon the young women were required to use to tie back their netted hair.

At this hour, the place was packed. Passengers like Buckner, who had gotten off in-bound trains, passengers waiting to board out-bound trains. Buckner found a seat among a crowd of men and women in business wear quite as uniform as the Harvey Girl outfits, people who ate hurriedly, glancing at wrist watches, gulping their food and then rushing off.

Eventually a waitress, smiling cheerfully, one thin dark curl of hair escaping the hairnet, took Buckner's order of coffee and a biscuit. Her failure to persuade him to get the full Businessman's Breakfast did not dent her radiant smile. She even brought him a copy of the *Globe-Democrat*, which he read until the editorials made him laugh out loud. Refills of coffee kept him there until eight o'clock, when he paid up and left.

Buckner stepped through the front doors of the station. As always, the noise and pulse of the city struck him like a physical blow. The wind drove thin rain against his face. Traffic rattled and thundered along Market Street. Grim-faced pedestrians, ducked under umbrellas or huddled down into rain coats, hurried to work, weaving and jostling along the sidewalks. Fifteen minutes dodging through it all took Buckner to the *Post-Dispatch* building. In the foyer, stairs to the right and left led up. He climbed the left set.

On the second floor, double glass doors opened onto a large room full of people sitting bent over typewriters, pounding on them energetically. A thick fog of tobacco smoke hung over their heads. Young men with stacks of paper draped over their arms darted between the rows of desks. The sign on the glass door said "City Room." Buckner went in. At the far end of the room, he saw a glassed-in office. Standing in the doorway, leaning against the door jamb, stood a short, red-faced man smoking a pipe and surveying the room with a scowl. The typewriters and the teletype machines clattered deafeningly, but there was little speech beyond the occasionally shouted "Boy!"

Buckner headed for the pipe-smoking man, who watched him come, puffing on his pipe, curiosity on his face.

"I'm James Bolivar Buckner, and I'm looking for my sister."

"Pleased to meet you. I'm Quinn Flaherty, city editor, and I wouldn't mind laying eyes on her myself."

"What does that mean?"

"It means Marty came barreling in here at some ungodly hour of the morning yesterday, left me a note about being on a story, and took off again. I haven't seen or heard from her since."

"What story?"

"Well, she's always got several going at once, sometimes connected, sometimes not." Flaherty thought a moment, casting his eye over the room. He spotted his prey and shouted, "Wieczek! Get over here."

A young woman with flame-red hair popped up from behind a typewriter and hurried over. She had one pencil behind an ear and another clutched between her teeth. Her hair was cut short and she wore a loose cardigan over a pleated skirt that just brushed her trim, silk-stockinged knees.

Men stopped pounding their typewriters to watch her stride down the aisle of desks.

She took the pencil from her mouth. "Yeah, chief?" she looked Buckner up and down with skeptical eyes.

"What's Marty working on, her main thing right now?"

"Cops," the young woman said.

"What, police corruption, that kind of thing?"

"Nah. Bigger. Way bigger. Something to do with the gang wars. That's all she'd tell me, anyway."

"Like what?"

"Like that's all she'd tell me. You know how she gets when she's on the trail of something big."

"I do indeed."

"Do you know where she is?" Buckner asked.

"What's it to you?" she returned sharply.

"This is her brother," Flaherty explained. "He's looking for her."

"Oh, yeah. The brother." Wieczek scanned Buckner from top to toe once again. Much more slowly this time. She barely came up to his chin. Her smile beamed up at him, full of friendliness, eyes sparkling. "She mentioned you. She said you used to be spoken for, all wrapped up by some little schoolteacher down there in the back woods. But not anymore. She said you were available now. That true? You available now?"

"Uh, listen, Miss Wieczek--"

"Rebecca."

"All right, Rebecca. Pleased to meet you."

"Friends call me Becca." She held out a hand.

"And don't call her Becky. Not if you want to go on living," Flaherty said.

"Fine." Buckner shook the offered hand, which held his warmly. "Do you know where I can find her, Becca?"

"You tried her place?"

"I'm guessing she's not there. I think she's gotten herself into something serious, and she's smart enough not to go home to hide out."

"Well, I can't help you, then," she said, finally, and with obvious reluctance, releasing Buckner's hand.

"How about you?" Buckner turned to Flaherty.

"Nope. Marty's as independent as a hog on ice. I've come down hard on her before this, but she keeps producing great copy, so I usually let her run."

"Trying to rein her in wouldn't do any good anyway," Buckner said.

"You're right about that," Flaherty agreed. "It's interesting, though."

"What's interesting?"

"There was fella up here yesterday looking for her, too. Colored fella. Mighty slick looking."

"Oh, he's more than just slick looking," Buckner said.

"Well, I told him what I've just told you, that I don't know where she's gone off to."

"Did he say where he was headed next?"

"Not to me."

"All right. Thanks." Buckner turned for the door.

"Come back this afternoon when we've put the paper to bed and I'll help you look for her," Rebecca Wieczek called after him.

Buckner stopped and turned. He opened his mouth to say something, changed his mind, and waved briefly before continuing through the door and down the stairs. She was very pretty, he acknowledged. Also very young.

Besides, he just didn't have the time right now.

He took out the envelope Buster had given him and showed it to the doorman.

"Do you know where this is?"

"Yes, I do," the doorman said. "Who wants to know?"

"I'm James Buckner. I'm Martha Jane's brother. I'm looking for her. She's in some kind of trouble."

"I 'spect she is. Night man told me she come running in here around two in the morning yesterday, talking about somebody with a shotgun looking for her. Then she took off again. He said he thought she was kidding him."

"I don't think so," Buckner said. "What about this address?"

"You know the city?"

"Not really," Buckner admitted.

"Well, that's up in what they call 'the Ville.' Mostly colored folks living up that way. You sure you want to go up there?"

"I'm hoping to find a friend of mine up there who might know where my sister is. He's looking for her, too."

"This'd be that colored gentleman come looking for her? Snappy dresser?"

"Yes, it would."

"All right. It's quite a walk up there, more'n an hour. I catch the streetcar out here on the corner, takes me right up there in no time." The doorman pointed.

"Thanks." Buckner looked at his watch. He guessed the store Dutton's cousin owned would not be open yet. But it would be in an hour. "I think I'll walk."

The doorman shrugged and gave him directions. On the street, he turned north, continuing to Easton, where he turned left. As he walked along Easton, he did, in fact, begin to see more black faces, but other than a few puzzled looks, most people ignored him. The light rain drizzled fitfully, and the chilly breeze made him pull up the collar of his trench coat against it. This did no good at all.

The walk didn't take him an hour, and he found the address at once. An OPEN sign hung in the window. A salesman was showing a young couple bedroom furniture. Several other customers wandered the aisles of tables and chairs, bureaus and cabinets. A tall man in a brown suit and vest spotted him immediately, came from behind the counter at the end of the showroom, and headed quickly toward him. Buckner waited until he arrived.

"May I help you, Officer?" the man asked with a carefully balanced tone of polite deference and suspicion.

Buckner smiled.

Buckner thought he had a pleasant, friendly smile, a smile that put people at their ease. This was not the case. His smile resembled a teeth-baring grimace. But nobody was willing to tell him that.

The tall man froze in place, deference giving way to suspicion tinged with fear.

"I'm James Buckner. I'd like to speak with Mr. Gordon if I may."

"You want to buy furniture?"

"No. I just need to talk to Mr. Gordon for a minute. Are you Mr. Gordon?"

"No."

"I'm sure he's busy, but it won't take a minute. Barely that."

Leaving a final suspicious glare in his wake, the tall man turned, hurried back down the aisle, and disappeared into an office behind the counter. All the other customers, plus the salesman, had stopped whatever they were doing and waited quietly, casting careful glances. Buckner was sure he heard someone whisper "Police."

He wondered how they knew. Was he wearing a sign? He had long ago stopped wearing his old cavalry campaign hat. Now he wore a gray fedora to go with his conservative charcoal gray wool suit and dark green tie. Michael Mullen's father, who had sold him all this, assured him it was what your average young businessman was wearing currently.

"You'll fit right in," Mr. Mullen had said.

"That's what I'm hoping for," Buckner replied.

But somehow people always knew.

The tall man returned with another man, not as tall, graying at the temples, working to adjust his salesman's smile.

"May I help you, sir?" He asked. The tall man remained a watchful two steps back.

"I hope so. I'm James Buckner. I'm from--"

"From Corinth. Yes." Gordon reached out and shook Buckner's offered hand. "Elroy's, ah, friend." He was smiling for real now.

"Yes, sir. I understand he's in town. I need to talk to him. Can you tell me where I might find him?"

"Yes, as a matter of fact, I can. He's in jail."

"Jail? Well, I guess I'm not surprised. There've been a couple of times I've wanted to put him in jail myself. Where is he being held? And what for?"

"Eleventh District station. And I don't know what for, exactly. He got here yesterday, asked to stay with us here, and then took off again right away. I guess I was his one phone call." Gordon hesitated. "Do you know why he's up here? He just said something about a friend in trouble."

"Yes. My sister, Martha Jane. She's the one in trouble."

"Oh. The reporter for the *Post-Dispatch*. His—uh—yes." Gordon stopped, puzzled.

"Yes. Exactly," Buckner said. "Where's the Eleventh District? They're probably holding him there."

"Right up close to Forest Park. On Newstead north of Laclede."

Gordon gave direction. "I don't know what he was doing out there, that neighborhood. He should have known better."

"Yes, he should have, but him knowing better and him doing better are two different things."

"Yes. That's always been his way."

"All right. Thanks." Buckner turned for the door.

"What are you going to do?" Gordon called after him.

"Get him out of jail. I'm going to need his help."

"They've set his bail at two thousand dollars."

"I don't plan on going his bail."

CORINTH & ST. LOUIS

Michael Mullen found the body during his lunch break.

"Shotwell," he said as he returned the telephone receiver to its cradle. "That was my daddy. He needs me over to the store. He's just got a big shipment, mostly bolts of cloth, and he wants me to help store and stock them. Can you watch the place while I'm gone?"

Buckner had left him in charge before when he had been away for any length of time, but Shotwell refused to sit in his office. When he was in the department, like now, he usually sat in a chair at the end of Mullen's desk.

"Sure. I thought you had gotten out of the dry goods business for good."

"I thought so, too. But somehow he finds something he needs help with at least once a week, and Ursel Hinkle's gone off to St. Louis to look for work, so he calls here because he knows I bring my lunch from home and eat it by the telephone. So he just calls."

"Well, he's getting on, isn't he?"

"He's not even fifty. He's not that old."

"Maybe he just wants company, then. Anyway, it's nice of you to pitch in."

"I suppose so, but, well, dammit, this is why I got into police work in the first place. I grew up at the store, weekends, afternoons after school, doing anything and everything that needed doing. I still live upstairs, in my old room. I wanted to get out and I thought police work would be more, I don't know, exciting."

"Adventurous?" Shotwell was smiling.

"Yes! And sitting at this desk may not be all that adventurous, but it's a lot better than waiting for some little old lady to make up her mind about which spool of thread to buy."

Mullen rose, pushed through the doors and stomped up the stairs.

He had been too young for the war, in his last year of school when it ended. But he was just the right age a couple of years later, when James Bolivar Buckner took over as chief of police and began rebuilding the department from the ground up. And he was proud of being the first new officer Buckner hired. But he still helped his father when called upon. His mother had died several years ago, and he was pretty sure Shotwell was right; his dad just wanted some company, especially as it had become clear that Mullen wasn't going to return to a career in dry goods. But, damn it, he lived just down the hall, and they often had breakfast and supper together. Wasn't that enough?

"Hey, Daddy!" Mullen called as he entered the store.

"I'm back here!"

The work turned out to be easy, and his father was glad of the help. He chattered away as the two of them moved from loading dock to storeroom and back. They finished quickly, and Mullen was just sweeping the loading dock when he saw the feet, in polished black shoes, sticking out from behind a stack of abandoned pallets.

He hopped down to look. He didn't have to look very closely to see the young man lying there on his back was dead. His eyes stared blankly at nothing, and flies were settling on them, and strolling in and out of his open mouth.

Mullen looked down at his own feet and backed carefully away. His boss, the old cavalry scout and Indian tracker, raised hell when bone-headed investigators contaminated crime scenes.

He jumped back onto the loading dock and hurried into the store. An elderly couple bickered softly over kitchen ware. Mullen's father waited expectantly by the cash register.

"There's a dead body out back of the store," Mullen whispered harshly into his father's ear. "Don't touch it, don't move it, don't go look at it, don't tell anybody about it. I'll be right back." He rushed through the door, across the square and up the town hall's steps.

Shotwell was relaxing with the newspaper at Mullen's desk.

"Dead body," Mullen said as Shotwell glanced up at him.

"Where?" Shotwell put the newspaper down and got to his feet.

"Behind the store."

"All right. You go get Peck and meet me there," Shotwell said. He saw Mullen's hesitation. "Start at his office."

"Then the Dew Drop Inn, I know. I mean the Corinthian." Mullen turned and ran back up the stairs.

Shotwell scooped up a notebook and got the camera from the storage cupboard. He put these into a paper sack, along with several smaller bags and a pair of gloves. Then he picked up the telephone.

"Mae, it's James Shotwell over at the police department." He tried to sound calm. "Could you ring up Bill Newland and tell him to come on over here and keep an eye on the place for a while? Tell him it's important and he should hurry." He ignored the operator's question, hung up the receiver, and hurried up the stairs and out.

He crossed the square, moving briskly but not running, working at not attracting attention. He succeeded. People paid no attention to him at all, except to nod the occasional greeting. Perhaps, at one time not long ago, pedestrians in Corinth might have been startled at the sight of a black man in a police uniform. But, regardless of how they might feel about it, Shotwell realized, it certainly did not surprise them.

He rounded a corner and came up behind Mullen's Dry Goods Everything on the Square. The alley ran between the backs of shops and a sagging board fence. Shotwell was alone. The body was not visible until he was almost upon it. When he could see it fully, he stopped and looked at the ground leading up to it. The weather had been wet lately, and two sets of footprints were clear in the wet dirt. One set certainly was Michael Mullen's. A quick check of the corpse's shoes confirmed the source of the others. There were no more. Shotwell knew those prints would provide volumes of information to Buckner, but to him they meant little.

He had to move the pallets to get close to the body. Once he had done that, he knelt down and put his fingertips to the cool, gray, putty-like flesh over the carotid artery. The muscles under the jaw were stiff and, as he expected, he found no pulse

He opened his notebook and sketched the loading dock, the stack of pallets, and the body wedged between them, noting the two sets of footprints and his own. At some point Mr. Mullen, a long gray apron over his white shirt and tie, came out and watched him work, saying nothing at all. After a few minutes, he went back inside the store.

Shotwell got out the camera, pulled it open, and began taking pictures. Full-length at first, then closer, different angles, until he had shot up the entire roll of film. He closed the camera and put the notebook in his pocket and waited for Mullen and Dr. Peck.

*

In St. Louis, the rain had picked up, so Buckner took a streetcar from the corner back into the center of the city. The federal appeals court was on Tenth. Buckner took an elevator to the top floor. The office he wanted was at the end of the hall. A sharply dressed young fellow with an even sharper center part, dark hair slicked down on each side, raised his eyebrows as Buckner stepped in.

"Yes?"

"I'd like to see Judge Long."

"Do you have an appointment?"

"Nope. Just take a minute. Promise."

"His Honor is very busy." The young man opened a notebook. "If you'd like to leave your name, I'll see if we can make an appointment for you." Without bothering to look at the notebook, the young man added, "I'm afraid His Honor won't be available until sometime late next week."

"Get on your squawker and tell him his favorite nephew needs his help. Right now."

The young man hesitated.

"The name is James Buckner." He stepped toward the young man's desk and smiled.

The young man immediately pushed the button on the gray metal box that sat beside his typewriter.

The machine crackled and screeched.

"Go right in," the young man said, looking relieved. He indicated a door. Buckner thanked him, opened the door and went through the doorway.

He was in an office paneled in dark wood, with a deep, dark green carpet and heavy dark red drapes that shut out light and sound. A tall man with a lion's mane of white hair brushed back and a broad face dominated by a prominent Roman nose stood and came around a large desk to greet him.

"Hello, Buck. I haven't seen you since Elizabeth's wedding. That's kind of the way of it, isn't it? Weddings and funerals."

"Yes, sir, I'm afraid it is."

"And how is my little sister?"

"Just fine, Uncle Will. Just fine."

"And since I don't have either a wedding or a funeral on my schedule, what can I help you with?"

"It's about my little sister. She's in some kind of trouble and she's gone to ground, and I need to find her."

"I suppose that comes as no surprise to me." The judge frowned. His white, beetling eyebrows almost hid his eyes. "Her working as a crime reporter and all that. It had to come to this eventually. I've read her pieces in the paper when they're pointed out to me. Evidently she doesn't have her own byline as yet. And they are very good, but obviously her work puts her in close proximity to dangerous, even murderous people."

"And she loves it."

"I don't suppose she'd just settle down, get married, have babies."

"Well, maybe someday, but not any time soon."

"All right. What can I do for you to help her?"

"I need to get a man out of jail. He's a friend of ours and he came up here to help Martha Jane, and he got himself arrested out in the Central West End. I think he might've been trying to get in touch with Fred and Doreen, maybe hoping she was staying with them, or they might know where she was."

"I always thought Fred and Doreen were her least favorite cousins."

"Oh, they are, no question about that."

"So how did visiting Fred and Doreen get your friend arrested?"

"His liable to get kind of aggressive when he wants something. And he's a Negro."

"Good grief. Is that that saloon-keeper friend of hers your mother writes me about?"

"Yes, I'm afraid so."

"Good grief," the judge repeated. "Well, Buck, I don't know what I can do, or, in fact, what I should do. I mean, getting this man out of jail … from what your mother tells me that might just be the best place for him. Since apparently the police department down in Corinth shows no inclination to interfere with his illegal activities."

"Uncle Will, you're right. I should have arrested him years ago. But right now I need him out of jail. His name is Elroy Dutton, and if Martha Jane is in trouble serious enough to ask him to come up here to help her, then whatever it is has to be pretty serious." Buckner shrugged helplessly.

"I don't like it any better than you do, believe me, but I need that man's help, and he can't help me from jail."

"All right," the judge grumbled. "You realize this is pretty high-handed on my part, intervening in a local matter like this."

"Yes, I do. But I'd be willing to bet you Dutton was arrested mostly because he's black and obnoxious and his only real crime was being both those things in a wealthy white neighborhood."

"This is a pretty risky move. If the people who arrested want to challenge this, your whole plan to get him out of jail could land you in it with him."

"I know that, too."

The judge pushed a button on a small gray box, and spoke into it.

"Could you come in here for a minute, please, Mrs. Cohen?"

A door on the opposite side of the room opened and a tiny women in black came in, a notebook and pencil in her hand.

"Yes, Your Honor?"

"Mrs. Cohen, I'd like you to take a letter, and then type it up, one copy, no carbons, and then immediately forget what you have just written."

"Certainly, Your Honor." And she sat in a chair in front of the judge's desk and waited, pencil poised.

Half an hour later, Buckner was headed back to the street with a document, signed and sealed, folded into his coat pocket.

A street car took him to the Eleventh District headquarters. The mostly red brick building with sharply peaked gables occupied the entire corner. Buckner took the seven steps to the arched entry and entered the double doors. He turned right. Behind an elevated desk, a uniformed sergeant pecked hesitantly at a typewriter. The sergeant ignored Buckner, as the typewriting obviously required his full concentration. Buckner waited. He could hear other typewriters clacking and people talking, and occasionally a police officer would walk by, but no one spoke to him. Finally, the desk sergeant sat back and sighed. He rolled the completed form from his typewriter, separated the copies and the carbon paper, and slipped the copies into various files. He put the carbon paper carefully into its own file folder. Then he looked down at Buckner.

"Help you?"

Buckner showed the sergeant his badge.

"I'm here for a prisoner you have in one of your cells," he said. "Name of Dutton, Elroy."

"Dutton. Hmm." The sergeant squinted at Buckner's badge, then at Buckner. "Colored, right?"

"Yes."

"Hang on." The sergeant opened a drawer and took out a file, opened it, and skimmed what he found there. "Got smart with an officer over by Portland Place."

"Sounds like him."

"What do you want him for?"

"Federal charge. Volstead Act. Down in Highland County. Corinth."

"Hmm. Well, I don't know as I'm interested in … where, again?"

"Corinth. Highland County."

"Highland County. That's pretty far south of here."

"I guess so."

"You said federal. Your badge says chief of police. How's that your business?"

Buckner took out the folded sheet of paper and handed it to the sergeant.

"As you will read there, I am responsible for taking him into custody and locking him up. In Corinth. In Highland County. South of here. Where he will be put on trial for a whole bunch of things. That there is an order from a federal judge regarding a federal crime, and I hope that outweighs him upsetting a police officer here in St. Louis. How is that a crime, anyway?"

"Depends on who's doing it."

"I expect it does, him being colored and all."

"Look, I don't know how you handle things down your way, but up here we make 'em walk the line. You gotta keep an eye on 'em. Can't let 'em think they can just go anywhere they want, do whatever they want. Specially in that neighborhood."

"Uh-huh. Well, you go right ahead and read that court order and then we'll see about what we can do."

The sergeant turned his piercing gaze on the document in his hand. He frowned as he read. The more he read, the more he frowned, until, by the end, he was positively gloomy.

"I can't understand all this damned lawyer talk," he said at last. "I better show this to the watch commander."

"That's what I'd do, I was you," Buckner said. "I'll wait right here."

"Might take a while," the sergeant said. He smiled the confident smile of an entrenched bureaucrat whose only real power lay in the ability to prevent things happening.

"Do you think it'll take long enough for me to call the judge's office?"

The sergeant's frown returned. He pushed a button on the intercom on his desk. It squawked at him and he responded, explaining the letter from the judge, and asking for Captain Plunkett. The box squawked again.

"He'll be right along."

Within minutes, a trim man in a uniform with gold eagles on the shoulder tabs came bustling from somewhere behind the booking desk.

"Hello there, Chief Buckner. How are you?"

"Just fine, thanks," Buckner said, shaking the captain's hand. "I don't want to interrupt your schedule here. I just need to pick up a prisoner."

"This is Dutton, right? Federal rap?"

Buckner nodded.

"I called the judge's office, just to make sure. Spoke to the judge himself."

"Of course," Buckner said. "Chain of custody."

"Right. Don't want him to get mislaid," the captain said. "Well, a federal charge takes precedence over a misdemeanor charge of failing to move on, and I don't need him cluttering up my cells when I've got real criminals to put there, so I've sent a turnkey down to get your boy. Volstead Act, it says here."

"Believe me," Buckner said. "Volstead Act is the least of it, really. It just happens to be the one we were able to get a warrant on."

"Causing you a lot of trouble down your way."

"You have no idea," Buckner said. "Bootlegging. Gambling. I could go on. Volstead charge is just the hook we needed to reel him in."

The captain nodded sympathetically. Just then, another officer came down a corridor with Elroy Dutton. Dutton's natty gray suit was badly wrinkled and smudged with dirt, and his tie was askew. One eye was swollen shut, and his face on that side was all puffy. Spots of blood dappled his white shirt.

"Got his property?" the captain asked the desk sergeant.

The sergeant held out a paper sack. Buckner took it and looked inside.

"This isn't everything," he said. "Dutton always carries a matched pair of .32s in a double shoulder rig. I need them for comparison with some bullets we took out of a fella down in Corinth."

"You all sound pretty much up to date," the captain said.

"Have to be, these days, or the lawyers will eat you alive in court. Just got the comparison microscope a couple months ago. It's going to mean convicting Dutton here on a whole lot more than the Volstead Act. And prove to the city fathers it wasn't a big fat waste of money."

"Right." The captain turned to the sergeant. "Well?"

The sergeant reached under the desk and pulled out Dutton's double shoulder holster, complete with two ivory-handled Colt .32 Police Positive revolvers. He held it out to Buckner and watched mournfully as Buckner put it in the paper bag.

"That'll be all," Buckner said.

"You got cuffs?" the captain asked.

"Right here." Buckner patted his jacket pocket.

"Okay." The captain gestured to the turnkey. When Dutton had been re-cuffed, Buckner signed the offered form and took his copy.

"Captain, thanks for your help. If you like, I'll let the judge's office know how helpful you've been here."

"Much obliged," the captain said. "Can't hurt having a friend downtown."

As Buckner and Dutton descended the steps outside, Dutton snarled, "You gonna take these damned cuffs off me?"

"Not just yet," Buckner said.

They walked south on Newstead to Laclede, where Buckner took off the handcuffs. Dutton held out his hand and Buckner gave him the paper bag.

"You might want to wait till you're someplace more private before you finish getting dressed."

Dutton said nothing, just pocketed his possessions, leaving the pistols in the bag.

"Looks like they roughed you up some," Buckner said.

"I've been smacked harder by a couple of ex-girlfriends," Dutton said.

"You going to tell me what's going on?" Buckner asked. They resumed walking.

"You first. What are you doing here? Buster talk?"

"Of course he talked. He's worried. Me too, since I saw that telegram. Where's my sister?"

"I don't know. I haven't seen her or heard from her since the telegram, so I don't know any more than you do."

"How'd you wind up in jail?"

"I got up here as quick as I could, stopped in to see my cousin, nail down a place to sleep, then went looking for Marty. Tried her apartment and the newspaper, no luck. Then I remembered she told me about these cousins of yours that live out in Portland Place, so I thought I'd try them."

"Did you talk to them?"

"Hell no. I never even got past the gate. Only Negroes they let in there are the help."

"Yeah, and you don't exactly look like the help. Or act like it."

"Damned right I don't. Anyway, how'd you manage to get me out of jail back there?"

"Oh, they didn't really want you all that bad, and I gave them an excuse to turn you over to me." Buckner explained about the letter.

"So this federal judge is your uncle?"

"My mother's older brother."

"But, was all that back there even legal? Can he just do that? Spring some guy whenever a relative asks?"

"Not usually. But he had his office make a few telephone calls, find out how you got arrested. He said it sounded phony as a lead dollar to him, so he just had that letter written out and signed it."

They reached a corner with a streetcar sign and waited. Passersby gave them a wide berth, two rough looking men, one of them looking like he'd been knocked around, the other grim-faced and glowering, looking as though he might have done the knocking. Otherwise people ignored them.

"So he was running a bluff. And so were you."

"Afraid so. If that police captain back there had challenged that letter, or called up a superior officer, or even a municipal judge, you'd still be sitting in a cell. And most likely with me right there beside you. But, like I said, they didn't really want to keep you all that bad."

"Must be nice," Dutton said. "Being able to work the system like that. Comes of having important kinfolk."

"Yes, it does. And if that's what it takes to get my sister out of whatever kind of stupid jam she's got herself into, then I'll work that for all it's worth."

"How many relatives you got in this town, anyway?"

"Oh, I guess if you count second and third cousins and what not, it'd run into some numbers. Of course, not all of them could've sprung you from jail. And a couple of them I know for a fact are sitting in cells up in Jefferson City right now. So I don't exactly count kin any more than I have to."

"And now, thanks to you and your kin, the St. Louis police think I'm some sort of gangster from down in Highland County."

"Not just some sort of gangster, *the* gangster. The head man, like Holmes called him, the Napoleon of Crime."

"Swell. I'll never be able to show my face here again."

"You have all my sympathy. But none of that gets us closer to finding out where my sister is."

"No, but while I was sitting in that cell, I had a chance to do some thinking about where she might be."

"All right, what did you come up with?"

"The one person in this town she can barely stand the sight of, and the last person anybody would think she would go to for help."

"Harris."

"Right. On account of he arrested her in Corinth back when Bushyhead was still chief and was trying to put pressure on you."

"Just the man she would go to."

"Do you know where to find him?"

"As a matter of fact, I do. At least I know where he had an office last year."

"That's a start," Dutton said as a streetcar squealed to a stop at their corner. They boarded and Dutton took a seat directly behind the motorman. Buckner sat next to him, a look of surprise on his face.

"Nothing to worry about," Dutton said. "Union Army veteran named Tandy raised hell about it back fifty, sixty years ago. He must've been one tough old cob, worked as a deputy US Marshal out in New Mexico in the bad old days. Anyway, the streetcar companies got tired of him pestering them, stopping their cars, complaining about making black people sit in the back, so they finally gave in. We sit wherever we want now. Some of the good white folks in this lovely city tried to change all that so they wouldn't have to sit next to us on the cars, but they haven't had any luck so far."

"Fine with me," Buckner shrugged.

"You really got a comparison microscope?"

Buckner just laughed.

*

Robert Shotwell paced the alley before the loading dock and the pallets. And the corpse. A few people came along. None paid him more attention than a nod. None demonstrated any curiosity at his presence. The position of the corpse allowed him to block easy sight of it simply by standing in front of it.

He did not have long to wait before Mullen came trotting down the alley with Dr. Peck, bag in hand, shambling along after. The two policemen then stood back and let the doctor get close.

Peck stood over the body, glaring down at it as if somehow it offended him by being dead.

"Young," Peck muttered.

He knelt down, his face close, barely inches away. Shotwell and Mullen watched, vaguely horrified, as Peck sniffed at the body, face, clothing, hands. Then he felt around the corpse's jaw, arms, and hands, all the way down to the feet, touching lightly, gently, almost caressing it. After a moment, he stood up.

"Alcohol poisoning," he said. "Sometime late last night, early this morning."

"That's it?" Shotwell asked. "No other cause of death?"

"No other obvious cause," Peck answered. "I'll know for sure when I can get a closer look at him. But I'm betting on the booze."

"You can tell that from the smell? Alcohol?"

"Hell yes." Peck pointed. "Roll him over. See if there's a bottle under him."

They did that, and there was. Shotwell put on the gloves he'd brought and, using only thumb and forefinger, picked the bottle up by the neck and held it out to Peck, who sniffed and nodded.

"Smell it yourself," Peck said.

Shotwell held the brown pint bottle under his nose and inhaled cautiously. He jerked the bottle away and gasped.

"Lord that is terrible. What is it?"

"Wood alcohol, along with some other stuff for flavor and color," Peck said. "Mainly, anyway. It usually takes more than a pint for this stuff to kill you. But if he was drinking some better quality stuff before he got to this, his liver was already working overtime, so maybe this just hurried the process along. Won't know for sure until I open him up and take a look inside."

"How'd he get ahold of it?" Mullen asked.

"Oh, I don't know for certain," Peck said. "I expect originally it came courtesy of the U.S. Government."

"The government?"

"I'm guessing neither of you young fellows is a drinker, am I right?"

"Absolutely not," Shotwell said. "Maybe once or twice when I was in the army, but not now. Augusta won't have it. Says it's a white plot to poison our people."

"She might have a point there," Peck said. "Look what it did to the Indians."

"Me neither," Mullen said. "My dad's dead against it."

"That's right," Peck said. "He's head of the local chapter of the Anti-Saloon League here in town isn't he?"

"Yes."

"Well, I'm what you might call an expert on the subject," Peck said.

"All right," Shotwell said. He carefully put the empty bottle into the paper bag. "You're the expert. How, exactly, is the government involved?"

"Simple. The more they crack down on bootleggers and moonshiners, the more the price goes up, so your average drinker is priced out of the market. Starts drinking stuff made with a combination of methyl alcohol and ethyl alcohol, a combination ordered by the government, with much fanfare, to warn people off. But people keep making it and people keep drinking it. Hell, twenty-nine people died in the past couple of months up in St. Louis, and plenty more sick. I'm pretty sure the government expected folks would learn the stuff was bad and stop drinking it."

"In other words, expecting people to be sensible," Shotwell said.

"Yep."

"But this is the first time somebody's died from it here in town," Shotwell said.

"The first that we've heard about," Mullen said.

"That's mostly because here in Corinth, in Highland County, if you want a drink, you can get one that isn't poisonous," Peck explained. "Most people can. I expect you'll find this fellow isn't from around here. I sure don't recognize him anyway. Probably came in on the train sometime yesterday and brought that bottle with him."

"Well, I don't recognize him," Mullen said.

"Me neither," Shotwell added.

"So you two fellows are going to have to find out who he is, where he's from, and how he came by that bottle. I'll get the body up on the table, do an autopsy, see if I can find out anything more."

"I'll go get Murtaugh's wagon," Mullen said.

"I guess that means I'll have the pleasure of going through this fellow's pockets, see if I can find some identification."

"Isn't that what being in charge is all about?" Mullen said with a grin.

"I guess it is."

"Well, I'll do the autopsy at Murtaugh's, and you can go through his clothes more thoroughly there," Peck said.

"Fine."

Peck sauntered off down the alley.

"Is it my imagination," Mullen said. "Or does he seem to perk up when we ask him to do some detective work?"

And he too was gone.

ST. LOUIS

Alonzo Harris, one-time Corinth police detective working for Baxter Bushyhead, now worked as a private investigator out of an office on South Wharf Street, near the corner of Rutger, up against the skein of rail lines that crowded the Mississippi River. The river, nearing flood stage, had already submerged some of these tracks.

St. Louis was no longer the booming metropolis it had once been, the "Gateway to the West," as it called itself. But as a place where major rail lines crossed the country's biggest river, and as a major port on that river, it still did a lot of business. Hundreds of boats still loaded and unloaded along the riverfront. Towboats pushed barges, massive engines hauled long lines of freight cars. Trucks, automobiles, horse-drawn wagons, peddlers' pushcarts all competed for space along the narrow riverfront streets. Warehouses lined the streets, huge open doorways revealing the nation's goods piled to the ceiling, awaiting transshipment somewhere else. Everybody, men, women, children seemed to be rushing, working, buying, selling. The everlasting roar of trucks, boats, and trains all converged on a squat, four story brick building with warehousing at the ground level, offices and apartments above. Dutton and Buckner climbed the dark, narrow staircase. At the first landing, Dutton took his pistols out of the paper bag. Buckner held his coat while he shrugged into the rig. After checking the loads, Dutton put his coat back on.

"Ready now," he said.

"You think he's going to give you trouble?"

"No. I just like to be fully dressed."

Harris's office was an outer room with a bare and unoccupied desk and chair and a door leading to an inner room. Buckner and Dutton found

Detective Harris standing at the room's single window, looking down at the boats on the river. He turned around as they walked in.

"Some folks knock first," he said, evidently not surprised to see them.

Harris was a thick, squat man with a mostly bald head traced by a few strands of hair carefully flattened into place with oil. He seemed to Buckner always to be sweating, and his face wore a permanent look of discontent. Buckner had never seen him in a suit that fitted him properly. Today the jacket was tight across his chest and his wrists protruded, while the trousers bagged over his shoes. A cigar angled up from one corner of his mouth.

"How are you fellows?" he said. "I been expecting you."

"Other business," Buckner said.

"Where is she?" Dutton demanded.

Harris took the cigar from his mouth, chuckled, and replaced it. It had gone out, and he relighted it before answering, enjoying his guests' impatience.

"She's at my place," he said, puffing billows of smoke. He even managed a smug smoke ring.

"Is she safe there?" Dutton asked.

"Safer'n anyplace else in this town right now, I expect."

"What in hell is going on, exactly?" Buckner said.

"Best I can tell you, she's in some kind of trouble with the police department."

"Police department? What's that all about?"

"She told me she was working on something to do with crooked cops in with the gangs somehow. She was meeting some cop was gonna fill her in on all the details, names and everything, only he got killed and whoever shot him took a shot at her, too, so she went to ground. Showed up here crack of dawn yesterday morning demanding I hide her."

"And you agreed to that?" Dutton was surprised.

"Sure. Hell, I got nothing against her, though I gotta admit, I was kinda surprised she come to me to hide her out." Harris laughed. "On account of what you might call our history and all."

"Yeah, that's a surprise all right," Buckner said.

"Well, hell," Harris said. "That's why I quit Bushyhead, come up here. I don't go with beating up on women. So you could say she's kinda responsible for me getting a new start in life."

"You're a prince," Buckner said. "So who was the cop that got killed?"

"A lieutenant named Morris, she said. Some friend of yours."

"I know him," Buckner said. "Not real well, but I know him."

"Huh. So how did you two get here so fast? The papers didn't mention her name in their stories about the shooting, since they didn't know about her being there. Just a police lieutenant dead in an alley."

"She sent Dutton a telegram."

"Right. She would. And told you to make sure not to tell the Chief, right?"

"Yes," Dutton said.

"But you had to tell Buster where you were headed, and Buckner here wormed it out of him and took the first eastbound through town.

"That's right."

"You want to see her?"

"Damned right."

"Let's go, then."

They followed Harris through the door and into the outer office.

"You're not worried about missing customers?" Dutton asked.

"Nope." They walked through into the hall. Harris locked the door behind them. "I generally get a dozen or so a day. If I ain't around, they just toss the bags of money over the transom."

He led them down the stairs and into the street. A short walk took them to Chouteau Avenue and another red brick building with storage space on the ground floor. Like the others, it had offices and apartments above. Harris led them up to the third floor, where he knocked on one of the four doors off the hallway.

"It's me," he growled, and unlocked the door.

He ushered Dutton and Buckner into a narrow corridor that opened into a living area with a sofa and several chairs. Two windows overlooked the alley behind the building. A kitchen stood to the right.

Buckner had met Harris's wife once before, when the family still lived in Corinth. She was a well-upholstered woman and no great beauty, but pleasant enough given her choice of husband, and the noisy, rambunctious children they shared. All of whom were out, perhaps at school. Buckner struggled to remember. Two girls and a boy, he thought.

Mrs. Harris sat at a table in the kitchen drinking tea. Martha Jane Buckner stood at the kitchen sink, wrapped in a too-large flowered apron, washing dishes. She glared at the visitors.

"I told you not to tell him," she snapped.

"He didn't," Buckner said. "I pressured Buster into showing me the telegram."

"Ha! You probably didn't even have to break a sweat." She looked closely at Dutton. "What happened to you?"

"He went looking for you at Fred and Doreen's place," Buckner said.

"Never got past the gate." Dutton rubbed his bruised face and smiled. "A little lesson from the local police."

"Stupid," Martha Jane muttered. "How'd you figure I'd be here?"

"I tried the newspaper first," Buckner admitted. "We both did. No luck there, of course. But that Wieczek is a real fireball isn't she."

"She's a damned fine reporter, and a friend of mine," Martha Jane said. "Play your cards right, and I might be persuaded to put in a good word for you. Maybe set you up with her."

"I don't need you—" Buckner began.

"I don't mean to interrupt," Dutton said. "But is there any chance of an explanation of what's going on?"

Martha Jane hesitated.

"Go ahead, honey," Mrs. Harris said, getting to her feet. She took the apron from Martha Jane. "I'll finish up here."

"This way," Harris said.

He led his guests down another narrow corridor to a small room and closed the door. The room contained a chair and a side table and a small desk with a lamp and a typewriter on it. There was a chess set on the side table, a game in progress. Harris turned on the lamp. It illuminated the chess set and little else. A piece of paper lay next to the chess set with what looked to Buckner like code writing on it.

"Who are you playing?" Dutton asked.

"Guy in London. Russian. We play by mail. He got chased out by the Reds, works in a restaurant there. Used to be a duke, or so he claims. You play?"

"Only a little," Dutton admitted. "Picked it up from the French during the war."

"I never could figure it out," Buckner said. "It just confuses me."

"I know how," Martha Jane said. "But he beat the tar out of me last night."

"That's all right," Harris said. "I've never beaten the Russian."

"Could we get back to the main point," Dutton interrupted. "What kind of trouble are you in, exactly?"

Martha Jane leaned against Harris's desk and told them about the shooting in the alley.

"So you're doing a story on police corruption, and you figure Johnny Morris was going to give you a list of names, right?" Buckner said when she finished.

"Not exactly. He told me a couple of weeks ago that there was something going on and it was way more than the usual stuff. A whole lot more. He wouldn't tell me any more at that point. We were talking on the phone, and he said he didn't trust it. Which was why we were meeting in person in that alley. He was finally going to give me names and details. He did give me a list, but I lost it somewhere. It's probably still in that alley."

"And you figure somebody shot him to shut him up," Dutton said. "And you wound up being a target as well just because you happened to be there."

"It sure as hell felt that way." Martha Jane shuddered, remembering the sound of 18 pellets of 00 buckshot hitting the shop window across the street, reducing it to fragments.

"And you never got a look at who it was that was doing the shooting?"

"No. Not a glimpse. I was too busy running away."

"How well did you know this Morris?" Harris asked.

"I met him when I was up here a couple of years ago," Buckner said. "The police department was giving classes on fingerprinting, how to write up accurate reports, maintaining a chain of evidence, things like that. He was in charge of the classes. And he helped me out on a couple of cases with St. Louis connections."

"You getting all up to date in sleepy old Corinth?"

"Sure. Have to. Police work has to move into the twentieth century. Lawyers are getting trickier all the time. Criminals, too."

"I got to know him when he was on the deputy mayor's crime commission," Martha Jane added. "They were trying to clamp down on the gang wars, and they wanted as much good press they could get."

"All this doesn't exactly solve the problem, though," Dutton said. "Did Morris's killer get a good look at her, or did she get shot at just because she happened to be there? If he did get a good look, then she's in serious trouble. How do we protect her? Do we try to get her out of town and back to Corinth? Would that work?"

"Well," Buckner said. "We could try."

"I'm standing right here," Martha Jane said with an edge in her voice.

"Yeah, and you know running back to the Lead Belt is no guarantee," Harris said. "You figure whoever shot Morris was one of these cops he was there to tell you about?"

"Sure," she answered. "Who else? We gave the crime commission all the coverage they wanted and we played Johnny Morris up in it. Plus, he was already well known for what he did taking down a local gang, Reagan's Rats. This was a couple of years ago. So, yeah, that's who I think it was."

"If there really are cops looking for her," Harris said, "they've got ways to find out who Morris's contact was and where she lives, and if they're serious about eliminating her as some kind of threat to them, they'll just follow her down to Corinth and take care of her there."

"Hold on a minute," Marty said. "What makes any of you think I'm going to run away and hide out in Corinth? I've got hold of a piece of a great story, and I want the rest of it, all of it. That's the only way my editor will accept it."

"Why are you so hell-bent on following this story?" Buckner asked. "Can't you drop it, move on to something else? Something a little safer?"

"No, I can't. And why the hell should I? I've got competition in this town, damn it, even at my own newspaper."

"Competition for what?" Dutton asked.

"Competition for stories, for a byline, for better pay. That's why I've got to get this story down and file it."

"But you can't exactly go back to work as usual and expect to survive," Dutton said. "Whoever killed this Morris also tried to kill you. Whatever information he had must have been pretty serious. You say you lost it, but for all the killer knows, you still have that information and plan on using it. You have to assume you're still a target."

"Do you know what the information was?" Harris asked.

"That's what I'm trying to say. Johnny never got that far. He had a piece of paper he gave me. I think I took it just as he was shot. But I haven't got it, and I honestly don't know what happened to it."

"All right," Dutton said. "If you can't go back to Corinth, and you can't go back to the newspaper, we need to find out what the hell is going on. And if there's some way to fix it, we have to fix it."

"How?" Harris demanded. "Investigate the police department? Not a chance. I've gotta work in this town, and I need to have the cops at least tolerate me if I'm gonna make a living. They'll never like me, but they let me work, so me going up against them is just not in the cards."

"Well, I'm not exactly in a position to take them on, either. Colored man against the police in this town? I wouldn't last ten minutes. Especially now they know who I am." Dutton gave Buckner a glance.

"All right," Buckner said. He had been standing a long time, and his leg hurt. He wanted to move but the four of them filled the gloomy little room to bursting. "It looks like we have to do several things. We need to find out what Johnny was trying to tell Martha Jane. And we need to find out who killed Johnny and tried to kill her."

"And figure out if there's some way to fix it so Marty can go back to work without having to worry about getting arrested, or shot, or both." Dutton added.

"Where are we supposed to start?" Harris asked.

"I can think of one place," Marty said. "The whole thing started, for me anyway, with the death of Robert Hanley a couple of months ago."

"I remember that," Harris said. "Deputy Mayor in charge of that crime commission Morris was part of."

"Yes," Marty said. "The state board put in a new chief of police. He's only been here a couple of years. And there've been months of local gang warfare, lots of killings on all sides, including a lot of police officers killed."

"What're they fighting over?" Dutton asked.

"Control of the local liquor trade," Harris said. He chuckled. "Things up here aren't as, let's say, regulated as they are down in Corinth, where the bootleggers and the moonshiners pretty much have free run of the place."

"That's horseshit and you know it," Buckner said.

"Whatever you say, Chief," Harris continued. "It's just you, chief of police, and the town's leading purveyor of booze palling around together."

"We do not pal around together," Dutton snapped.

Harris raised his hands in mock surrender.

"We also don't have gang warfare and police officers getting shot," Buckner added.

"I guess that counts as law and order," Harris said, still smiling broadly.

"If you gentlemen don't mind," Marty interrupted. "As I was saying, the new chief turned to Hanley right after he took the job. Hell, I don't think he'd even unpacked his bags and he was on this. Hanley had a reputation as a gang buster from when he was in the district attorney's office a few years back, and he'd pushed hard to hire the new chief. Now, Hanley was supposed to head up the commission looking into improving the operations of the department, making them better able to deal with the gangs. Johnny got in touch with me to tell me this. He said Hanley had come across some serious illegalities committed by some officers, and he wanted Johnny to look into it. But about the time Johnny started sniffing around, Hanley died in an auto accident out in the County. That's when Johnny got in touch with me. He was afraid the whole thing would get swept under the rug, and he thought maybe if the paper did some work on it, maybe shine a light on whoever these officers were, something might get accomplished."

"Did Johnny think Hanley's death might not have been an accident? Might have been because he was investigating all this?" Buckner asked.

"Yes, that's exactly what he thought."

"Well, maybe that's one place to start." Buckner turned to Harris. "Could you look into that without jeopardizing your relations with the department?"

"I guess I could find out if anybody's investigating it at all," Harris said.

"All right. Could you talk to your cousin?" Buckner asked Dutton. "He's been doing business here for a while, hadn't he?"

"Twenty years and more."

"Ask him about the gangs, see if he knows anything about that just from living here and paying attention. Oh, one more thing. Are there any Negro officers on the force?"

Harris and Marty both said "Yes."

"Maybe you could see if there's a way to get information from one of them," Buckner said. "I doubt if the rest of us could make any headway down there."

"I'm not sure why you think I'd have any more success just because I'm black," Dutton said. "But I'll talk to my cousin and see."

"Oh," Marty said. "There's going to be a service for Johnny tomorrow. Sort of a wake at his house. It'll be full of cops."

"And reporters?"

"I doubt it. When one of their own gets it, they like to keep it strictly among themselves."

"I'll go to that," Buckner said. "A friend and fellow officer paying his respects. I'll see what I can pick up."

"So I'm still stuck here," Marty grumbled.

"You can start writing up what you have so far," Buckner said. "And then you can add whatever we dig up. That way, you'll be ready to put it all together when we're finished and you're out of danger.

"Assuming that's going to happen," Dutton said.

"You can use my typewriter," Harris said.

"Where are you going to stay?" Dutton asked Buckner. "This place isn't big enough for the both of you."

"What about your cousin's place?"

"You mean both of us? Some pistol-packing ofay holed up in the Ville? Word about that would be all over the city by nightfall, and there's be cops climbing all over the place."

"I can't go back to my apartment," Marty said. "Why don't you stay there?"

"Last time I stayed at your place, I couldn't get any sleep, what with gentleman callers knocking on the door at all hours."

"One caller, one time," Marty said, ignoring the looks of the others. She dug a key out of a pocket and handed it to him. "Just don't answer the door. And don't make a mess."

"All right. Can we meet back here tomorrow?"

"My office would be better," Harris said. "It was already running a risk, having Dutton here."

"All right," Dutton said. "The office, say tomorrow afternoon around four."

They all agreed. Marty returned to the kitchen with Harris. Buckner and Dutton went down the stairs and out onto the street. Traffic rattled noisily past, ignoring the light mist that threatened to turn into real rain. The two of them took refuge at a fruit peddler's canopied cart. Dutton bought an apple.

"Just a minute," Buckner said. "Why does everybody keep calling her Marty?"

"Because that's what she wants to be called now."

"Since when?"

"Since I don't know. A while now."

"She didn't say anything to me about it."

"Well, maybe she figured you'd tell her it was silly and what was wrong with 'Martha Jane' anyhow."

"It is silly. And what's wrong with 'Martha Jane?' Or 'Marthy,' like I used to call her when she was little?"

Dutton did not say anything, just shook his head and walked off down the street.

CORINTH

James Shotwell was alone again with the corpse. It wasn't exactly his first time with a dead body, but it was the first time he was in charge of finding out how the body got that way. He went to work at once, carefully slipping his hands into pockets, trying hard not to touch the body itself, as though that touch might somehow disturb its repose. The pockets in the jacket and the trousers yielded scraps of paper and a few coins and nothing else. One scrap of paper had a telephone number written on it in careful, elegant script. And there were train ticket stubs, one from the Wabash Line, one from the Missouri Pacific. Shotwell saved all of it, folding it into a new envelope he carried specifically for at purpose, as required by his boss.

A strip of pale skin on the left wrist suggested a wrist watch, now missing.

A more thorough examination, to include shoes, socks, underwear, would wait until the corpse was on the table at Murtaugh's, and under Dr. Peck's care.

In the meantime, Shotwell prowled the alley from beginning to end, poking into dark corners, under and behind trash bins, even looking into the two or three outhouses that sat there, mostly unused now that indoor plumbing had spread through the town. And the prowling paid off when he found what had been missing from the corpse's pockets.

The wallet was made of smooth, soft leather, with none of the bulges and indentations a well-worn wallet develops over time. The letters W, A and L were stamped in gold in one corner. Thinking the leather might take fingerprints, Shotwell handled it carefully. It contained no money, just a piece of paper with a list of what appeared to be dates and letters: "10/12

I St; 10/19 Drake; 10/26 Neb; 11/2 K St; 11/9 Wash; 11/16 NYU; 11/23 K; 11/28 OU."

None of it made any sense to Shotwell. Were K St. and I St. addresses? The only K Street he knew about was in Washington, D.C. But what about the others?

He found no wrist watch.

He put the wallet and the piece of paper in his pocket and returned to the corpse. Mullen had arrived with the truck from Murtaugh's Funeral Parlor. For more formal occasions, Murtaugh's provided an elegant, long black hearse made by Cadillac, but for simple body removal, the flatbed truck would do. To Shotwell's surprise, a woman was driving instead of the usual acned young man. It was Mrs. Murtaugh. She set the brake and got down, brushing off the front of her black wool dress.

"What're you gaping at?" she demanded.

Mullen also got down and came around the back of the truck. He was smiling as he got the stretcher down.

"I was just wondering," Shotwell said.

"He's poorly," she said, answering his question. "You gonna help, or you just gonna stand there with your mouth open?"

"Right."

With Mrs. Murtaugh directing, Mullen and Shotwell put the corpse on the stretcher and the stretcher on the truck bed. They folded a tarp over the body, securing it with belts provided for the purpose. Mrs. Murtaugh folded her arms and watched them with a critical eye. When they were done, she got back into the truck and started the engine.

"You coming?" she asked.

"Yes, Ma'am," Mullen said. He winked at Shotwell. "See you there," he said as the truck moved away down the alley.

Shotwell completed his search, finding nothing that seemed connected with the dead young man. He got to the funeral parlor as Dr. Peck was beginning to work. Highland County possessed a coroner with a laboratory, but it was in the county seat and Corinth's chief of police refused to delay an investigation while the county's machinery creaked into gear. Murtaugh's was the closest thing the town had to a laboratory where Peck could perform the autopsies Chief Buckner occasionally demanded of him when somebody had met death by violence. Abel Murtaugh was only too happy to bill the town for its occasional use of his facilities.

Black victims of violence were, of course, dealt with at Proudfoot's

Funeral Parlour located over on the other side of the town. Dr. Peck autopsied all equally. Mrs. Proudfoot equally billed the town for the service. James Buckner ensured she was paid the same as Murtaugh.

Shotwell and Mullen hung back. Peck and Mrs. Murtaugh had already stripped the corpse, which lay on a stainless steel table. The table was built with gutters to channel fluids, which drained into containers underneath.

"Are you boys too delicate to help?" asked Mrs. Murtaugh.

"Delicate or not, I don't want their clumsy fingers messing up my work," Peck said.

When the body was naked, Peck handed the clothing to Shotwell, who headed into another room. Mullen turned to follow.

"Hold on, there, Officer Mullen," Peck said. "Get your notebook out. You do shorthand, don't you?"

"Yes, sir."

"Pitman or Gregg?"

"Gregg. Learned it at school. Nobody does Pitman anymore. There's supposed to be a new kind, 'Speedwrite,' invented by some woman in New York, but I haven't seen it yet."

"Gregg will do fine," Peck said. "I usually have to do this myself while I'm working, which is inconvenient as hell, so you are going to save me a lot of work. Pull that chair over and sit down and start taking down what I say."

Mullen sat with his notebook in his hand, pencil poised, as Peck began: "The corpse is that of a young white male who appears to be approximately 20 to 25 years of age."

Shotwell, in the outer room, began examining the clothing. He found nothing in the pockets beyond what he had already found. All the labels were from stores in St. Louis. Including the underwear, which was not the standard union suit, but the more fashionable undershirt-and-shorts combination young men had taken to wearing lately. Each piece had a label carefully hand sewn into it, a label with a name printed on it.

Shotwell returned to the examination room. He stopped abruptly and clapped a hand over his nose and mouth. Mullen was scribbling with one hand while the other pinched his nose shut. He kept his eyes resolutely on his notebook and breathed mostly through his mouth. Shotwell kept his gaze directed at the corner where the far wall met the ceiling, but he was still able to see far more than he wanted to see.

Peck and Murtaugh worked around the body, ignoring them.

"I found a name," Shotwell was able to say at last. "William A. Lance, according to the labels on his underwear. And that matches the letters on the wallet."

"Assuming he was wearing his own underwear," Peck muttered.

The two young men looked at him in horror.

Mrs. Murtaugh laughed.

"Well, it's a start," Mullen said. "What else?"

"The ticket stubs from the Wabash and the MoPac, an empty wallet, a telephone number, and this list of dates and, I guess, addresses."

"What's the phone number?" Peck asked, still concentrating on his work. He removed something wet and glistening from the corpse and placed it on a scale.

Shotwell read out the number.

"That's Mrs. Belmont's number," Peck said. "You know—"

"I know," Mullen said without removing his hand from his nose. "Buck told me once when he was over there and said I might have to telephone him." He quickly added: "He was over there investigating something, I mean."

"I'm sure he was," Peck said. "Maybe this young fellow paid Mrs. Belmont a visit for reasons of his own. So you two are going to have to look into that."

"What about this list?" Shotwell said. He experimented with taking his hand away from his nose and mouth, hoping he might have gotten used to the smell. He hadn't. He pinched his nose once more and read from the slip of paper.

Peck and Mrs. Murtaugh began to stitch up the long Y-shaped incision that ran from the body's shoulders to the pubic bone.

"I'll finish," Mrs. Murtaugh said. "I'll give him a nice, tight seam."

Peck pulled off rubber gloves and his long rubber apron and dumped them into a barrel. He washed his hands at a sink against the wall.

Shotwell read aloud again.

"Those are schools," Peck said, turning and drying his hands with a towel. "Colleges. NYU is New York University. The others are, I'm pretty sure, Iowa State, Kansas State, Oklahoma University, and Nebraska University. Drake is up in Iowa. Wash is probably Washington University. I was in medical school there, about a thousand years ago."

"And the dates?"

"Those are all Saturdays," Mullen said.

The others looked at him in surprise.

"Can't help it," Mullen confessed with a shrug. "I just kinda know about dates."

"Ah," Peck said. "More hidden talents. Well, then, that is probably a football schedule."

"Who's the home team?"

"Again, I'm guessing, but I'd bet it's Mizzou, Missouri University, up in Columbia."

"All right," Shotwell said. "Thanks. I guess we'll have to hold onto the body until we can locate next of kin, all that."

"You finished with me?" Mullen asked, getting to his feet.

"Yes. Type that up for me and I'll drop by and pick it up. I'm confirming death due to alcohol poisoning."

"How many carbons will you need?" Mullen asked.

"Shouldn't need more than three or four," Peck said, winking at Mrs. Murtaugh.

"Two," Mullen said with conviction. "And bring your bill."

"Don't worry about that."

"One more thing," Mullen said. "How do you stand the smell?"

"Around here, Bub, that's the smell of money," Mrs. Murtaugh said, smiling grimly.

Mullen and Shotwell returned to the department, taking the clothing and other evidence with them. Shotwell sent Bill Newland home. Mullen filled two cups with coffee and the two of them sat at the desk.

"I think we have to assume William Lance is a student at the university," Shotwell said. "Until we find out otherwise."

"And probably from St. Louis, judging by the labels on his clothes."

"That's probably a safe bet as well."

"All right," Mullen continued. "And it looks like he got here by train, but there's no direct line between here and Columbia. He'd have to take the Wabash to St. Louis and change to the Iron Mountain."

"Unless he drove down here in an auto."

"I think he'd still have to go through St. Louis, then come down Highway 61. Otherwise, it's 63 to Rolla and back roads from there. Is there a date on those stubs?"

Shotwell took them out and looked.

"Yesterday. But no return tickets, nothing of value in the wallet at all."

"You found it farther down the alley, cleaned out."

"Sure. And anybody planning on paying Mrs. Belmont a visit would have to bring plenty of money. If the rumors are true." Shotwell looked at Mullen, eyebrows raised in question.

"Don't look at me like that," Mullen protested. "I make the same as you and I'm putting what I can into the stock market. You won't catch me at Mrs. Belmont's."

"The stock market? Really? Is that safe?"

"Don't you start in on me," Mullen said. "Buck's already been riding me about it."

"Right. Sorry." Shotwell smiled.

"So unless this Lance fellow had already been to Mrs. Belmont's and spent all his money there, somebody must've found him, taken his wallet, and cleaned it out."

"And we stand no chance of finding whoever that was."

"And we still need to find out how he got hold of that bad liquor and then ended up dead in the alley."

"Right. That's a lot of questions we need answers for. How does Buck do it?"

"Beats me," Mullen said. "Most of the time he just sits there in his office and drinks coffee and glares at the wall. Then he comes gimping out here and tells me he's headed off someplace, and a while later he comes back and explains it all and you fellows go out and arrest somebody."

"Well, we are going to have to find out everything we can about William Lance. So it looks like a visit to Columbia to find out whatever we can there, and another to St. Louis to find and inform his next of kin. Parents, I guess. And they'll have to make a formal identification."

"Right," Mullen agreed. "Columbia first. They'll have an address for Lance's family. It'll take a while to get up there, so we better leave now."

"You mean you better leave now," Shotwell said. "That's called 'Little Dixie' up there for a reason. I don't believe they'll be much interested in helping a Negro policeman. It's a Jim Crow town and a Jim Crow university. I show up there in uniform and start asking questions, I'll just get my head busted."

"I expect you're right about that. All right, then. I'll go to Columbia. But that means you're going to have to follow Lance's comings and goings here in town. Which will include, first of all, a visit to Mrs. Belmont's."

"Of course," Shotwell sighed. "Maybe getting my head busted in Columbia would be better than having to explain to Augusta what I'm doing at Mrs. Belmont's. Because people will see me and she will find out. Besides, Buck says trying to get information out of Mrs. Belmont is like pulling teeth. And she's not afraid of the law, not with the protection Buck says she's got."

"And not with Isaac Joe standing right there, watching every move you make." Mullen was laughing. "You might just get your head busted either way."

"While you're enjoying that thought," Shotwell said, "Who's going to watch the desk while we're both gone?"

"Not Carter."

"No," Shotwell agreed. "Not Carter. Willet?"

"Durand?"

"Willet," Shotwell said.

"Okay. Willet."

"I'm going to talk to Augusta about what I'm about to be doing." Shotwell got up and started out.

"Hang on while I put this stuff away."

Mullen went down the hall and put the clothing in a cupboard, keeping the wallet and scraps of paper, which he put in a large brown envelope from his desk. Then he and Shotwell went up the stairs and out.

"I'll round up Willet. He's patrolling over on the west side of town. Then I'll head for the train station and get a ticket."

Mullen found Willet strolling casually down Maple, humming to himself and twirling his nightstick by its leather strap.

"If you have a moment, Officer Willet."

"Sure, Mike. What's up?"

"You're on the desk for the rest of the day, till Bill Newland comes on."

"I am?"

"Yes, you are. I've got to go to Columbia and Shotwell's in the middle of a serious investigation over on the other side of the tracks." Mullen explained about the dead body in the alley.

"Gosh," Willet said. "I hadn't heard about that."

"I found it during my lunch break. Young fella. We think he might've been a student at the university. Now, Shotwell's still in charge, but you're on the desk till I get back."

"You sure Durand wouldn't be better for that?"

"Yes, I am sure. Get on over there now."

"Right." Willet started off.

"Don't go rearranging anything on or in my desk."

"Right."

"And don't make a mess."

Willet waved and kept walking.

At home, Mullen packed a small bag, including the brown envelope, and changed out of his uniform and into his everyday suit. He was careful to pocket his badge and department identification. Then he headed for the station.

"That'll be fifteen dollars, Officer Mullen," said Young Clarence, the aged clerk.

"Fifteen dollars? To go to Columbia?"

"Yes. You see, you've got to go to St. Louis on the Iron Mountain, then switch to the Wabash, and that'll take you to Centralia, then you have to change to the Wabash shuttle that'll take you on into Columbia. That right there is where your cost is."

"All right." Mullen put money on the counter. "And I'll need a receipt."

"Police business?"

"Of course. When's the next eastbound?"

"In about an hour and a half." Young Clarence had worked for the Line since he had actually been young and learned the trade from Clarence, his father. The Line's schedule was imprinted on his brain.

"Thanks." Mullen hurried to the department, where he shooed Willet away and sat at the desk. He typed up his notes from Dr. Peck's autopsy and filed a copy. Then he took another copy to Peck's office, where Peck gave him a certificate of death.

"That makes it official," the doctor said.

"You don't need these notes I took?"

"Not unless the case ends up in court for some reason." Peck held out his hand. "But I'll take that copy anyway, since you took the trouble. And I'll let you have this, too." He gave Mullen a hand-written bill.

Mullen went carefully down the rickety stairs that led from Peck's office to the empty yard behind Coy's Drug Store and crossed to the train station. The eastbound arrived a few minutes later.

Robert Shotwell, sitting in the small living room of his home a few yards east of the station, heard the train's whistle as it pulled in. His wife, Augusta, sitting opposite him on the sofa, seemed concentrated on the sewing in her lap, though she wasn't actually stitching anything. The two of them sat like that until they heard the train pull away.

"I think you absolutely must go right ahead and do your job," she finally said.

"You do?"

"Yes. Of course. You swore to uphold the law."

"You don't mind? I mean, what people are going to say?"

"Of course I mind. People will see and people will talk, and I expect I will have some explaining to do. At church. To my mother." She gave a little sigh. "I knew there would be some things about police work I wasn't going to like, and I decided I would deal with them as they came up. They," and here she tilted her head just slightly to the west, "seem to have grown accustomed to a Negro policeman, just as we have here." She smiled. "And I think some of us are proud you're the one Chief Buckner leaves in charge when he goes away."

"Yes, but this is going to set tongues wagging for certain. Me paying a call on Mrs. Belmont, going in and out of drinking establishments, Dutton's, the Corinthian, every blind pig, dive, and speakeasy in town."

"Do you have to go to all those places?"

"Well, Michael and I figure this young fellow came to town to have himself some fun, which included a visit to Mrs. Belmont's. And he probably did some drinking while he was here, if what Dr. Peck says about how he died is true. So, yes, I'll be trying to find out where he went and if that contributed to his death."

"All right. If anybody says anything to me about it, I will simply tell them you are doing the job you signed up to do." She picked up a tiny pair of silver scissors and snipped a thread. "And it will be just too bad if they don't like it."

"All right, then." Shotwell got to his feet.

"I've met her, you know."

"Who? Mrs. Belmont? You met her? How?" Shotwell sat back down.

"Oh, various things around town, women's work, charity work that sort of thing. Of course, whatever she does, she has to do on her own. None of the ladies in town, here or over there, would be seen in public with her. But, last winter she sent that man of hers over to the church with a pile of nearly new blankets."

"That was nice of her. I hope they were clean."

"Don't be unpleasant, dear. She is a remarkable woman in many ways. On the one hand, a hard-headed business woman who, quite frankly, takes advantage of the weaknesses of men."

"Some men."

"Yes, of course. Some men. But she has a reputation as a decent, reliable employer who devotes a great deal of time and money to the well-being of her employees." Augusta threaded a needle and took up her sewing again. "She is a complex person, very smart, from all I hear. So you watch yourself over there."

"I promise."

"Why do you suppose he does that?"

"What?"

"Leaves you in charge when he goes away. Chief Buckner."

"I don't know. Maybe because I'm a good officer. I believe he served alongside Negro troopers when he was in the cavalry, before the war. So he must have gotten used to working with blacks on an equal footing."

"He's a very strange man, isn't he?"

"Yes, he is."

"He's is always so very polite to me. On those few times he's actually spoken to me. Takes his hat off, yes-ma'ams and no-ma'ams."

"I'm sure he'd do the same if you were white."

"Mm."

"He just seems so angry."

"Angry?"

"Yes. Furious. And just barely holding it in." Shotwell thought a moment. "His sister is in some kind of trouble in St. Louis."

"How do you know that?"

"Elroy Dutton keeps Buster informed."

"And you will talk to Buster."

"Sure," Shotwell said. "Part of being in charge. Anyway, that's what happened last time."

"What last time?"

"When those hoodlums from St. Louis came down here and got mixed up with Chief Bushyhead. I think the county had let Buck go as deputy sheriff, but that didn't stop him when Bushyhead and his gang killed Buck's friend from his army days, then kidnapped Buck's sister."

"The papers never explained exactly what happened."

"The town fathers hushed it up," Shotwell explained. "What happened was Buck took on the whole police department and Bushyhead's hoodlums. He killed about half of them, including Bushyhead. Dutton told me he jammed a metal spike into his throat." Shotwell smiled grimly. "Whoever's been causing Buck's sister up in St. Louis better watch themselves, or they could wind up the same way."

"Well, go pay your visit to Mrs. Belmont. You wouldn't want him angry at you."

Shotwell left his house wondering if he would ever completely understand his wife.

Chief Buckner had taken the trouble, years before, to learn all he could about Mrs. Belmont. She had been born Sadie Munch in a sharecropper's shack outside Memphis. There was not, nor had there ever been, a Mr. Belmont. But when the Corinth city fathers decided to give traveling men a reason to stop off in Corinth, they didn't care what her real name was. They had heard about her famous establishment in New Orleans. Several of them visited and asked around town about her. Hearing nothing but good reports, and after paying brief visits to gather firsthand information, they brought her upriver from New Orleans and set her up in business. They took a significant percentage of the business's gross, and they had never had reason to regret the decision. Their profits protected her from the wrath of the community, and from any snooping by the police department. Buckner accepted the situation as a reality he could not change. It also meant there were no free-lance prostitutes working Corinth; any that tried to open up shop were encouraged to move on. But Buckner still kept an eye on the red brick building with its green shutters.

That building, located so conveniently close to the train station, was only a short walk from Officer Shotwell's front door. He climbed the front stoop and used the brightly polished brass knocker. A large black man in a black cutaway and striped trousers opened the door and greeted with slightly raised eyebrows.

"I need to speak with Mrs. Belmont," Shotwell said.

"Police business," Isaac Joe said, nodding confidently.

"Of course." Shotwell wore his sternest, most official expression. Isaac Joe's fierce, scarred face opened in a broad smile. "Step right in, Officer Shotwell," he continued, stepping back and swinging the door wide.

Shotwell nodded curtly and stepped inside. He'd heard of the gilt mirrors, the flocked burgundy wallpaper and the thick red carpet, but the real thing amazed him. No wonder this was such an expensive place to visit.

Mrs. Belmont herself came down the hall, bright red lips smiling graciously. She held out her hand.

"Good afternoon, Officer Shotwell. How can we help the police? And how is your lovely wife?"

"Very well, thank you." Buckner was right. The woman could unsettle you with a glance. "Thank you for asking."

"I'm delighted to hear it. Please give her my regards."

Mrs. Belmont wore a light gray outfit cut like a man's business suit, with vest, watch chain, and tie; the skirt stopped modestly at her knees. Her shoes were square-cut brogues. Her short hair was a gleaming black helmet that framed her pale face, tapering along her jaw line into sharp points. Her dark eyes, set wide apart, gazed warmly at him from under long lashes. If she had really begun life in that sharecropper shack in Tennessee, she showed no signs of it now.

Shotwell explained about the body in the alley and the telephone number on the scrap of paper he had found in the wallet.

"The young man's name was Lance. We think he was a student at the university up in Columbia. And I just need to know if he was here last night, and, well, anything else you can tell me about his visit here."

"Lance," Mrs. Belmont said. "The name isn't familiar, but we usually just stick to given names here. Our customers seem to prefer it that way."

"His name was William." Shotwell gave a quick description of the young man.

"There was a bunch of them," Isaac Joe said. "Four of them."

"Four?" Shotwell said.

St. Louis

Buckner returned to the *Post-Dispatch*. At the desk he asked for Becca Wieczek.

"Well, hello," she said as she came down the stairs. She quickly took the pencil from behind her ear and shoved it in a pocket. "Come back to have me show you around town?"

"Not right now. I really need to read up on that accident the deputy mayor had. Hanley."

"Great! I'll take you down to the morgue." She looped her arm through Buckner's and led him down to a basement office where a man behind a counter greeter her with a scowl.

The morgue deserved its name. Dimly lit and chilly, it contained shadowed rows of filing cabinets cordoned off by a long counter. From behind the counter, a gaunt man in shirtsleeves, a green celluloid eyeshade on his head, watched them with silent disapproval.

"Relax, Mitch," she said. "I'm not here on my own account. This here is Marty Buckner's big brother, and he'd like to look at the stuff we did on the Hanley accident."

"Mph," Mitch replied. He turned and trudged heavily down an aisle of filing cabinets. He stopped at one, opened a drawer, and took out a thick file folder. This he brought back to the counter at the same languid pace. "For employees only," he grumbled.

"Right, right. I know." Wieczek handed Buckner the file and said, "Help yourself."

"Is there someplace I could set down?" Buckner asked. "Looks like this might take a while."

"Oh, right," Wieczek said bluntly. "Your bad leg. Marty told me." She pointed him to a desk in a corner. "I'll watch him like a hawk, Mitch. Promise."

She showed Buckner to the desk and sat opposite him. Buckner embarrassed by her comment, sat and began going through the clippings. The wound in his leg, despite the talents of French and then Canadian doctors, had never fully healed. The limp that resulted seemed to mock him, demonstrating a weakness he did his best to conceal. Wieczek watched with open curiosity as he read quickly through the clippings the file held. He jotted brief comments in his notebook. When he had finished, he asked, "Does Mitch back there have clippings from the other papers in town?"

"Oh, hell yes." She got up and took the file to the desk, returning shortly with another fat file folder. Buckner hurried through it.

There wasn't much to the story, in fact. It had been a routine motoring accident that happened to involve a major city employee. His car had run off a section of road in rural St. Louis County and overturned. The deputy mayor had died of a broken neck. There were hints that he may have been drunk at the time, and that he kept a woman in a remote hideaway out there. Nobody could say for sure, so the implications hung in the background, where they damaged Hanley's reputation and causing his survivors anguish while actually proving nothing at all. In any event, the particular section of road was notoriously dangerous and had accounted for several accidents over the years.

Buckner noted that some of the papers initially included coverage of Hanley's work with the crime commission, but only the *Post-Dispatch* had suggested there was any link between Hanley's work and Hanley's death. The paper hinted that several local gangs had put their sights on the deputy mayor. The paper also pointed out that since his death the work of the crime commission had slowed to a walk.

One article, however suggested that Hanley was following a lead he'd picked up in his work. The lead was one of the major gang leaders who had a woman out that way, and that was who Hanley was hoping to talk to.

Buckner showed the article to Rebecca Wieczek.

"Is this Martha...Marty's work?"

Rebecca Wieczek glanced at it. "Yep. That's hers. She never told me, but the word in the City Room is that she had a contact in the police department that was feeding her information in drips and drabs. She wouldn't confirm that when I asked her, but she did say the information was coming piecemeal and very slowly and whoever it was had to stay in the shadows, police officer or not."

Buckner read a few more articles.

"Is this everything?" Buckner asked.

"St. Louis papers, yeah," she said. "The small town papers out in the County will have run stories on it, especially out around Chesterfield, Ellisville, where it happened. But they won't provide more information than what you've seen here. Most of it relies on the reports issued by the sheriff's office, anyway, so that's the angle you're getting."

"All right. Thanks." Buckner returned the files to Mitch at the counter. Mitch leafed through them suspiciously until satisfied Buckner hadn't pocketed anything. Meanwhile, Wieczek again looped her arm through his.

"Now's your chance to let me show you around town," she said, walking him upstairs to the door.

"Thanks, but the only sleep I got last night was this morning on the train coming up here, and I'm pretty sure I wouldn't be much fun on a tour of the city right now. Besides, shouldn't you be at work?"

"Paper's on the street," she said. "So I'm free for the rest of the day. And on into the night." She grinned at him. "If you're interested in a late supper."

"Thanks," Buckner repeated. "Right now all I'm interested in is sleep." He thought a minute. "If I come back tomorrow morning, could you persuade Mitch to let me look at how the paper covered the gang wars the city's been having?"

"Sure. But you'll be on your own. We're an afternoon paper, so mornings are pretty busy for me."

"Just get me started."

"All right." She smiled. "But I'm going to make you buy me dinner tomorrow night."

"Oh, well, I guess I can afford that."

"Perfect. I'll see you tomorrow." She disengaged her arm, smiled again, and hurried up the stairs to the City Room.

Buckner took the cars to Delmar, jamming himself and his bag into the mass of commuters. His smile broadened, thinking of Becca Wieczek, amazed at the bubbling self-confidence of modern young women.

A woman, neither modern nor young, glared at him as the car bumped to a halt, slamming him and his bag into her.

"Watch it, Bub," she snapped.

Buckner apologized and concentrated on not disturbing his fellow commuters for the rest of the ride.

Buckner expected that, as usual, his sister would have nothing edible in her apartment, so he made a few stops after getting off the car. Nor had she relocated to a larger flat on a lower floor, so he lugged his bag and his groceries up the flights of dark stairs. The various cooking smells he encountered on the way up stirred his hunger. He hadn't eaten since early morning.

His sister's apartment, just one large room with alcoves, was as cramped and cluttered as he remembered it from his last visit. One alcove held a bed that could be screened off with a curtain. Another held a wooden icebox, an electric hot plate, and a shelf with mismatched plates and utensils. An empty saucepan sat on the hot plate. The same odorous sofa still squatted in the bay window overlooking the street.

Buckner sat on the sofa and ate some of the food he had bought, kosher salami and challah, and drank some of the milk. He left enough for morning. He cleaned up and lit a cigar, mostly as relief from the cat smell the sofa emitted. His sister owned no cats. She told him she had acquired the sofa second-hand and insisted the smell never bothered her.

Her small bookshelf held a collection of Sherlock Holmes stories. Buckner read several of them as he smoked, and enjoyed them as much as ever. The plots were ridiculous, but it didn't matter. Holmes was routinely bristly and brilliant, Watson was forever nonplussed, and the cops were stumblebums.

He finished his cigar and the story about the "speckled band." After a quick trip to the bathroom at the end of the hall, he undressed to his underwear, wrapped himself in a blanket, and drifted off to sleep wondering how you could train a snake to do anything, much less slither down a cord.

A grating sound in the door lock brought him instantly, sharply awake. He rolled off the sofa, pulled the .38 revolver from his bag and knelt behind the icebox. The strip of illumination from the hall light that showed under the door went dark with the sound of breaking glass. The door opened slowly. A figure, black against the blacked-out hall, stood in the doorway. At first he thought it was his sister, and then he saw the pistol turn his way.

He eased back the hammer of his .38, metal sliding against metal as the cylinder revolved. The figure in the doorway fired at the sound, the bullet thumping into Marty's icebox. Buckner, blinded briefly by the muzzle flash, fired back. There was a sharp cry of pain, a thump as the pistol fell on the floor, and the shooter turned and fled.

Buckner listened to feet clattering down the stairs, waited behind the icebox for several minutes, finally stood and stepped into the room. There were no other sounds. No one demanded to know what was going on, nobody complained about the noise. Perhaps his sister's neighbors were accustomed to small arms fire in the early hours of the morning. Or maybe they were extravagantly polite. Or just scared.

Buckner, ignoring the remains of the shattered light bulb on the floor, closed and relocked the door. He turned on the light. A quick glance at the lock assured him he could pick it with a soup spoon. The pistol lay on the floor. It was a .38 Smith & Wesson, identical to the one in his hand. He found a clean dish towel and picked it up, wrapping the towel around it. He put it in his bag. A check on his sister's icebox revealed the perforated wooden case and zinc lining, and a bullet, badly mashed, lying in a saucer of spoiled carrots. The bullet looked too badly damaged for any kind of close examination, and it had obviously come from the pistol in his bag, but he tossed it in with the pistol anyway.

He lay back down on the sofa. He pulled the evidence tag off his .38, but kept it on the floor by his hand. Sleep seemed unlikely, so he thought about what had just happened. Pretty clearly, his sister was in mortal danger. With that comforting thought, he fell asleep.

St. Louis

A thin, gray morning light through the window above the sofa woke Buckner. The bathroom at the end of the hall was unoccupied, and Buckner used it, returning clean, freshly shaven, and wide awake. He ate some of the bread he had saved from the night before, then dressed and went down to a shop on Washington, where he got a large mug of coffee and a refill for a nickel and spent two cents on a newspaper. He lingered over the second cup. The shop was not full, and the few customers concentrated, like Buckner, on their coffee and their newspapers.

Local sports fans were disappointed because the chilly, rainy weather had put off the Cardinals' season opener, while the Browns began their season on the road. The police department was taking the latest death of one of their own very seriously. A spokesman for the chief was quoted as saying "the perpetrator of this foul murder, a high-ranking officer shot in the back by a coward, will not escape justice. The department is putting every available man on this."

Buckner finished his coffee and took a car to the *Post-Dispatch*. Becca Wieczek, in a blue blouse and matching blue, very short, skirt, hustled him to the morgue and turned him over to Mitch with a brief explanation of what he wanted.

"Let me know when you're finished," she said, and rushed out.

"Gang wars, huh?" Mitch said. "Been plenty of that around here lately." He went to his filing cabinets and returned with two bulky file folders. "This is just for 1926."

Buckner took the files to the desk he had used the day before.

Just skimming the two files revealed the serious nature of the local gang wars that had plagued the city for the past several years. According to one story, some three dozen police officers had been killed in the line of duty. Buckner asked for, and received, the files for 1927 and 1928. He noticed that recently the in-fighting among the gangs seemed to taper off toward the end of the year, thanks in part to the death or disappearance of several of the more notorious gang leaders. The new chief was claiming success for the work of the department and assuring the public that the work would continue until the gangs had been completely routed.

At eleven, Buckner returned the files to the counter. Mitch sat on a high stool and sipped coffee.

"Did you find what you were looking for?" he asked.

"Yes, thank you."

"Got enough? Or do you want more?"

"I've got enough," Buckner said. "Looks like the police here have their hands full with the gangs."

"Scum of the earth," Mitch responded vigorously. "The sooner they kill each other off, the better off the rest of us will be."

"Well, they seem to be working in that direction," Buckner said.

He thanked Mitch again, and left.

In the City Room, Becca Wieczek, scowling ferociously, pulled a sheet from her typewriter, inserted another, and resumed typing. She glanced up as Buckner walked into the room and waved him over to her desk.

"I'm jammed up with this," she said without stopping. "There's a joint around the corner. Chinese. Meet me there at eight."

"All right."

A streetcar took Buckner to Lafayette Square. Johnny Morris had lived on St. Vincent, just west of the Square. The house was a small, two-story brick cube in a street lined with identical cubes. Autos, many of them police patrol cars, were parked along both sides of the street. Buckner's knock on the door was answered by a beefy man in a police dress uniform. He glowered at Buckner over a cup of coffee. He had lieutenant's bars on his shoulder.

"Yeah?"

"I'm James Buckner."

"So?"

"I heard about Johnny. I wanted to offer my condolences."

"Uh—huh. What're you to Johnny?"

"I'm chief of police down in Corinth, in Highland County. I've known

Johnny for a while now." Buckner groped in his pocket for his badge, and showed it to the lieutenant. He was not impressed.

"Who is it, Robby?" A woman came up behind the policeman. She was taller than he was, with dark hair pulled back into a severe bun and a round, pale face. She had large, dark eyes that seemed pinched against pain as they contemplated Buckner from under level brows. She wore a black, light weight woolen dress and stood slightly bent forward, arms folded across her breast, hands holding her elbows as though hugging herself. Or holding herself together.

"Says he's a friend of Johnny's," the policeman said without taking his skeptical eyes off Buckner. "From some hick town down south."

"James Buckner, Ma'am." Buckner took off his hat.

"Oh, yes. Johnny mentioned you. I'm Johnnie's—I'm Mrs. Morris. Come in."

Buckner deposited his hat on a table holding many others, and continued into the house. The lieutenant remained, a one-headed Cerberus, at the door. Buckner pocketed his badge and offered Mrs. Morris his hand, but she was already turning away, back into the crowd.

The small house seemed full to bursting with police officers, all in dress uniforms, from patrolmen to commanders. In a bay window overlooking a tiny side yard and the house next door, stood a small table with a framed picture of the deceased, also in full-dress and taken years before, judging by the broad smile on Morris's unlined face. Sprays of lilies in urns flanked the portrait. From time to time an officer would walk over to it, gaze at it, shake his head, and walk away.

"Would you like something, Chief Buckner?" Mrs. Morris asked over her shoulder. She indicated another table, this one with a large coffee urn and scattered cups and saucers. It was tended by a woman in black, approximately the same age as Mrs. Morris.

"I would love a cup of coffee," Buckner said.

"Charlene?" Mrs. Morris said. The woman looked up and smiled wanly. "Of course."

"Black," Buckner said.

"Sure." Her smile broadened. "I never knew a cop that took it any other way." She poured and handed Buckner a cup and saucer. "Friend of the family, me," she added. "Just another cop's wife." She scanned the crowd and pointed out a tall, gray-haired captain. "His, to be exact."

"Thank you," Buckner said.

Mrs. Morris gave Buckner a thin smile and drifted off, making her way through a sea of blue uniforms.

"If you want to—ah—fortify that, Chief," the captain's wife said, "It's just in there." She pointed to a doorway through which Buckner could see a kitchen, also filled with police officers.

"This will be fine, thank you, Ma'am."

"Sure."

"I remember you," a voice said. Buckner turned and confronted a lieutenant with his hand out. He was tall and red-faced, with thinning blond hair. "You were up here a couple years ago for those lectures on fingerprinting. I'm Tom Connell." They shook hands. "You any kin to that girl crime reporter on the *Post*?"

"She's my sister."

"Thought she might be. She's been getting a bit too big for her britches here lately."

"Life-long habit with her."

"Well, she oughta watch herself, or it won't be a habit much longer."

"Oh, she can usually take care of herself."

"She's been trying to dig up a lot of stuff about police officers, pointing fingers at some fine men. Word is, Morris was feeding her information, evidence, documents, that sort of thing."

Buckner shrugged. "Don't know a thing about it. Maybe that's what got Johnny killed."

"What? You think a cop killed Johnny? You better watch that kind of talk." Connell's face flushed redder still, and he talked through gritted teeth. "Johnny's made a lot of enemies with the gangs around here. Any of them would've been glad to blow him down for nothing."

"That'll happen," Buckner agreed. "Any police officer doing his job is going to make enemies."

"You're damned right. So you tell that sister of yours to back off. Stop making trouble."

"I'll be sure to pass the word along. If I see her."

"I hear she's gone to ground," Connell said.

"Couldn't tell you. I haven't seen her this trip. I had to come up this way to pick up a prisoner. He's in a holding cell down at the court house. I've just stopped here to pay my respects to Johnny's widow. I'm headed back home this afternoon."

"Well, she's not at the newspaper offices, some people asked around, and she's not at her place. And nobody's seen her for a couple days now."

"So you've been looking for her."

"Yeah. We think she might've been a witness to Johnny's murder, so, yeah, we're looking for her. She ain't done any real harm, not yet. Just a bunch of newspaper stories, after all. If there ain't any more along those lines, I expect it'll blow over. But in the long run, she'll be better off if she comes in on her own. You know, just to talk, tell us what happened in that alley."

"Like I said, I'm just here to pick up a prisoner and pay my respects, and then I'm headed back home. But if I hear from her, I'll pass along what you're told me."

Buckner sipped his now cold coffee. The lieutenant, looking dissatisfied, nodded curtly and moved off.

A grizzled sergeant came over. He held a coffee cup that reeked of sour mash.

"You're Buckner. I heard you talking to Connell."

"That's right."

"Well, don't believe everything he tells you about Johnny Morris."

"Oh?"

"Yeah. He's got a grudge. He thinks his wife had a little fling with Johnny here about a year ago."

"Did she?"

"Oh, hell, I don't know. Might've. Johnny had a reputation." The sergeant sipped from his cup and scanned the room. "Johnny probably had flings with the wives of half the guys here. Or tried to, anyway."

"I only know Johnny from the job," Buckner said. "I was up here for the lectures a few years back, and then he helped me out on some cases since then, information, suggestions, back when one of your gangs up here tried to move in on my town. I don't know anything about his personal life."

"Oh, Johnny was one hell of a cop," the sergeant said. "He was behind them classes the department does. Got the idea from other departments around the country. He was a big believer in, uh, lessee, 'inner-departmental coordination' he called it. No, wait, '*inter*-departmental.' That was it. Thought cops around the country ought to work together more, swap information on a regular basis, that sort of thing."

"That's a pretty good idea. We had trouble along those lines a while ago. Killer was living in plain sight. Departments down south knew about him, where he'd been, had their suspicions, but never bothered putting the word out."

"You get the guy?"

"Eventually, yeah, but not before he killed several young women."

"Yeah, that's the kind of thing Johnny was always talking about." The sergeant emptied his cup. He grinned at Buckner and winked. "You want me to stiffen yours up a bit? Gotta pretend we're drinking coffee so long as the brass is around." He glanced toward the kitchen. "But it looks like the Chief has left, so bar's open."

"He's new, isn't he? Your Chief?"

"Couple years."

"How's he doing?" Buckner remembered his own first years as chief of police in Corinth, discarding dead wood, building the department from the ground up. That had been no picnic. But taking over a major municipal department with hundreds of officers had to be far more challenging.

"Well, you know. He come in talking about a new broom, clean up the place. And I gotta admit, he's done all right. Got rid of a lot of cops that were crooked. Or just coasting along, collecting paychecks. And he's come down pretty hard on the free lunches and the parking tickets, too. Course, they never go away completely." The sergeant changed the subject. "So, you want something in your coffee or not?"

"Bit early for me," Buckner said.

"Not for me." The sergeant headed for the kitchen.

Buckner sipped more of his cold coffee and watch the room. Officer after officer spoke to Mrs. Morris, offered to shake her hand, to comfort her, patted her shoulder, head down, leaning close, talking softly, seriously.

Another lieutenant, having parted from her, turned toward Buckner. His step was unsteady, and the whiskey smell preceded him. Buckner suddenly realized, if this wake didn't end pretty soon, most of the St. Louis police force would be too drunk to do their job.

"Tony Marconi," the lieutenant said. "Tony Macaroni to these lunkheads." He sighed. "Johnny was a great cop. One of the best. We're gonna get whoever done this, you can bank on it. One of our own gets it, we don't rest until we find the bastard and put him down. You understand?"

"I do," Buckner said.

"Chief assigned me and four other dicks to work it full-time."

"I expect you'll get him."

"Damn right we'll get him." He indicated Mrs. Morris. "We owe it to her."

"Do you have any leads?"

"Just some ideas, you might say. Back in twenty-four, Johnny took out the Reagan mob."

"I read about that. Hoover's bunch were in on that, too, weren't they?"

"Oh, Johnny had his own crew, and it was them did the work. Johnny was the connection with the federal boys." Marconi made a face. "Bunch of overdressed kids, think going to law school qualifies you to take on goons like the Reagan mob. Hadn't been for Johnny, they'd never've gotten to first base."

"I met one of Hoover's agents a few years ago," Buckner said. "All he cared about was Reds. Didn't seem interested in law enforcement at all."

"They oughta stay out of it, then, and leave law enforcement to the professionals."

"Johnny got some good press on that Reagan investigation," Buckner said.

"Yeah, he did. That was that sister of yours wasn't it?"

"Yes, it was, but she wasn't the only one. Johnny told me it was embarrassing, all that attention."

"I'll bet," the officer scoffed. "Anyway, it looks like your sister's gone and painted a big red bull's eye on her back lately."

"That so?"

"Damned right it's so." Marconi was weaving slightly, and his words came out slurred. "Writing all that crap about cops on the take. That don't make her no friends in the department, I can tell you that. If there's anything like that going on, and I ain't saying one way or the other, she oughta let us take care of it ourselves. The new chief's dead set on cleaning up the department. Says people gotta trust the police or we can't do our jobs, which is protecting them, after all. But stories like the stuff she writes just makes things harder."

"You're not gonna get any argument out of me about that," Buckner said. "But I've never been able to get my sister to do what I tell her to do as long as she's been alive."

"Sure. I know. Got a sister of my own. Don't know what's got into women these days. Still, a little bit of that crusading journalist crap goes a long way. Hell," Marconi said with a laugh. "Folks around here still spit when they hear Lincoln Steffens's name, just on account of that piece he wrote. 'Tweed Days in St. Louis.' Boy, that ruffled a lot of feathers."

"It was twenty years ago," Buckner said.

"Over twenty-five, but folks are still plenty mad. And some of them see your sister heading down the same road."

"All right. If I see her before I head back home, I'll tell her what you said."

"It's for her own good."

"Sure."

Buckner noted the crowd was thinning. The gang in the kitchen were still in full force, but the ones who had taken their coffee straight were paying last respects, making their excuses, heading for the door. Charlene, the captain's wife, had stopped serving and was now cleaning up, taking used cups and saucers to the kitchen, telling the men in there to go home. Or to work.

One of them, a young patrolman, wasn't ready to leave just yet, and he made his point loudly.

People shushed him.

"I don't care what you say about honoring the dead. I just know he made a play for my wife, and I don't go for that sort of thing."

Charlene put down her load of cups and saucers and spoke softly, urgently to the young man.

The young patrolman listened, head down, shaking his head, but he said nothing more, just walked out.

Every person in the room had heard him, and everyone had ignored him.

"Good luck with your investigation," Buckner said to Marconi. "Not a good idea, hoodlums thinking they can kill cops and get away with it."

"You're damned right about that."

They shook hands, and Marconi made his tottering way to the kitchen. Buckner waited until Mrs. Morris was free.

"Thank you for letting me stay," he said.

"Thank you for coming. Johnny had a lot of respect for you. He said you were the future of police work."

"I don't know about that," Buckner said. "But thank you."

As he offered his hand, she turned away with the same sad look of pain, and walked to the far corner of the room. Buckner put his cup and saucer on the small table, grabbed his hat, and left. He walked to the streetcar stop. The next car took him downtown.

Columbia, Missouri

The University of Missouri was the first university established in the Louisiana Purchase. As a result, someone thought it would be a good idea to honor Thomas Jefferson, who actually signed off on the sale, and who was a famous advocate of education. And so, the tombstone of Thomas Jefferson, instigator of the Purchase, sits in a prominent spot on the campus, a gift from his descendants, despite the fact that full enrollment of white women only began in 1871.

*

Michael Mullen woke up when the train stopped in Columbia. His watch told him it was almost seven. He got up and stretched, grabbed his bag, and stepped down onto the platform. Young men and women carrying book bags, plus a few older men with briefcases, got off with him. Most of them hurried down the street. Several men in suits got on.

Mullen thought of himself as a man of some experience. He had, after all, served briefly as a rookie police patrol officer in St. Louis before deciding big city life was not for him. And he was a committed child of the new century, a firm believer in the automobile and the airplane, the modern corporation, and the exciting opportunities offered thanks to the stocks those corporations sold. As bright as today might be, sloppy weather notwithstanding, Mullen knew tomorrow would be brighter.

But he had never been more than a hundred miles from Corinth, making this train ride the longest of his life. Certainly the worst.

The run up to St. Louis had been familiar, and quick, the train pulling in at a decent hour. But the wait in St. Louis persisted into the night, and the Wabash train to Centralia had stopped in every village and crossroads along the 130-mile route. There followed another wait in Centralia, a small town offering nothing at all during the early hours of morning. The shuttle, the Columbia Branch, ran eight trains a day to and from Columbia, but the first one didn't leave for more than an hour, and it seemed to stop wherever a light shone.

As Mullen waited, a few autos pulled up and passengers got out and joined him in the barren waiting room. At one point a wagon stopped outside and a young man hopped down and waved to the woman driving as she pulled away. The young man a came into the waiting room as well.

When the train pulled in, Mullen was surprised to see it was hauling freight and cattle cars as well as passenger cars.

The train quickly filled with students, yawning hugely in the dark car. The older men must be the teachers. Mullen learned there were actually two other colleges in Columbia besides the university, and the Columbia Branch made it possible for many to live in the surrounding area and still get to school. But everyone looked exhausted, and Mullen wondered how much learning would get done today.

The cars emptied quickly when the train finally reached Columbia.

Mullen walked through the Wabash station, a gray limestone block, and crossed to a coffee shop on Tenth Street. He had a light breakfast and got directions to city hall and the university from the woman behind the counter. He didn't hurry, assuming no offices would be open until eight. The university had a famous journalism school, and it published the *Columbia Missourian*. Copies were available, stacked by the cash register. Mullen picked up one and read it with breakfast. He was expecting to find stories about football games and other campus doings, but was surprised to find the newspaper covered national and international news, stories from the United Press and Associated Press, just like the papers in Corinth. Patriotically, Mullen concluded that the writing in the Corinth papers was just as good, if not better.

When he finished reading and eating, he paid his bill and folded the receipt into his notebook. He left the paper on the table for the next customer. He decided it was still too early for offices at the university to be open, so he paid a courtesy visit.

City hall was just around the corner, and the police department was on the ground floor. An officer stood behind a booking desk piled high with files and ledgers. Pencils rolled to the floor as he sifted through papers, searching for something and not finding it.

"Help you?" he said to Mullen without stopping his frantic search.

"Yes, I think so," Mullen said. The disordered counter horrified him. Every fiber of his being demanded he help the officer, but he stuck to business by force of will. He identified himself and showed his badge. The officer, both hands full of paper, stopped and looked at the badge then at Mullen.

"All right. What?"

Mullen told him about William Lance.

"All right," the officer repeated. "What am I supposed to do about it?"

"Nothing, I guess," Mullen said. "It's just my boss, Chief Buckner, always says if you're in somebody else's jurisdiction, you have to check in with them before you do anything else. So I'm just checking in."

"Fine," the officer said. "You've checked in. Thank you."

Mullen hesitated.

"Go away," the officer said. "I'm busy."

Mullen went away.

He walked to Ninth Street and turned south. Jesse Hall, the administration building, was easy to find, as its dome rose above virtually every other building in the town. Anybody viewing Columbia from a distance would see immediately what mattered in Columbia. Jesse Hall shared space on the David R. Francis Quadrangle with the Jefferson tombstone. The quadrangle was named for Missouri's former governor and Wilson's minister to Russia. Red brick buildings made up the sides of the quadrangle, enclosing a grassy lawn. Jesse Hall had replaced an earlier building that had burned down before the turn of the century. All that remained were six Greek columns standing alone in a line. Mullen looked up at them and wondered what the point was.

A wide staircase led up to the imposing front doors of the building. Once in, Mullen found a directory on the wall just inside the door. Stratton Brooks was the president, and his office was just down the hall. Mullen decided to start there.

"I'm sorry, but President Brooks is in Jefferson City today, preparing to testify before the education committee of the legislature. He isn't due back until sometime tomorrow."

The smiling woman at the desk in the president's outer office seemed genuinely sorry she couldn't be of more help. She wore her gray hair in a neat bun and reminded Mullen of his mother. Her steel-rimmed spectacles were identical to ones she had worn. The name plate on the desk identified her as Emma Doddy.

Mullen showed her his identification.

"I don't really need to talk to him personally, Miss Doddy," he said. "I really just need some information about someone we think is a student here. William A. Lance."

"What's he been up to now?" the woman said. "And it's Mrs. Doddy." But she smiled when she said it.

"Has he been in trouble before?"

"Him and that gang he runs with, yes, often."

"Gang?"

"Oh, I don't mean a criminal gang or anything like that, Officer. I suppose it's not much more than high spirits, but they do cause their share of trouble. Has Mr. Lance gotten himself into trouble in—where was it, again?"

"Corinth, Ma'am, and not exactly. I mean, he's not in trouble, he's dead."

"Oh, dear. Oh, no. Oh, I'm so sorry. What happened?" The woman suddenly burst into tears.

This was not what Mullen expected. He didn't know what he expected, but it wasn't this. She was so upset, and she had hardly known the boy. And he was supposed to find out who his family was and tell them. What was that going to be like?

Mullen didn't say anything for a moment, and he and the woman collected themselves.

"That's just it, Ma'am," he said. "That's what I'm trying to find out. You see, I found his body lying in an alley behind my Dad's store. He owns a dry goods store in Corinth, my dad does. And the doctor down there says he died of alcohol poisoning. William Lance, that is. Not my dad. But that's about all I know, except for his name and that he's probably a student here, and you just told me that. Oh, and we think he's probably from St. Louis."

"This is very sad," said Mrs. Doddy. She had taken a handkerchief from her sleeve and was dabbing at her eyes, her spectacles in her other hand. "We lost so many fine boys in the war, of course, but that was for a good cause. It's so sad to hear one of our boys dying in this way."

Mullen wondered if Buckner thought it had been a good cause.

"Yes, it is," he said. "I don't know if Mr. Lance was part of a gang or anything like that. He was alone when we found him, and his wallet had been emptied of cash and any identification." Mullen decided to skip over the phone number of a prominent whorehouse. "I was hoping to talk to some of his friends, maybe they could tell me what happened."

"Yes, I see that. But, Officer Mullen, I'm not sure I can give out personal details about students without permission. I'm pretty sure President Brooks would be glad to give his permission, under the circumstances, but, as I said, he's away."

"I see. But maybe you could give me the boy's parents' address. I have to inform the next of kin in something like this."

"Oh, yes. Of course. I see that. It must be very difficult for you."

"I've never done it before," Mullen said. "This will be my first time."

"Oh, dear." Mrs. Doddy thought a moment, then got up and opened a filing cabinet, returning moments later with a file folder. "Here," she said. "Take this down." Mullen took out his notebook. "Richard and Annabelle Lance, University City, Missouri." She added a house number on Waterman Avenue.

"University City?" Mullen said. "I thought he was from St. Louis."

"Yes. That's a town in St. Louis County, not in the city at all. It's where Washington University is. That's a private university." Her tone implied the superiority of her employer.

"Thank you," Mullen said. Where Jeff Peck had gone to school, Mullen remembered. He put away his notebook. "Maybe his parents will know something, or can tell me who some of his friends are." He thanked Mrs. Doddy. "I guess it's back on the train for me."

"There is one more tiny bit of information I think I might be able to give you," she said. "Since I've already, ahem, exceeded my bounds."

"Anything will help me find out how William died." Mullen's freckled face gathered in a sincere frown of concern.

"Mr. Lance and his friends are all members of the same fraternity."

"Great. Which one?"

Mrs. Doddy gave him the name of a prominent national organization.

"The house is on Rollins," she said, and gave him the address. "They all live there, so I'm sure William did as well."

Mullen thanked her and went out onto the quadrangle. The day had not brightened, and the sky looked full of rain. A short walk took him to Rollins Street.

He saw that several of the big, old rambling houses had large Greek letters posted prominently. Mullen didn't know Greek, and relied on the address Mrs. Doddy had given him. The house had a wide gallery with pillars and a few scattered chairs. The front door was open, so Mullen walked in. Looking around the small entryway, Mullen guessed the building must once have been a single family home, but no longer. To the right, stairs led up. To the left was a large room with overstuffed chairs along the walls and a large pool table in the middle. A young man in flannels, collarless striped shirt, and a boater stood chalking a cue and staring at the balls on the tabletop. An unlighted cigarette dangled from his lips. Straight ahead was a dining room with lights on and people moving around. Mullen decided that was his best bet.

Several young men sat at tables, eating, drinking coffee, smoking. There was little conversation. A sideboard held platters of food and a large coffee urn. Mullen's entrance attracted a few glances, nothing more. At the nearest table, a young man sat alone, peering intently at a thick book that lay open next to a cup of coffee. A plate with the remains of breakfast sat nearby. The young man wore a blazer and a white shirt, and his tie hung loosely around his neck. A Greek letter pin gleamed from his lapel. He held a lighted cigarette in one corner of his mouth.

"Excuse me," Mullen said. The young man squinted up at him through thick smoke. "I'm looking for someone that might be a friend of William Lance." Mullen showed his badge to the young man, whose gaze flickered over it, then back to Mullen. "Is there someone in charge here?"

"Well, I'm recording secretary," the young man said. He quickly scanned the room. "Yeah, I guess I'm in charge. What did you want again?"

"I need to talk to someone who knows William Lance."

"I know him," the young man said with exaggerated patience. "Everybody here knows Bill. He's a brother."

"Uh—huh." Mullen sat opposite the young man and took out his notebook. "Who are you?"

"John Craig," the young man said. He eyed the notebook suspiciously. "What's this about? Why do you need my name?"

"Can you tell me why William Lance would take the train from here to Corinth?"

"Corinth?"

"Corinth, Missouri. South of here." The young man stared blankly at Mullen. "In Highland County. Why would William Lance go there?"

"Well, I don't know, do I? And just why do you need to know? Is he in some kind of trouble down there?"

"I found his body in an alley in Corinth yesterday. He's dead."

"Dead? Oh, Christ! What happened?"

"That's what I'm trying to find out. Do you know why he might have gone to Corinth?"

"What happened?" Craig repeated. "Did someone kill him?"

"I'm hoping if I can find out why he was in Corinth in the first place, I might learn how he wound up dead in Corinth," Mullen replied. He wondered if Buckner had to put up with this kind of thing when questioning people. And how he dealt with it.

"Oh," the young man said after a moment. "Well, I don't know if I can help you there. I'm a senior and Bill's a sophomore, uh, was a sophomore, I guess. We don't have any classes together or anything like that, and, really, I don't hang around with sophomores."

"Can you tell me someone who might know him better? Another sophomore maybe?"

"Well, yeah, there's his roommate. That's Chuck Haase. He could probably answer your questions."

"Where would I find him?"

"In his room. Where else?"

"And where is his room?" Mullen folded away his notebook and pushed his chair back.

"Hold it just a minute," Craig said. "I'm not sure you've got the right to just come barging in here and start ordering us around."

"I'm not ordering anyone around," Mullen said. "A friend of yours has died, one of your so-called brothers. I'm just trying to find out what happened to him. But that's all right, if you don't want to help." Mullen got to his feet. "I expect somebody over in Jesse Hall will be glad to help me out. Or maybe the Columbia police department."

"That's all right," Craig said, holding up a hand. "I can take care of this. Really, I can." He suddenly bellowed, "Pledge!"

A harried-looking young man in a filthy white apron came rushing through a door at the end of the room and hurried over to John Craig.

"Yes, worthy sir?" he said.

"Pledge, go wake up Brother Haase and tell him to get out here."

"Yes, worthy sir."

As the boy hurried away, Craig gave Mullen a satisfied smile.

"It'll be a couple of minutes. You want some coffee? Something to eat?"

"Not right now, thanks," Mullen sat down.

Craig shrugged. He stubbed out his cigarette in the remains of the food on his plate, lit another, and returned to contemplation of his thick book. A few minutes later, the boy returned with a sleepy-eyed, scowling young man in pajamas and a blue terry cloth robe thrown over his shoulders.

"Jesus Christ," he muttered. "I was up all night working on my damned poli-sci paper. What's going on that is so goddamned important at this hour of the morning?"

"Sit down, Haase," Craig said. He glanced at the aproned boy, who hovered expectantly. "Pledge, bring Brother Haase coffee."

The boy dashed to the sideboard, got coffee, and returned. He placed the cup before Haase and hovered until Craig dismissed him with a wave of his hand.

"Haase, this policeman needs to talk to you."

"Policeman?" Haase sipped coffee carefully and stared at Mullen. "I'm not talking to any policeman."

"Haase, do you want the whole house to end up on academic probation for another semester?" Craig asked.

"No."

"All right, then. Now answer the man's questions."

"Do you know why William Lance might go to Corinth?" Mullen said, adding, "I'm from Corinth."

Haase looked at Craig.

"Lance is dead," he said.

"What? He can't be. He was all right when we left him," Haase said, biting off the last words, suddenly aware he had said too much.

"Left him?" Mullen said. "What do you mean? Were you in Corinth, too?"

"Yes," Haase said after a moment. He turned to Craig and pointed to the pack of cigarettes on the table. "Mind if I have one?" Craig shook his head. Haase took out a cigarette and stuck it in his mouth. He took a box of matches from the pocket of his robe but the first match he took out broke in his trembling fingers. The next one wouldn't strike after several tries. He dropped the third into his lap. Finally, Craig used his lighter to help Haase get his cigarette going. After inhaling deeply and expelling smoke, Craig nodded his thanks and turned back to Mullen. "Yes," he said. "We were all there."

"Who is 'all'?" Mullen asked.

"Me and Bill and Dave and Stan."

"Dave Enslin and Stan Vesey," Craig said, watching Mullen record the names in his notebook.

"Why were you all in Corinth?"

Hasse looked at Craig, then back at Mullen.

"Just tell him," Craig said.

"Well, you see, we went there for a little fun. There's this place we'd heard about, run by some woman."

"Mrs. Belmont?"

"Yeah, that's the one. It's pretty famous, and we thought we'd go down there, see if it was all it was cracked up to be."

"Pretty expensive fun," Mullen said.

"Well, yes," Haase agreed. "Very expensive." He waved his cigarette in the air jauntily. "But, you know, when you want to have a really good time, price is no object."

"So you fellows bought train tickets to get to Corinth just to spend a night at Mrs. Belmont's?"

"Yeah. And it wasn't all that expensive, really, on account of Dave's dad is on the board of the Wabash, or something like that anyway, and he got us the tickets for free. And we'd been saving up for the trip, so it didn't set us back that much."

"I see. And this is Dave Enslin?"

"Yeah."

"All right. Now how long were you at Mrs. Belmont's? And did you go anywhere else in Corinth?"

"Now long? Hell, we weren't there any time at all."

"What do you mean?"

"I mean we got thrown out. We hadn't been there five minutes, and we were just waiting for the girls to come downstairs, when this woman comes in with this great big—ah—colored man. Meanest looking buck I've ever seen, scars all over his face. And they threw us out."

St. Louis

"I'm not so sure the cops are working very hard at finding out who killed your pal," Harris said. He had his cigar going, and it left a plume of smoke behind him as he walked along the sidewalk.

"This Marconi said he and some other detectives have been working on it," Buckner said. He and Dutton followed Harris through the heavy traffic, weaving their way through the tangle of vehicles and jostling pedestrians.

"He may think he's been assigned, I don't know about that," Harris shouted over his shoulder. "But nobody's turned up anything so far. Besides, the new chief's coming down hard on the gangs, says he's gonna clean 'em out."

"I may have something on that," Dutton said.

"Hang on a second." Harris stopped at a corner. A large truck, too big to make the sharp turn into Miller from Third, had blocked both streets in both directions. Autos and pushcarts and other trucks sat stalled while their drivers shouted and cursed and waved useless fists. Pedestrians worked their way through and around. Harris turned west for Broadway. Dutton and Buckner hurried to catch up.

"The other thing going on here," Harris continued. "Is that your friend Morris wasn't all that popular with a lot of guys on the force. For one, the papers, your sister's included, made him out the big hero when they busted up Reagan's Rats, and some of the boys figure they did as much work as Morris did but he got all the credit. So there's that. And he's been known to turn in other cops, report them for stuff they thought was pretty small potatoes, penny-ante stuff. Usually nothing happened to them, but they resented it. And then there's his reputation with other guys' wives."

"That came up at the wake," Buckner said. He asked Dutton, "What did you find out?"

"Not a lot. But whatever Marty's been working on with Johnny Morris, it was bigger than free lunches."

"Did you find out what?"

"No, not exactly. Mostly rumors. Nothing solid."

"About what?" Buckner insisted.

"Hold it a minute," Dutton said, grabbing Buckner's sleeve and stopping him. "I don't want to be shouting this on the street."

"All right." Buckner stopped. Harris, noticing he was no longer leading the parade, also stopped.

"There's a rumor going around about a bunch of cops going into business for themselves," Dutton said.

People pushed past them, muttering curses. Harris pulled the other two over against a store window displaying electrical fixtures, fans, toasters, percolators, all in bright metal.

"What, exactly. Bootlegging?" Harris asked.

"I'm not sure what it means," Dutton said. "But there's a fellow going to talk to me tonight about it. You can come along if you want."

"Not me," Harris said, and resumed walking. "I got business."

"I'm in," Buckner said. He and Dutton moved along, keeping up. "Do either of you know anything about this deputy mayor, Hanley, that got killed in an auto accident?"

"Not much," Harris admitted. "Just what I read in the papers. He was heading up this crime commission, working with the new chief to break up the gangs, crack down on the violence, close the speaks. Morris was one of the lead investigators."

"So anybody wanting to stop the commission's work had a pretty good reason to go after Hanley and Morris both," Dutton said.

"Yeah, sure."

Harris angled suddenly into a small shop. A man in a black satin kippah stood behind a counter, engulfed in heavy smoke and the dense, almost palpable smell of tobacco. The counter, glass-topped, held large jars of tobacco and cigars. Shelving behind the counter held more, plus cigarettes, lighters, papers, and matches. At the back of the shop, men stood smoking. A rack of magazines with titles like *Pep!* and *Spicy!* and *Wow!*, along with the more sedate *Black Mask*, and *Ace High*, took up one entire wall. Occasionally one of the smokers would take one down, flip it open, and replace it after a quick scan, only to pick up another.

The man in the kippah watched them suspiciously.

"But there's gotta be plenty of guys in town fit that description," Harris continued. "And, like I said, that commission hasn't been making much noise lately."

"Well, somebody still takes it seriously. Maybe seriously enough to kill Johnny, and to try to kill my sister. Serious enough to try again last night."

"What? Last night?"

Buckner told them about his visitor. As he talked, the man behind the counter, without a word, handed Harris a box of Judge's Cave cigars. Harris handed him money and turned for the door. The three of them stepped out into the relatively cleaner air of Broadway.

"You gotta admit," Harris said. "You've made a few enemies over the years. There's fellas in this town remember real clear what happened when they tried to move in down there in Highland County. I expect some of them you killed down there got kin up here and would be happy to take a shot at you, should the opportunity arise."

"I suppose that's true," Buckner said.

"Of course it's true," Dutton said. "But would they know he was in town, or recognize him on the street? I doubt it. No, it sounds to me like whoever killed Morris and took a shot at Marty in the alley the other night was just trying to finish the job at her place last night. It was where he expected to find her, instead he found you, loaded for bear."

"Seems obvious to me we have to find out who's out to kill my sister."

"Yeah," Harris said. "But you've given me an idea. There's a couple guys I know that're pretty well-connected. Maybe we could pay them a visit, see if any of your Sicilian friends are gunning for you."

"All right," Buckner said. "When?"

"Now's as good a time as any."

"Where?" Dutton asked.

"I know for sure where one of them is. Not far from here," Harris said. "Only take a few minutes. You got someplace important you gotta be?"

"Not at the moment."

"He reliable?" Dutton asked. "Is he going to know anything worthwhile?"

"If somebody's painted a bullseye on her back, or yours, this guy'll know it."

"Let's go, then."

Harris led them north, paralleling the river, moving quickly, the other two hurrying behind. Thirty minutes of this took them to a narrow street of boarded up windows and locked doors. Harris stopped at one and banged on it. When nothing happened, he banged again.

A door on the opposite side of the street cracked open slightly.

"Yeah?"

"Open up," Harris said. "It's me."

"So?"

"So I just wanna talk to Ed."

"Who's your friends?"

"Nobody at all. I just need to talk to Ed."

The door closed. Nothing happened for several minutes, then it opened and a man in a black suit and bowler hat emerged. He crossed the narrow street and unlocked the door. He returned the way he had come.

"You're on your own, Harris," he said, closing the door behind him.

Harris tossed his cigar into the street and pushed open the now unlocked door. The three men walked in.

It was just a pool hall. Four tables under low hanging lamps that illuminated the tabletops and little more. Men smoked and played pool and chatted quietly. They glanced in the direction of the newcomers and quickly returned to their games and their conversations.

Harris continued to the back of the room, where men sat on tall stools and watched the games. He stopped in front of a man in a dark suit and bow tie, thick, graying hair curving over one eye, a thick black moustache hiding his mouth, from which protruded a fat cigar butt.

"Got a minute, Ed?" Harris said.

Ed did not answer, only leaned slightly to one side to watch the pool tables around Harris's bulk.

"No games, Ed," Harris said softly. "I just need to talk to you for a minute."

Ed did not move.

Harris tucked his box of cigars under one arm, grabbed Ed by the back of his collar, jerked him off his stool, and began marching him in the direction of the door. When a man with a pool cue raised over his head moved to block him, Dutton took it away and jammed the butt of it into the man's face. He staggered back, his hand going under his jacket. Dutton's left hand suddenly held one of his ivory handled revolvers.

"Go on," Dutton said, smiling. "Go for it."

The man's hand dropped to his side. He muttered dark curses.

"You two through fooling around?" Harris called from the open doorway.

Buckner's .38 was down by his leg, pointed at the floor. The men around the pool tables watched him closely but did nothing else. Dutton tossed the pool cue onto the table, scattering balls, and joined Harris at the door. They went through. Buckner, walking backwards, his pistol still pointed at the floor, followed them out and closed the door behind him.

Harris had his man up against the wall, and with one hand, lifted him by his shirt collar until his feet brushed the ground.

"Tell me again, Ed, that there's nobody in town would have an interest in gunning down Johnny Morris."

"You gonna hit me again?" Ed bleated.

"That was just a love tap, Ed. You'll know for sure when I hit you." Harris laughed. "Keep talking."

"Look, there's plenty of guys was glad to see Morris go down, but if one of them took him down, I haven't heard anything about it. Honest."

Buckner watched as Harris eased Ed to his feet.

"What about his work on the crime commission?" he asked.

"Hell, nobody's afraid of those guys since Hanley crashed his motor. He was the juice on the commission." Ed added hurriedly, "But I never heard nothing about that, either. Story was he had a woman out that way that he visited now and then. Everybody says he just drove off the road one night."

"What about the *Post's* crime reporter?" Dutton asked.

"You mean that girl? Hell, nobody's afraid of her either, believe me."

"All right, Ed," Harris said. "One last thing. What do you know about a bunch of cops running a little side operation?"

For the first time in the conversation, Ed looked scared. He clamped his mouth tight and shook his head.

"Nothing," he said softly. "Nothing at all."

"Ed?" Harris said, tightening his grip on Ed's collar. He too spoke softly. "Don't be holding out on me now. We been friends too long."

"Listen," Ed whispered urgently. "You wanna keep clear of that. I ain't fooling."

"So you have heard something," Buckner said.

"What I've heard is that I wanna live a long, quiet life," Ed insisted, still speaking softly. "And the best way to do that is keep my mouth shut about…about…whatever it is you're talking about."

"So there is something to that," Buckner said.

"You can pound on me till I'm black and blue, but you ain't never gonna hear a word from me about those boys. No offense, Harris, but they scare me more than you and your friends here."

Harris sighed and released his grip. He spun Ed around and shoved him toward the street. "Go carefully, Ed, cause if I hear you been handing me a line, I'll find you. You know I will."

"Go to hell," Ed shouted over his shoulder. And started running.

Nobody chased him.

"That was no help at all," Dutton said.

Harris shrugged. "Tells us a bunch of stuff we already knew." He opened his box of fresh cigars, took one out and lighted it.

"Look," Buckner said. "I don't care what your friend Ed there said. It seems clear to me somebody's out to get my sister, and right now that bunch of rogue cops look like the candidates for the job."

"Well, I sure as hell can't keep hiding her forever at my place. She's no trouble, helps the wife, the kids love her. Ruthie thinks she hung the moon. Big-shot girl reporter, short hair, shorter skirts, all that. But she's getting restless. Says we're keeping her in prison, keeping her from getting her work done."

"I'll talk to her," Buckner said.

"Why don't you let me try it first?" Dutton said. "Her natural reaction to your advice is to do the exact opposite."

"Fine," Buckner grumbled.

He remained furiously puzzled about what was going on between Elroy Dutton and his sister. It didn't matter how many times he asked her, the reply was always a sharp suggestion he mind his own damned business.

"Fine," he said. "You talk to her. And when are we meeting this contact of yours?"

"Tonight."

"What about you?" Buckner asked Harris.

"I run a business. I gotta work to support my family. Your sister's paying me rent, despite what my wife told her, but I have to work. Unless one of you wants to hire me, I'm really not in a position to do much more."

"All right, I'll hire you," Dutton said. He took out a wallet.

"It'll cost you five dollars a day and expenses. What are you hiring me to do?"

"Keep an eye on Martha Jane Buckner."

"I thought you meant investigate who's trying to kill her. Hell, I'm no bodyguard. And she don't like me all that much anyway, mostly just puts up with me."

"Go home," Dutton said. "Make an excuse. And try to keep her there. That won't be easy. And if she absolutely has to go out, tag along. Keep her safe."

"Jesus, you don't want much."

"But I will pay you." Dutton handed Harris two ten dollar bills.

"She's my sister," Buckner said, and he took out his own money. He peeled two tens off his roll and handed them to Harris. "There. That should cover the time she's been hiding out with you up to now. If we can't get this cleared up in the next couple days, we'll have to come up with something else. Maybe she'll have to leave town for good."

"Then we better get to it," Dutton said. "Because I don't want to be the one has to tell her that."

"All right," Buckner continued. "I want to take a quick look at this road accident that killed the deputy mayor. The fact that he and Johnny wound up dead just strikes me as too convenient. Anyplace around here I can hire a car for the day?"

"Sure." Harris gave him directions. "I guess I'll lock up and go on home, since all of a sudden I'm rolling in money."

Buckner glanced at his watch, then at Dutton.

"It's too late to look into that car crash. Let's go talk to this cop."

CORINTH

"You threw them out?" Shotwell was writing in his notebook.

"Oh, yes, Officer," said Mrs. Belmont.

"Why?"

"They were drunk, rude, loud, and thoroughly unpleasant. Four young men in nice clothes with a lot of money who thought that gave them carte blanche. It did not. They were pounding on my new Bechstein. I couldn't have that."

"Bechstein?"

Mrs. Belmont drew back the burgundy red curtain that hung in the archway to the left. When Shotwell hesitated, she led him in. It was laid out like a living room, a very ornate living room, with the same deep red carpet as the foyer. Elegant armchairs and a pink satin sofa lined the walls under discreetly suggestive drawings of young women in various stages of undress artfully entwined with each other. A piano took up most of one corner, giving the room an odd domesticity.

"Bechstein," Mrs. Belmont said.

"Bechstein." Shotwell copied down the name.

"Isaac had to show them out."

"All four of them? Did they give you any trouble at all?"

"They was pretty drunk," Isaac said. "They wasn't no trouble at all."

"Do you know where they went after leaving here?"

"They were talking about going on to Dutton's," Mrs. Belmont said.

Shotwell thanked them both and left.

A small red brick church stood across the dirt road from Mrs. Belmont's. It had the same green shutters and doors as Mrs. Belmont's. Both had originally been built as homes by the same man at the same time many years before, a major share-holder in the Iron Mountain Railroad who wanted to keep a close eye on his investment. When the Missouri Pacific bought the Iron Mountain, the man had sold out and moved on. If it had amused him to see one house become a brothel and the other a church, nobody ever heard. The windows in this building were now decorated with brightly colored paper cut out to resemble stained glass. They would effectively prevent anyone inside from looking out at the nearly identical building opposite, while reducing the likelihood of anyone mistaking the one for the other. This building an African Methodist Episcopal church. Shotwell was a Baptist, but he certainly knew the woman who came through the church's front door and turned in his direction. And she knew him.

"Good day, Miz Da Silva," he said from the top of Mrs. Belmont's steps, tipping his uniform cap politely.

Mrs. Da Silva nodded curtly, her face glowing with righteousness.

Shotwell thought briefly about trying to explain what he was doing at Mrs. Belmont's and decided there was no point. As he descended the steps and turned east, heading for Dutton's, Mrs. Da Silva crossed to the other side of the road, clipping along, keeping up with him, watching him intently. When Shotwell turned into the barbershop, she stopped, nodded grimly to herself, and walked on.

Shotwell decided he, and more likely Augusta, would have some explaining to do.

Fleming Gaylord sat at his ease in the barber chair. He got up when Shotwell entered.

"Don't believe I've ever seen you in here before," he said.

"Strictly business, Mr. Gaylord."

"Oh, I know that. It way too early to go upstairs."

"You know I'm here on business, Mr. Gaylord."

"Yes, sir. I do."

Shotwell asked about four young white boys, noticeably drunk. Gaylord knodded.

"Mist' Elroy don't like folks like that coming in. We keeps a nice, quiet place here."

"And Mr. Dutton doesn't like having his customers disturbed."

"That's right. Bad for business. So those boys never got past the door."

"Did they give you any trouble?"

"Well, couple of 'em thought they might like to try. But I showed 'em the shotgun and they decided to go someplace else."

"Did they say where they were going?"

"Not where I could hear, no, sir."

"All right. Thank you, Mr. Gaylord."

Shotwell returned to the street. He knew of small drinking establishments on this side of the tracks, but he guessed the white boys with money to burn would want someplace more stylish. He turned west, headed for The Corinthian, the town's best hotel, which also housed a very nice, very quiet little saloon in the basement.

Columbia

"A shotgun?" Michael Mullen said.

"Yeah. What kind of town you got down there? We've been hearing about Corinth ever since we got to school here. Hell, I'm from Sikeston, and I'd already heard about it. About how it's a wide-open town, you could do anything down there if you had the money. But, hell, it wasn't like that at all. Niggers running things."

"That's enough of that," Mullen snapped. He'd grown up with that word but his boss wouldn't tolerate it, said only white trash used it. That was enough for Mullen.

When the young man stared at him in disgust, Mullen continued. "Where did you go after you got run out of the barber shop?"

"We tried a couple of places, wound up at a joint called The Corinthian, but it wasn't so much either. There were whole families in there, children, people singing, having a rare old time. But not the sort of fun we were looking for, so we had a couple of drinks and moved on." Haase stopped a moment. "But you never said what happened to Bill. He's dead?"

"Yes. He died of alcohol poisoning."

"Alcohol poisoning? Goddammit," Haase said. "But how the hell did he—oh, I know. Hell, I told him. I warned him."

"You'll have to stop cursing in the house, Brother Haase," Craig said. "You know that's not permitted."

"Yes. Of course, Brother Craig. I'm sorry. But I warned him not to buy that stuff."

"What stuff?" Mullen asked.

"This was going to be our big weekend before we had to start cramming for finals," Haase explained. "We had it all planned out, got the tickets, saved our money, like I said. All planned out. We'd even lined up the booze." Haase stopped suddenly. "Say, you're not a revenuer or anything like that, are you?"

"No. I'm a police officer investigating a suspicious death," Mullen said. His voice tightened as his patience slipped away. "Tell me about the booze."

"That's what I'm saying. We stocked up on the good stuff. Stan's dad, uh, he knows some people, and he told us how we could get hold of some really good Canadian. So we did. But Bill likes to drink." Haase stopped for a moment. "I mean, he liked to drink. Anyway, he ran through most of his share of the Canadian before we got to Corinth. And he was sitting there, moaning about running out when the trip was just starting. And he was pestering everybody to give him a drink, and nobody would, and then this conductor came by and told us he might be able to help us out."

"What conductor? Which line? Wabash or Iron Mountain?"

"Iron Mountain?"

"Missouri-Pacific," Mullen corrected.

"Oh. Missouri-Pacific. It was after we pulled out of St. Louis."

"All right. Anyway, he said he could help us out, and Bill said OK, and he bought a bottle from him."

"Did any of the rest of you buy from the conductor?"

"Hell no. I mean, no, sir, we did not. I took a sniff of it, and it was pretty rank, so the rest of us never touched it. Besides, we still had our Canadian. And we were told the stuff we'd find in Corinth was OK, too."

"But Lance drank it?"

"Yeah. Drank it slow, though, through the rest of the day, but he certainly finished that off, too."

"Then what happened? After you had finished your tour of Corinth's speakeasies?" Mullen didn't bother to hide the disapproval in his voice.

"Well, uh, we left The Corinthian and found a couple more places, here and there, you know. And the booze was OK, but there was nothing going on. I mean, after all we heard about that town of yours, it's really boring. There's nothing going on there at all. No fun, no girls. We just wasted our money."

"Too bad," Mullen said. "It may have been more exciting a few years ago, but nowadays we work pretty hard to keep it as boring as we can."

Mullen certainly knew the stories about Corinth back in those early boomtown years of lead mining when diamond-bitted drills, financed by big corporations in New York and London, had dug millions of dollars of lead from the region, made Corinth famous, and gave the whole region the name Lead Belt. Mrs. Belmont and Sheriff Bushyhead were products of that era. Buckner had replaced Bushyhead, and he tolerated Mrs. Belmont. But he worked hard at keeping Corinth quiet. If folks wanted to drink and fool around, that was their affair, as long as they kept it to themselves. His attitude was now department doctrine.

"Be sure to tell your friends that," Mullen went on. "Don't bother coming down there looking for fun, you'll just be disappointed. Now finish your story. What happened to your friend?"

"Well, we were all pretty drunk by that time, still moving along all right, but Bill said he wanted to find some more booze. We told him we were gonna be late for the train. We tried to get him to come with us, but he wouldn't. Flat refused. Started waving his arms around, claiming we weren't having any fun."

"What did you do?"

"We did what we had to do to catch the train. It's a long damn ride."

Mullen agreed with that.

"So you left him."

"He wouldn't move, dammit, that's what I'm telling you. We figured he'd be all right, maybe find someplace to sleep it off, catch the train back in the morning."

"Wait a minute," Mullen said. "Wasn't it raining that night?"

"Could've been." Haase shrugged. "I was pretty drunk, like I said."

"It was cold, too."

"If you say so."

"All right. Just so I have this straight, you left your friend in a strange town in the middle of a cold, rainy night and came back here. I have to ask, though: how could you do that?"

"Well," Haase said, cranky at Mullen's failure to get the point. "We had to get back."

"All right," Mullen said. "What can you tell me about the conductor that sold you the liquor?"

"Uh, he had a nameplate on his jacket, I remember that, because it was a pretty funny name. Pinch. His name was Pinch." Haase laughed to show how funny it was. "Bill even made a joke about it, getting pinched for buying booze from Pinch."

"Fine," Mullen said. "Thanks. Now, I will need to confirm William Lance's home address, his parents' name, all that."

"I'm not sure we are allowed to give you that," Craig said.

Mullen gritted his teeth and said, "Someone has to inform William Lance's next of kin, his mother and father, that he is dead and how he died. That is something I figured was part of my job, but if you want to do it instead, as recording secretary of this little boys' club of yours, tell them some of your 'brothers' left him to die in an alley, go right ahead. I'd be glad to turn that over to you."

"It is a fraternity," Craig said stiffly. "A brotherhood of gentlemen and scholars and athletes committed to service to the University Community. And I think you ought to do your job and take care of that yourself." And he got up and walked out.

Mullen, glowering, turned to Haase, who fidgeted uncomfortably, finally gesturing for Mullen's notebook. Mullen handed it over, along with his pencil. Haase scribbled it in and handed both back. There was an address and a telephone number.

"Thanks," Mullen said. He had already gotten the address from Mrs. Doddy, but compelling this smug boy to hand it over left Mullen satisfied.

He put the notebook and pencil away and went out, crossing the campus quickly and heading for the center of town. A telegraph office stood next to the Wabash station and Mullen went in.

St. Louis

They took a streetcar downtown, got off, and walked the last few blocks. Commercial Street was practically in the Mississippi. If the water kept rising, it soon would be.

A rooming house huddled on the corner of Mound. It was a two-story wood building amid the usual brick warehouses and businesses. It leaned precariously toward the water, an aging and tattered drunk about to topple over. Light came from one half-shaded window on an upper floor, a single half-closed eye.

The few people on the street seemed concentrated on their own affairs, studiously avoiding eye contact with anybody, keeping to shadows.

Dutton led the way through the door and straight up the flight of stairs that shared the entryway with a corridor leading straight back. Tiny bulbs barely illuminated four doors opening off a central hallway that ended in a window. Buckner could see the skeleton of a fire-escape just beyond.

The building smelled of boiled cabbage and tobacco smoke. Buckner could hear muttered voices and cushioned footsteps.

Dutton knocked on a door. It opened a crack. A single eyes inspected them.

Buckner looked down and saw a second eye, the barrel of a pistol, staring at them as well.

"You Dutton?" a soft voice asked.

"Yes."

"Nobody said nuthin' 'bout no comp'ny."

"I'll answer for him."

The door opened wider, and Dutton and Buckner stepped in slowly. A black man holding an automatic pistol closed and locked the door behind them, keeping the pistol tucked up tight against his hip, pointed in their direction the whole time. He nodded toward a lumpy gray sofa against a blank wall.

"Set over there."

Buckner and Dutton sat. The sofa's springs must have expired long ago, because the two men sank deeply into the cushions. Buckner decided that was probably the point, since it made it difficult to get up out of the sofa quickly. When the man with the pistol sat opposite them, a full eight feet away, in a ladder-back chair with no padding at all, he was sure of it.

Buckner could see two doors leading off the room. Both were closed, but light showed under one of them. He wondered if someone waited behind it. Two windows looked at a blank wall a few yards away. Last year's calendar hung between the windows. It assured you Fireman's Insurance was the best you could buy.

A single lamp lit the sofa and the men sitting on it. The light did not reach the man in the chair, but it did illuminate the pistol.

"This is Earl Reeves," Dutton said. "He's a sergeant out of District One."

"First, and so far the only, Negro sergeant in the department," Reeves said. He continued pointing the pistol at them. "There's a couple young fellers coming up behind me, but I got there first."

"Congratulations," Buckner said. "Why are we here? Are you going to tell us something useful, or just wave that .38 at us?"

"Right to business," Reeves said. "I likes that."

"Yes, my sister's life is in danger. So let's get on with it." Buckner told him Marty's version of what happened it the alley.

"Sure. You figure whoever killed Johnny Morris is after her, too."

"Yes. Whoever it was took a shot at her in that alley later came by her place to try to finish the job. My sister's hard to get along with, but I can't think there's two people in this town that want to kill her."

"I expect you're right," Reeves said. "What happened at her place?"

"Bumped into me instead."

"You get him?"

"Nicked him. Got the pistol, if there's any prints."

"Huh." The man with the pistol sneered. "Gotta have somebody on record to compare with."

"I'm not here to discuss proper procedure," Buckner said. "Why was Johnny killed? And is my sister a target because she just happened to be in that alley and the killer wants to clean up loose ends? Or is she involved in this for some other reason?"

"I can't say for sure about that," Reeves said. "But I'd guess it got something to do with what Johnny was working on."

"The crime commission," Dutton said.

"Part of it, yeah," Reeves said. He leaned back in the chair. The pistol's empty eye remained focused on Buckner. "See, a while back, we had some serious gang wars around here, make what's going on now look like a Sunday school picnic. The Irish and the Jews was on top, and the Italians and the coloreds was coming up fast. There was lots of killing going on. And then, in the middle of all this, and it's only been a year or so now, there's these guys that do killings for hire."

"A new gang trying to move in?" Dutton asked.

"No. They don't want a piece of the gambling, nor the booze, nor the whores. They work for cash money. They charge a lot, and they get it, 'cause they got the edge."

"Which is what?"

"They's police."

"Police officers operating their own murder squad?"

Reeves nodded.

"The rest of the department know about this? Does anybody know about this?"

"Sure, but, long as they was only killing crooks, nobody minded much. Doing us all a favor, far as most folks was concerned, so nobody's looking too close."

"Do they know who these officers are?"

"Oh, some do, yes. Lots more think they do, but they's wrong. Anyway, ain't nobody willing to say anything public about these fellers at all. It's just too damned dangerous."

"But if they're just killing criminals, why do you think they killed Johnny and tried to kill my sister?"

"I don't know what that was about. Honest," Reeves said. "What I know for sure, Deputy Mayor Hanley found out about this murder squad, and he had Morris looking into it. He knew Morris from before, when they busted up the Reagan gang, and he asked for him to be assigned to this new crime commission the chief's put together."

"So Hanley asked Johnny to look into the gang of cops killing for hire and they found out about it, and they killed Johnny for that, and my sister just happened to be in the wrong place at the wrong time."

"I'm telling you, I don't know about that," Reeves said. "For sure, Morris and Hanley was gathering evidence, gonna arrest these cops, bring them to trial, and get them convicted and sent to Jeff City for a good long spell. Then Hanley was killed in a car crash out in the County. Whether these boys is behind Hanley's car wreck and now that shooting in the alley, I just can't say. They ain't no evidence either way."

"Well," Buckner insister. "If the department's serious about that murder squad, they're going to have to start all over now that Hanley and Johnny Morris are dead."

"Yeah. They sure who these fellas are, but they can't move against them without rock solid evidence, and that's been hard to come by, 'cause they's cops and they know how to play that game. And, like I said, lotsa folks, including a lot of cops, figure these boys just doing us all a favor. What I don't get though, is what you think you gonna do. These is mighty rough boys, and they just as soon shoot you as look at you. Specially you." Reeves aimed the pistol directly at Dutton.

"Who are they?" Buckner asked. "What are their names and where are they stationed?"

"You gonna take them on by yourself?"

"He's not by himself," Dutton pointed out.

"Huh. Well, suit yourselves. They's all vets, served over in France. 'Cept for Pitaluga; he was too young. The jab him about that. Anyway, the man in charge is Lieutenant Thomas Kane, called Candy, but not to his face."

"I'd bet not," Buckner said.

"Then there's 'Shorty' Werner, Sergeant Daniel Werner. The rest are Arthur Pitaluga, Bernie Runge, and Robert McKinney, known as Red. All detectives."

"What district?"

"Kane's out of the Seventh. Pitaluga and Werner's at the Second. The others kind of scatter around."

"How'd they get into this line of work?"

"Hell, I don't know. Easy money, I guess."

"So they kill by special arrangement, like a contract?"

"Well, not on paper. But, yeah, I think they seen a situation where the gangs sometimes needed outside help, and they offered it. I hear the

Italians and the colored gangs use them most, cause they're the new boys on the block, might need a little help getting a leg up. These fellas are supposed to be pretty expensive, but if you can afford them, they's the best, on account of there's no comeback, no chance the Department's gonna get into it. And since they just been killing folks that's criminals, well, any investigation just chalks it off to the usual gang stuff."

"Except the Hanley killing."

"If he was killed," Reeves corrected. "You gotta know he was supposed to be a drinking man, so it could'a been a accident. And rumor was he had a little bit on the side out that way."

"Well, Johnny Morris was no accident."

"True. If they's the ones did it. Thing is, these guys are good. They know how to cover their tracks. And this Morris shooting just don't sound like them. Sounds sloppy." Reeves leaned forward. There was urgency in his voice. "Look, this been a couple tough years. The gangs been busy, they got organization, they got plenty of firepower, Thompsons, scatterguns, you name it, and they killed a bunch of cops, more in the past couple years than in the Department's whole history. So, honest, this bunch of cops going out on they own, most cops ain't gonna say too much about it."

"As long as they kill the right people," Dutton said.

"Yeah," Buckner agreed. "Only now it looks like they've killed a deputy mayor and a police officer. And when they went after my sister, that made them fair game. For me. Cops or no cops."

"That's how you figure it?"

"That's how I figure it."

"You best be sure on that. You might wanna think real hard before taking them on," Reeves insisted. "Might be best you take your sister and get on back down where you come from."

"I've been hearing that since I got up here, Sergeant. And if I thought it would do any good, I'd've done it already." Buckner pulled himself up out of the sofa's close embrace. The barrel of the pistol followed him up. "Thanks for your help."

Dutton also stood.

"You keep my name out of anything at all," Reeves said. He was on his feet now and moving to a corner of the room, giving Buckner and Dutton plenty of room to get to the door. The pistol never wavered.

"Thanks," Dutton said.

"Uh—huh. Just keep me out of it."

At the bottom of the stairs, Dutton held up a hand.

"I'll go first and head north. Give me five minutes, then you head west for Marty's place."

"You'll be at your cousin's?"

"Yes. And remember, someone took a shot at you last night."

"Don't worry. I'll be sure to lock the door tight and keep sleep with one eye open."

*

Dutton disappeared through the doorway. Buckner waited. He waited a long time, counting in his head, watching the street. Finally, reaching a slow one hundred, he stepped through the door. The street was completely empty now, still, dark, the infrequent street lights glowing feebly. Buckner could feel every nerve vibrating. He hesitated, measuring his breathing, looking, waiting. Then he moved. Along Mound quickly, heading for First Street.

As he reached the corner, a large black auto lurched to a stop just in front of him and four men jumped out. One struck him hard in the stomach, knocking the wind out of him, doubling him over, and another man tapped him on the head with something hard as he fell. The four men then scooped him up and heaved him onto the floor in the back of the auto. One of them sat on him while the others got in. The car drove off. Hands groped until they found his pistols and took them from him.

Buckner, gasping to catch his breath, and dizzy from the blow on his head, tried to shift his weight. This elicited only a growled "Be still." So he lay still and breathed carefully.

The car took many turns in the next five minutes before finally pulling to a stop. One of the men got out. A door rumbled heavily open, and the car moved ahead a short distance before stopping. The driver killed the engine and door rumbled shut.

"You gonna behave?" a voice asked.

"Do I have a choice?"

"Not really."

The man got off slowly, making sure to grind knees and elbows into Buckner on the way. Then he got out and waited expectantly, fists clenched tight, while Buckner sat up and got out. As he brushed himself off, he watched a short, gray-faced little man in a vested suit and brown hat step forward. He wore a yellow bowtie.

The little man watched Buckner in return, frowning slightly, curious, saying nothing. The four men, in long, dark coats, hats shadowing their face, fanned out behind him.

They were in a large room, bare except for empty wooden orange crates stacked high along one wall. Bright labels displayed the beauties of Florida. A half-dozen shaded lamps on long cords hung from a high ceiling, casting circles of light on the dusty concrete floor. The auto they had just exited was a big Moon touring model.

"Like it?" the gray-faced man asked. "Got eight cylinders and goes like a bat out of hell. Got it right off the factory floor not a month ago."

Moon was a St. Louis company.

"Comfortable," Buckner said. "Spacious. Convenient for kidnapping. Floor smells like somebody got awful sick back there."

"Damned right," the man said. "First arrest I made in the thing, the guy was so hyped up on rotgut, he puked all over the place. Brand new upholstery and everything. But don't worry, you ain't been kidnapped. We just need to have a little chat, you and me."

"And the four horsemen of the Apocalypse there?"

The man laughed and held out his hand.

"I'm Sweeney. Mike Sweeney. Lieutenant Mike Sweeney, to be exact. St. Louis Police Department."

"I'm—"

"I know who you are," Sweeney interrupted. "I saw you at Johnny Morris's wake. You're chief of police down in Athens, or maybe it's Sparta, somewhere in the Lead Belt."

"Corinth."

"Right," Sweeney said, indifferent to this information. He continued. "You're up here to rescue your little sister, Martha Jane Buckner, ace girl reporter for the *Post-Dispatch*, who somebody took a shot at the other night while she was sticking her nose where it don't belong. Now you're up here doing the same thing. Must run in the family."

"Family runs in the family," Buckner said. "And until I'm satisfied my sister is safe, I'm here taking care of it. And if I have to, I'll make a couple of telephone calls to make sure I stay here until the job is done."

"On account of you got an uncle that's a judge. Yeah, I know all about that, too. That's how you got your colored friend out of jail yesterday, using that letter from him. But believe you me, even the judge himself won't be able to save your ass if I decide it's time for you to leave. Which I have just about done. You and Dutton both. What the hell, I could arrest him right now on a half dozen charges, and he'd rot in jail waiting for a trial date, you can be damned sure of that. Federal charges for real, too. Do you have any idea of the kinds of operations he's got his fingers in?"

"Sure, sure. But he keeps his nose clean in my town."

"Just booze and gambling. Maybe that don't matter in your town. But you're in my town now, and you are interfering with my investigation. You are consorting with a known criminal, carrying concealed weapons in my town without a permit. In the long run, you might be able to dodge jail time, but you and the judge and all the rest of your kinfolk are gonna be pretty busy for a while, so the easiest way to save yourselves all that trouble is for you to go home. And take Dutton with you."

"What about my sister?"

"She's safe enough where she is. Harris can keep an eye on her, and if she stays out of sight for a while longer, until my investigation wraps up, she should be all right."

If he was surprised at the little man's depth of knowledge, Buckner didn't mention it.

"You'll have to excuse me," he said, "If I'm skeptical of your ability to keep her alive. There's a bunch of police officers in your town running a murder for hire racket, and I think they killed Johnny Morris and they're after my sister."

Sweeney was quiet for a while, just watching Buckner.

"So that's what you went to see Reeves about," he finally said.

"Who's Reeves?"

"Never mind. He's a good enough cop, hell, better than most or he wouldn't've made sergeant. But there's a lot of stuff going on he don't know about. As for those cops you mentioned, you really think I don't know what's going on in my town? In my Department? You think the Chief doesn't know? Christ, you must think we're as dumb as posts up here."

"As a matter of fact, I think pretty much everybody does know," Buckner said. "They just don't give a damn. Nobody cares as long as the hoodlums are killing each other and if a bunch of cops join in and start killing hoodlums, then that's all right, too. Just makes the good folks of St. Louis feel all the safer. But then Hanley and Morris started poking around, turning over rocks."

"Why the hell do you think they were poking around in the first place?" Sweeney said. He took off his hat and scratched his nearly bald head vigorously. He replaced the hat, pulling it down so that his eyes were just hard points of light glinting sharply under the brim. "Look, I'll keep this simple for you. The Chief knows all about it. And he put Hanley and Johnny, and me, to work on it. Us and my boys here, sort of a flying squad. A year ago this was. And it ain't been easy. A cop trying to put other cops in jail ain't gonna win no popularity contest, even if those cops are crooked as a dog's hind leg. Getting cops to swear to evidence, promise to testify, hell, even to give me the time of day, is damn near impossible."

"And it looks to me like they're still ahead of you. Hanley's dead, Johnny too, and they've targeted my sister. Hell, they even took a shot at me."

"When was this?" Sweeney demanded.

Buckner told him about the incident in his sister's apartment.

"What makes you think it was these boys?"

"I can't think of anybody else might want her dead. And I figure they were just cleaning up from the night before."

"You got any enemies in town?"

"None that know I'm here," Buckner said, sounding more certain than he felt.

"So, yeah, whoever it was probably was after her, not you," Sweeney said.

"I expect you're right. But, one way or another as long as my sister is in danger, I'm not leaving town. And I don't think Dutton feels any different. You can make life tough for us, run us in for minor violations of this or that. And it would be a nuisance, sure. But why don't you let us stick around, maybe attract some more attention from these boys? If they go after us, you might just be able to scoop them up before they do any real damage."

"Yeah, if I find them, in uniform, standing over your dead body with a smoking service revolver, that'd be interesting, all right. But they'd just claim they were doing their duty, and there you'd be, deader than hell."

"It might not turn out that way," Buckner said. "Anyway, what's it to you?"

"Right. What is it to me? And maybe that friend of yours will get himself killed at the same time."

"People have tried that before, including the Boche, and he's still walking around."

"Uh—huh. What exactly is it you think you're gonna do? Just so I have some idea of where to pick up the pieces."

"What I've been doing. Looking into the Hanley thing, see if anything comes of that.

But if you want to help me, there's one thing you might do. Tell me who Johnny worked with when they busted up the Reagan gang."

"Treasury people on that one. Very hush-hush."

"I thought it was Hoover's boys."

"Nah, they're not interested in bootleggers. Too busy sniffing out Reds. No, you want to talk to the Treasury people. They got Reagan and his pals on income tax, liquor tax evasion, Prohibition violations, that sort of thing. Revenuers doing their job."

"All right. I'll start there."

"They brought in people from Washington on that one. When it was done, most of them went back home. Fella to talk to is Casterman. Got an office in the Federal Building. He can probably tell you what Johnny's role was in that."

"I looks like I'm going to be around for a while, then," Buckner said.

"I guess," Sweeney conceded. "I don't have the manpower to assign people to keep an eye on you and your friend, so if things get dicey, you're gonna have to get in touch with me." Sweeney took out a notebook and pencil and scrawled quickly. "Here's a couple of phone numbers that ought to work."

Buckner looked at the paper, memorized the numbers, and handed it back.

Sweeney turned to his men. "Give him back his iron and let's get out of here."

In a moment, they had opened the big door and disappeared through it. Buckner holstered his weapons and left the same way, pulling the door closed behind him. He walked to the corner, which turned out to be Broadway and Cass, barely three blocks from where they had picked him up. A streetcar rattled to a stop a few minutes later, and Buckner rode it, the only passenger, to the Delmar Loop. From there he walked to his sister's apartment.

As he walked, he tried to sort out what had happened since he got into town. He had seen the St. Louis Police Department in various guises. The Eleventh District where Dutton had been held. The wake for Johnny Morris. The black sergeant scared of his colleagues. Sweeney and his mob.

He had come out of the army, US Army, Canadian army, but still army, a large, complex institution. He'd spent almost a decade in it, and it had fitted him nicely. He had been a good soldier. Then he became a policeman. The switch had been a shock because, though he had been a policeman now for a full ten years, he had always been part of small, simple organizations. Elmer Aubuchon's deputy in Corinth, where he worked alone, now chief of a tiny police department in the same town.

But even as chief of police, he was still a speck on the landscape of policing. His department was effective, efficient, it operated smoothly, handling the daily work of policing, with all the routine and boredom that implied. And he was proud of them. But they were all, himself included, very small time indeed.

And now he was caught up in something a whole lot bigger, a whole system, more like the army than his little department. Lots of different departments and different individuals pursuing their own ends within the larger thing that was the St. Louis Police Department. Somehow he was going to sort all that out.

As he climbed the stairs to his sister's floor, he realized he had missed dinner with Becca Wiezcek. Well, he had a pretty good excuse.

He slept undisturbed through what was left of the night.

The next morning, Buckner found the car-hire in a weathered board building the size of a coat closet, perched on the corner of a lot only slightly larger. A single auto sat there, a new Ford. A man in a suit, clean but well-worn, with a knit tie, sat on a high stool at a high desk. He had a newspaper folded to reveal a black and white grid, and he was writing letters in the white squares.

"That one of those puzzles?" Buckner asked.

"Yep. Been hooked on 'em for a while now." He stopped writing. "What can I do for you?"

"I'd like to rent your motor out there."

"Sure. Buck-fifty now and a buck-fifty if you bring it back by the end of today. Be another buck-fifty tomorrow morning."

"Right." Buckner gave the man money and walked over to the Ford. He looked inside and around and returned to the office. "Where's the crank?"

"Don't have to crank it. It's an A-Model. Got a starter motor. Button down there on the floor by your left foot. Just step on it."

"About time," Buckner said. "Everybody else's been putting them in for a while now."

"Well, old Henry J, he don't like to move too fast. They started rolling off the line couple years ago. They're even talking about bringing some out in different colors."

"That'll be the day."

"Sure. But starting one of those things ain't easy unless you know how." The man explained the process of starting a Model-A. "Just remember, once it's running, close the spark advance so it runs smooth."

"Sounds like it would be easier to crank it," Buckner said.

"I don't believe most folks would agree with you on that, especially the ladies."

"Have you got a map of St. Louis County I could take along? I've never been out that way before."

"There should be one in the glove box. City and county. It comes with the motor. And when you're done, just park it back here."

"Right. Thanks."

"Sure." The man looked at his newspaper. "Say, can you tell me two words for a Western Front battle, 1917? Nine letters. Third letter is an M."

"Vimy Ridge," Buckner said.

"Thanks."

Buckner sat in the auto and spent several minutes with the map before starting the engine. When it was running smoothly, he turned it toward the street. Just then, the man popped out of the doorway.

"Hey, that was the answer, all right. How'd you know?"

Buckner ignored him and pulled out into traffic. He drove west, then north, until he picked up Clayton Road and continued west into the county.

It wasn't all that long ago, was it? Maybe to some people. They took the ridge in April, but the Nivelle Offensive had collapsed by August and the poilus were refusing to attack. Buckner was long out of it by then, but the large, angry red mass of scar tissue that was most of the back of his leg was not likely to let him forget.

St. Louis County embraced the City of St. Louis to the north, south, and west. To the east was the Mississippi River and beyond that, Illinois. St. Louis, with a population under a million, would never acquire more acreage. Any new growth would have to be straight up.

The county was tree-lined streets and neat houses with carefully tended lawns that quickly gave way to farms and woods, crossroads with corner stores, gas stations still sharing space with blacksmith shops. When Buckner turned north onto Etherton Road, then onto Wild Horse Creek

Road, he might as well have been back home, driving the back roads of Highland County. Cattle gazed at him as he drove past. Fields lay muddy under the heavy gray sky, just waiting for sunlight to make them sprout green shoots. Houses, set well back from the road, showed smoke rising from chimneys.

Buckner had seen London and Paris during the war, Quebec and Montreal before shipping out. Over the years he had spent some time in St. Louis, visiting relatives, attending the weddings and funerals that gathered up the large clan, the in-laws, the second cousins once removed, people he never saw for any other reason. But he still felt lost in the city, disoriented. His sister seemed to have taken to it immediately. Marty, a new name for a new person? Anyway, a person who appeared a complete stranger to him, yet, simultaneously, completely familiar.

Out here, on this winding road with woods all around, familiar sights and smells and sounds, Buckner felt perfectly comfortable. Out here, he could find his way around with his eyes closed.

He had noted the crash site from the newspaper accounts, and with the help of the map, he found it easily. The scattered farms were open spaces amidst dense woods and thick underbrush. A long hill with a sharp left turn at the bottom before rising steeply again explained a lot. Mix in too much booze, add a blowout, and the whole think looked perfectly obvious. A stand of saplings recently sheared off near the ground marked the exact spot the car had gone off the road. Buckner pulled over.

The rain that had been intermittent all day had become a steady downpour. Buckner watched it from inside the Ford. When he decided it wasn't going to stop any time soon, he got out to have a look.

This place, at the bottom of a steep hill, surrounded by woods, seemed completely isolated, as though it was the bottom of a hole. Rain pattered on Buckner's hat and trench coat.

The auto was gone, of course, but he could easily see where it had come to rest. He looked around, not at all sure what he was looking for, and gave up after several minutes of finding nothing to attract his interest. He was walking back to the Ford when a car with a light on top and a star on the door came down the hill and stopped. A man wearing a deputy's badge and a large pistol prominent under a shining rain slicker got out.

"Help you?" he said. He stood with his feet braced apart, slicker pushed back and his hand on the butt of his pistol. He did not look like he wanted to help anybody.

"Just looking," Buckner said. He reached slowly into his shirt pocket and took out his own deputy sheriff's badge.

He had not been a deputy sheriff for five years, but he had kept the badge.

The St. Louis County deputy glanced at it.

"Uh—huh," the deputy said. He was not impressed. "You after anything in particular here?"

"No. Like I said, just looking." Buckner cast off from the truth. "Sheriff Aubuchon knew I was coming up this way to visit family in town, and he asked me to take a look on account of he knew the fella was killed here, knew him from a long ways back."

"Well, you've had your look."

"I heard he was drunk."

"Yeah. We got a telephone call, somebody driving by said there was a motor lying upside down on Wild Horse Creek Road, so I come on out and found it. He was dead as hell but still warm, so it couldn't've been too long before that he went off the road. Inside smelled of liquor, his clothes stunk of it." The deputy pointed up the hill. "We get one ever so now and then, folks coming down this hill too fast, the turn at the bottom surprises them."

"Who called it in?"

"Oh, I don't know. Didn't leave no name."

"According to the coroner, he died of a broken neck."

"I guess."

"Where'd the auto end up?"

"Junk yard. Wasn't no fixing that up after what it'd been through. Axel bent all to hell." The deputy pointed again. "We must've been going pretty fast. You can see how far off the road he came."

"Tire blew out?"

"That's how it looked. Anyway, him drunk, at that speed, he just lost control, the thing flipped over, looked to have rolled once at least, wound up with him over in the back seat."

"All right. Thanks. I'll tell Aubuchon."

"He must be getting on by now." The deputy thought a moment. "Say, I thought he retired."

"Yeah, he did. He just wanted to know about this fellow. Says everybody he knows are all dead now, friends and enemies both. I think that's why he wanted me to check on what happened here. Says he's going to be the last one left."

"Uh—huh."

"Thanks again."

Buckner got into his Model A, started it up, and drove up the hill past the deputy's vehicle while the deputy watched him leave. As he got to the top of the hill, Buckner realized not a single car had passed them the whole time they were talking. Not a well-traveled road, then, though the rain might be keeping people indoors. He wondered how much traffic it got at night. He also wondered what the deputy mayor was doing way out here in the first place, whether the rumors that he had a woman out this way might be true.

As Buckner neared the junction of Wild Horse Creek Road and Ossenfort Road a big Model A Ford, identical to the one he was driving, roared from out of nowhere, aiming straight for him. He braked and swerved off the road as the other vehicle swept past. The driver, face distorted with rage, shouted and waved a fist and was gone.

Buckner sat for a moment. The other vehicle had come from a nearly invisible dirt road that led to a large two story house barely visible through the trees. He could see a woman standing on the porch. After a moment, she disappeared inside.

Buckner looked at the map, then backed carefully onto the road and continued to the junction, turning left onto Ossenfort Road.

He turned south at the county road and then back the way he had come, watching both sides of the road carefully. The first place he found was no help, but the man working there told him where he could find two more. He found what he was looking for on the third try. It was a field packed with motor vehicles in various stages of collapse, laid out in long rows accessible by dirt paths, a field of catastrophes and failures. Buckner had never seen so many different kinds all in one place. Some looked undamaged, some were barely recognizable as autos, looking more like shapeless balls of crumpled, rusting metal. Fields of corn stubble surrounded them on three sides. These, Buckner suspected, would soon be filled with more rows of destroyed automobiles.

Buckner drove up to a tar paper shack.

"Howdy," said the young man behind the counter as Buckner stood in the doorway. He wore freshly laundered and starched overalls over a worn but clean plaid flannel shirt. Bright red hair stuck out in all directions from under a St. Louis Browns cap. "Looking for something in particular?"

"Sure am. I'm looking for a Chevrolet V-8 sedan, 1925 model."

"What for, exactly?"

"I need a rear door, driver's side."

"What color?"

"Doesn't matter. I'm just gonna have it painted to match."

The young man pulled a ledger from under the counter and consulted it. He ran a finger down a column of illegible scrawls.

"Yeah. Thought so. Got one."

"Can you show me?"

"Sure. Come on."

As they passed Buckner's Model A, the young man said, "I thought you were looking for a Chevy."

"That's the rental I'm driving for now. Can't go out on the road without a door."

"Right."

The young man led him along a corridor of wrecks until he stopped and pointed at one.

The newspaper stories had called Hanley's auto the "Car of Death," and included a description of the badly crumpled rear door on the passenger side. The rear door on the driver's side had only minor scrapes and dirt smears.

"Hmm," Buckner muttered.

"Feller got killed in this one," the young man said. He seemed to consider it a selling point.

"Doesn't matter to me," Buckner said.

He continued to survey the auto. The entire body on the right side was scored and streaked. Twigs hung from it, and the roof was caved in. But all four tires were in perfect condition.

"All right," Buckner said. "I'll get on home and pick up some tools and come back. How much do you want for that door?"

"If you're gonna take it off yourself, call it two bucks."

As they walked back to the shack, they met the deputy sheriff coming toward them.

"You looking for anything in particular?" the deputy demanded. "What's he been looking at, Phil? What've you been showing him?"

"Chevy there," said Phil, aiming a thumb over his shoulder.

"I think," the deputy said to Buckner, "that you better get yourself back down there to Highland County right now before you run into trouble up here that you won't like at all."

"I'm on my way, Deputy," Buckner said.

He started to walk to the Ford, but the deputy grabbed his arm and spun him around.

"Don't come back here poking yer nose in," he said, his face close, his breath heavy with the licorice sent of Sen-Sen.

"Of course not," Buckner said, smiling, waiting, not moving.

The deputy let go of his arm and stepped back, his hand going to the butt of his service weapon.

"Thanks again," Buckner said. He got into his rented Ford and drove off, making a wide U-turn between the rows of cars and accelerating past the deputy and the puzzled-looking Phil.

"So," Buckner muttered as he drove. "No flat tire, unless Phil back there put fresh tires on a wreck."

But he also admitted to himself that it meant nothing. Every other single fact he knew about the incident could be completely true except that one. He just didn't think so.

But he wanted to satisfy his curiosity, so he headed back for the junction of Wild Horse Creek and Ossenfort Roads. He pulled his Ford well off the road and walked until he could see the two story house at the end of the dirt road that had yielded up that angry, cursing driver. He picked a spot and watched the house, listening for traffic on the road that was out of sight off to his east.

Nothing happened for an hour except that Buckner got wetter as the rain picked up. Finally, the back door opened and a woman in a long slicker, collar up around her face, and a head scarf hurried to the outhouse just across the back yard. She reappeared a few minutes later and dashed back into the house. Buckner couldn't tell if it was the same woman he'd seen earlier.

Buckner went back to his Ford and drove to St. Louis.

St. Louis

The car-hire office was closed when Buckner got back to town. There was another Ford parked in the tiny lot. Buckner was just able to squeeze in next to it. He pushed the ignition key and a five dollar bill through the mail slot in the office door and caught a streetcar to the Ville. The address Dutton had given him was on Cottage Avenue. He found Dutton sitting at a table looking out at a red brick high school across the street. A waitress brought him coffee and pie, delivering it with a warm smile. When Buckner asked for the same, the smile faded, and all he got was a quick nod as she walked away.

"You and your fatal charm," Buckner said.

"Can't help it, I guess." Dutton smiled complacently.

"Seems to work on my sister," Buckner said.

"Look," Dutton said, leaning forward, speaking softly, his voice tight. "Marty and I are friends, have been friends ever since we took turns sitting and waiting to see if you were going to die, and we've never been anything other than friends."

"Fine. My mistake. Forget it. What information have you got and what are we going to do about it?"

The waitress brought Buckner's food, set the plate and cup heavily on the table, and walked away.

"Mostly what I have is stuff you probably already know. The papers are up in arms, and there's reporters down from Kansas City and Chicago. Morris's killing looks to them like part of the long-running gang wars over the making and selling of booze. This town hasn't had so much publicity since the Cardinals won the pennant. But it's not the kind of publicity the city likes. The police department keeps making statements about bringing the gangs to heel, punishing evildoers, solving Morris's murder. They say it's all because of the gangs. Trouble is, there doesn't seem to be much going on. The latest theory is that, since Morris was responsible for getting a lot of the top gangsters put away, some second-level hood killed him to make his mark, demonstrate leadership skills, allow him to move up."

"But that stooge Harris rousted yesteerday said he didn't know of anybody like that, gunning for Johnny Morris as a way up."

"Yeah, but that could just mean the gangs weren't after him, nothing formal. Some loner might have decided shotgunning a man from behind in a dark alley would show everybody how tough he is."

"We're still no closer to knowing who that was."

"How did your trip to the country go?" Dutton asked.

Buckner told Dutton what he had found at the accident site and the scrap yard.

"No evidence of the blowout that was supposed to have caused the crash?"

"None." Buckner then said, "I was almost in an accident myself out there." And he explained the encounter with the speeding model A and the woman in the house.

"Any idea who they were?"

"No. The driver just flashed past. And the woman was completely covered up."

They ate slowly, silently. When they finished, Dutton left a dollar on the table.

"That's a pretty big tip," Buckner said. He had slid a quarter under the edge of his plate.

"I liked her smile."

"You want her to remember you next time you come in here."

Dutton just grinned happily.

*

On the street they conferred briefly. Dutton would continue looking into the murder squad.

Buckner headed for the Harris apartment. He found his sister on the sofa reading *Just–So Stories* to the little boy. In the tiny kitchen, Mrs. Harris put a mass of freshly kneaded dough into a large bowl, covered it with a cloth, and but it on top of the stove to rise.

"Coffee?" she asked Buckner as she washed her hands. She was thoroughly dusted with flour and looked to Buckner like a large dumpling.

"I believe I will thank you." He took the offered cup and sat in a chair at the end of the sofa.

"Do you know how the elephant got his trunk?" the boy asked. Buckner struggled to remember his name.

"It got pulled on by an alligator, didn't it?"

"Crocodile," the boy corrected smugly.

"Oh, right. Crocodile. I forgot."

"I seen an elephant," he said.

"'Saw' an elephant," his mother said.

"Saw an elephant. At the zoo. My daddy took us there last year. Elephants are really big."

"I guess," Buckner said. "I've only seen pictures." He said to his sister, "How are you making out? Where's your bodyguard?"

Heavy footsteps coming up the stairs caused them both to be very still. Buckner's hand eased toward his hip.

"It's just him," Mrs. Harris said.

The little boy knew those steps as well, and stood waiting by the door as his father came in.

"Checking up on me?" Harris asked. He handed his hat to his son, who hung it on the coat tree in the corner.

"Just stopped by for coffee. And to check in," Buckner said. "What happened to your hand?"

"Just business," he said. He sat and rubbed battered knuckles. "I thought I'd check around some more, see if anybody's out to get Marty here." He shrugged. "Not everybody was happy to help me out." When his wife brought him coffee, he thanked her and went on. "How did the rest of your day go?"

Buckner gave a brief account of his meetings with Reeves and Sweeney and his explorations in the County.

"I know 'em," Harris said. "By reputation, anyway. Reeves is supposed to be good. Probably be the first colored detective on the force someday. Sweeney's supposed to be as straight as they come, which not everybody is happy about. When the new chief put him in charge of internal investigations, his popularity dropped to just about zero."

"As far as I can tell, he doesn't care much about his popularity."

"Well, he's not going to get very far getting any solid evidence on that murder gang Reeves says is going on inside the department. Nobody'll testify against them, and none of them are gonna testify against each other."

"No reason why any of them should."

More footsteps clattered up the stairs. Harris got up and unlocked the door just in time for it to burst open and admit his two daughters, each carrying books strapped together. They tossed the books unceremoniously into a corner and sat next to Marty.

"Home for lunch?" Marty said.

"Yeah," said the oldest, sighing dramatically. "I can't wait for it to be over. I'm in the eighth grade, and once I'm done, I'm done for good."

"Me, too," said the younger. "I'm in sixth grade."

Both girls watched Marty with shining eyes. If it made her uncomfortable, she didn't let it show.

"You both better go on and finish high school," she said. "You want to be a newspaper reporter, you'll need that diploma."

"Don't worry about that," Mrs. Harris said from the kitchen. "They're going to keep right on through twelfth grade. Now get in the kitchen, all three of you.

"Aww, Ma!" the girls groaned. They trooped into the kitchen and sat at the table. Their brother followed.

"Is that lipstick you're wearing?" Harris demanded.

"It's just strawberry Twizzlers, Dad." The older girl sighed again and rolled her eyes.

"Uh—huh."

"She's sweet on Jimmy DiCarlo," said the younger. "That's why she wears it. She hopes he'll notice her."

"I do not!"

"Eat your lunch," Mrs. Harris said, gently but firmly. The children obeyed.

"All right," Buckner said, getting up. "I just wanted to check in. I've got work of my own that needs attending to." And, ignoring the pleading look on his sister's face, he turned and fled.

He found the Seventh District police station easily and walked straight in. The place was quiet. The desk sergeant dozed over a newspaper; the few officers passing through the foyer paid him no attention. It occurred to him that looking like a police officer came in handy sometimes.

A bulletin board hung to one side. It held the usual mix of wanted posters, safety tips, and departmental announcements. One of these congratulated the district's championship bowling team, complete with a photo of the grinning officers. One of them, a cheerful looking young man with mean little black eyes under heavy brows and a nose like a small potato, was Arthur Pitaluga.

Confident he could remember that image, Buckner left the station house and crossed to the coffee shop on the other side of Grand. He took a window seat and ordered coffee and pie from a tiny woman in a crisp apron. The place was full of policemen, most in uniform, a few in plain clothes but clearly policemen.

Buckner sipped coffee and toyed with the pie for an hour, until four men carrying bags and laughing came around the corner from Magnolia Street and went into the station. They came out a few minutes later, without their bags, three in uniform, one, Arthur Pitaluga, in a light-colored suit. After much back-slapping and hand-shaking, they split up. Pitaluga headed west on Magnolia.

Buckner put a dollar on the table and left. He let Pitaluga get a block away and fell in behind. Pitaluga sauntered along jauntily, hands in his pockets, taking his time. He walked for forty minutes, nodding occasionally to people on the street, who seemed to recognize him.

Tower Grove Park was to the left as Pitaluga and Buckner walked. As Pitaluga passed Tower Grove Avenue, a man leaned out from behind a tree in the park. When Pitaluga had gotten a block away, the man stepped out and began following him. Buckner, who had slowed when he spotted the man, let him get ahead and then he, too, followed along. This new shadow concentrated all his attention on Pitaluga, paying Buckner no attention at all.

But Pitaluga must have begun to feel the heat of all that concentrated attention, the sense of being at the head of a parade. He turned down Hereford Street and stopped under a sign saying "The Garibaldi Club." He took out a cigarette and lit it, glancing casually back the way he had come. The follower, a slim man with pale blonde hair and wearing a long overcoat, turned the corner, jamming his hands into his coat pockets as he did so.

Buckner hurried and rounded the corner right behind him.

He was just in time to see another man come rushing through the door of The Garibaldi Club and head for Pitaluga. As the slim man pulled revolvers from his coat pockets, Buckner grabbed him from behind and slammed him into the brick front of The Garibaldi Club, causing him to drop his revolvers. Buckner spun him around, rammed his fist into his belly, and stepped back as the man folded forward. Buckner then spun him back around and shoved him headfirst into the brick façade. His head thudded wetly against the wall.

The slim man collapsed to the sidewalk. Blood was already coloring his blonde hair, staining the sidewalk. He didn't move. Buckner scooped up the fallen revolvers, .38's, and turned to help Pitaluga.

Who did not need any help. The other man, the one who had come from inside the club, lay on the ground, moaning softly as Pitaluga knelt over him and punched him alternatively in the stomach and the face.

"I think he's done," Buckner said. He opened the revolvers and ejected the rounds, putting them in his pocket.

"And I think he ain't," Pitaluga said without looking up.

"Sure." Buckner leaned against the wall to wait.

Pitaluga stopped eventually and stood over the man, who now lay silent and still on the sidewalk. Pitaluga's cigarette had been broken at some point, and he threw it away. He took another from a silver cigarette case, stuck it in his mouth, and lighted it.

"I got these off this fella over here," Buckner said, holding out the confiscated .38's. He indicated the slim man, who remained motionless on the sidewalk. Blood seeped from his scalp onto his face and ran down into his collar.

"I don't need them to take care of these two. And I don't need your help either, whoever the hell you are."

"You're welcome," Buckner said. "I think he was going to shoot you in the back."

"And now I'm gonna shoot them both." Pitaluga took a .38 from inside his jacket.

"Golly, right here on the street?" Buckner indicated several people who had stopped to watch the slow. They had kept a safe distance. None of them seemed startled when Pitaluga took out his revolver.

"Right," Pitaluga said grudgingly. He put his pistol away. "They know who I am and who these two punks are. I grew up in this neighborhood and so did they. Ain't nobody gonna say a goddamned thing. But you're right. No need."

"You gonna call a cop?"

"Hell no. I am a cop."

"Oh. So you're gonna arrest them."

"Nah. The hell with 'em." Pitaluga contemplated Buckner for a second. "So maybe I do owe you one. How about I buy you a drink, that way we can call it square."

"Sure. Fine. Here?" Buckner indicated The Garibaldi Club.

"Hell no. Much better place, few blocks over. Full of cops, though. You got a problem with that?"

"No. I'm a cop." Buckner took out his badge.

"Uh—huh." Pitaluga glanced at it. "You're not from around here, then."

"Down south a ways."

"What're you doing up here?"

"Looking for a fella."

"Local boy?"

"Home town boy, but he's got kin up here, and he sometimes hides out with them when things get too hot for him back home."

"Ain't you afraid he'll take off while you're having a drink with me and my friends?"

"Nope. He's got no place to go but here, and nobody to help him but those kinfolk. And I know where they are, so he'll keep for a spell."

"Fine. Let's go."

They walked to the corner of Bischoff and Edwards, to a place with no sign at all. Buckner stopped at a storm drain and tossed in the two pistol he had been trying to carry unostentatiously.

Pitaluga led the way into a long, narrow room. It was dark and smoke-filled, but not crowded. There was a door at the far end of the room. Three men sitting at a table near the door hailed Pitaluga. He crossed to them, Buckner following, looking for another way out. There wasn't one.

Pitaluga made the introductions.

"Shorty, Bernie, Red, this here's the chief of police from someplace down in the hills south of here."

"Jim," Buckner said, shaking hands all around.

"Pull up a chair, Jim," said Bernie, who was heavy and jowly and badly in need of a shave.

Buckner sat. The four men smiled at him, smiles that bared their teeth but didn't reach their eyes. They all wore suits that made no attempt to hide the pistols they wore in shoulder holsters. Except for Pitaluga, each man wore an identical multi-colored pin on his lapel.

"Beer OK?" Pitaluga asked.

"Sure."

"Hang on," said Shorty, scooping up the empty glasses on the table. "I'll come along."

Buckner watched Pitaluga and Shorty Werner, predictably much taller than Pitaluga, walk to the bar. As they waited for the bartender to fill their glasses, they talked quietly, heads together. Werner, looking back, nodded and smiled some more. When the glasses were filled, they returned to the table. Werner put a pint glass in front of Buckner.

"Where you been, Arthur?" Runge asked. "We been waiting on you for an hour."

"I had to deal with a couple fellas, Morasco's boys, thought they could ambush me." Pitaluga told them about the encounter outside The Garibaldi Club, relegating Buckner's role to that of interested onlooker.

"So what's he doing here?" McKinney asked. He was mostly bald, but what hair he had, a monkish fringe surrounding a bald and shining dome, was a dark rust color.

"Oh, he gave me a little help with those two boys."

"Well, thanks, then," McKinney said, clapping Buckner on the shoulder harder than necessary. "But I'm pretty sure Little Arthur here didn't need no help."

"Damn right I didn't," Pitaluga, flushing red with anger.

While they were joshing Pitaluga, another man came in and crossed to their table. Tall, in a suit and vest tailored to emphasize his broad shoulders, he nodded to the policemen.

"Hey, boss," McKinney said. "Have a seat. Weren't expecting you to drop by."

"Hadn't planned on it, then I found out Little Arthur here put a couple of Morasco's boys in the hospital. And that he had help doing it."

"I told 'em boss," Pitaluga protested. "I didn't need no—"

"I know, Arthur," the man said, putting a patronizing palm on Pitaluga's arm. "I know. And are you going to introduce me to your new friend?'

Introductions were made. Lieutenant Kane shook Buckner's hand, his grip firm but not crushing, his eyes cold gray. He didn't bother to pretend a smile.

Neither did Buckner.

"I see you fellas all served," Buckner said, indicating the pin on Kane's lapel.

"That's right," Werner said.

"All except Little Arthur here," McKinney said, ruffling Pitaluga's hair. "He was just a bit too young."

"Dammit, cut it out," Pitaluga said, pushing McKinney's hand away. "I signed up all right."

"Yeah," Runge confirmed. "But when they found out you was only fourteen, they sent you home to mama."

This brought more laughter.

"I don't see you wearing no Victory pin," Runge said to Buckner. "You a slacker? Get an exemption cause you're chief of police? Or on account of that bum leg you got?"

"I was in the cavalry before the war," Buckner said. "Joined up with the Canadians in '15, got invalided out in '17." Buckner smiled at Runge. "If it's any of your business."

"Canadians, huh?" McKinney said. "You that anxious to get blowed up?"

"Wanted to see the elephant," Buckner said. "You all in the same outfit?"

"One-fortieth Infantry," Runge said. "Missouri National Guard."

"Figured we'd never have to leave the country," McKinney added. "Protect the homeland and all that kind of crap, just like Wilson promised."

"It's what we deserved, believing government lies," Shorty Werner said. "They brigaded us in the Thirty-fifth Division, along with the Kansas Guard, sent us to Camp Doniphan ... Fort Sill, I guess, really."

"Been to Sill," Buckner said. "Before the war this was. I served with the last cavalry outfit posted there when the Army turned it into the artillery school."

"They crammed us all into the training camp, half of us got sick as hell," Werner said. "Went over there in May of '18. Attached to a British outfit for training."

"Lobsterback bastards," said McKinney.

"The British could be hard to get along with," Buckner agreed.

"At least they weren't gutless cowards, like the little Froggies," Werner grumbled.

"You served with the French?"

"We was attached to XXXIII Corps for front-line training, but all they knew how to do was hide out, or run away whenever the Huns attacked."

"Were you with the French the whole time?" Buckner wanted to defend the French, who'd been bled white by almost three years of fighting before the Americans bothered to show up. Instead, he let the insult go unchallenged. He needed these men friendly and outgoing.

"Nah," Werner said. "Pretty soon we got assigned to I Corps, U.S. We went over the top in the Meuse-Argonne Offensive, end of September."

"I remember reading about that," Buckner said. "Some fight."

"A real picnic," Runge said.

"What do you mean?" Buckner asked.

"Right," McKinney said. "Well, see, Pershing replaced our CG couple months before, him and the whole division staff. Hell, the new CG didn't have time to find his way to the latrine before we was in action."

"That's why we ran out of rations and ammo," Runge explained. "Wasn't nobody knew how to handle resupply, specially since we was moving pretty fast right there at first. Punched right through the Huns, then we got bogged down and they countered, and it was all we could do to hold them off."

"Then we was relieved," McKinney said. "Pulled us out of the line. But we was right back just a couple weeks later, and stayed there till the end."

"Were you all police before the war?"

"Hell no," Werner said. "When we got home, there wasn't much else to do. No jobs, all the war factories closing down. The department was looking for men, though. They lost some when the war came along, guys enlisting, going off to do their patriotic duty. Then there'd been a lot of strikes, stuff like that, all around during the war, and they wanted to clamp the lid down tight on any kind of Red activity like that."

"And some of the boys coming back, when they couldn't find regular work, got into what you might call other lines of endeavor. And there was a lot of that on account of Prohibition."

Everybody laughed at that. Except Kane, who had watched Buckner closely, smiling at the appropriate time, but saying nothing at all.

"Cops or crooks," Buckner said. "Yeah, we had some of that down my way. And you fellas were the cops."

"Beats going hungry."

"Man does what he has to do to … ah … augment his income."

"I suppose," Buckner said.

"So, what's a chief of police from down south doing up here in the big city?" Werner asked.

"Looking for a fella, like I told Officer Pitaluga here."

"What kind of fella?"

Buckner retold his tale of Elroy Dutton's wickedness, embellishing only slightly.

"Why don't you just shoot him?" Werner asked.

"Yeah, who'd mind?" Runge added.

"Well, I would," Buckner said.

"Well, maybe we could help you out," Runge suggested. "Where's this fella likely to hide out?"

"He's got kin here, someplace called 'the Ville,'" Buckner said, regretting it the instant he said it.

"Oh, colored fella," McKinney said. "You been up there looking for him?"

"Yes, but I didn't have much luck."

"No surprise there," Pitaluga said. "Excuse me for saying this, but what in hell made you think them folks up there would even talk to you, much less hand over one of their own to you?"

"Had to start someplace," Buckner said. He finished his pint and stood up.

"Where you going?" McKinney demanded. "We're just getting started."

"Yeah," said Runge. "We might be able to help you out, since we're more familiar with what you might call the lay of the land."

"I'd appreciate the help," Buckner said. "But right now you gotta tell me where the latrine is in this place."

"Out back," Runge said, pointing to the door at the end of the room.

"Thanks."

The back door opened onto a grimy alley. In the growing dark of early evening, a single lamp above the door cast a thin light, revealing an outhouse leaning against the wall opposite. Buckner started through when he heard chairs scraping and fast footsteps behind him. He slammed the saloon door and jammed his foot against it, looking both directions for a way out. Both ends of the alley were dark, offering nothing. It didn't matter anyway, because the weight of the men on the other side blasted the door open, knocking Buckner against the rough wood of the outhouse. As he fought to keep his balance, the policemen pushed through and spread out, blocking any hope of escape.

All of them except Kane. Buckner recognized him at once. It had been Kane behind the wheel of the Ford that ran Buckner off the road.

CORINTH

Shotwell sat at the booking desk and read Mullen's telegram. What it told him confirmed what he had learned following the trail of the four young men as they prowled the streets of Corinth, looking for a good time. They did not seem to have found it, at least not at Mrs. Belmont's or Dutton's. They had gotten stinking drunk, and one of them ended up dead in the alley behind Mullen's Dry Goods, the result of drinking booze poisoned by order of the federal government and sold to them by a conductor on the Missouri Pacific somewhere between St. Louis and Corinth. A conductor named Pinch. All Shotwell had to do was find that conductor and arrest him. Mullen, for his part, was headed for St. Louis to tell the family of William Lance their son was dead.

He left the department and walked to the train station.

"Good morning, Mr. Weiner," he said to the man behind the ticket window.

"Good morning," Mr. Weiner replied. He was bent over papers on his desk, frowning at them.

"I was wondering if you could help me with something," Shotwell said.

"I'm extremely busy, as you can see," Mr. Weiner said without looking up.

"It's pretty important, Mr. Weiner. It's about that young fellow we found behind Mullen's."

"I heard it was from drinking bootleg whiskey. Serves him right."

"We believe he got that whiskey from a conductor on the Line, Mr. Weiner," Shotwell persisted. He kept his voice even, respectful. "Somewhere between St. Louis and here."

"A likely story." Mr. Weiner still had not looked up from his work. He used a pencil to make check marks beside items in a column.

"Maybe so, Mr. Weiner." Shotwell plodded on patiently. "But I need to find out one way or the other."

"Well, go on and find out. I don't see why you're pestering me with it."

"I was hoping you could give me the name of that railroad detective who helped Chief Buckner out with one of his cases a couple of years ago."

"His name is Griswold, Officer Shotwell," Weiner said through gritted teeth.

"Can you get in touch with him, Mr. Weiner? The department would appreciate it."

"Where is Chief Buckner?" Weiner demanded, suddenly whirling to face Shotwell, his thin lips twisting in a sneer. "Why isn't he handling this? Why did he send you?"

"He didn't send me, Mr. Weiner. Chief Buckner is working on another case. I am in charge of this one, and I'm asking for your help as a courtesy to you, sir. I am perfectly willing to go straight to the head office of the Line if that's what it takes. Of course, they might want me to explain to them why I didn't start with their man on the spot, which would be you, and then I would have to tell them that you were unable, or unwilling, to help local law enforcement deal with a violation of federal law and the U.S. Constitution perpetrated by one of their employees, a violation which may have led to the death of one of their customers. So I'd appreciate it if you could give this a second thought and save me all that trouble."

"Why, you damned—"

"Careful, Mr. Weiner," Shotwell said, smiling pleasantly.

Weiner got up suddenly, fists clenched at his sides, and said, "Alleged perpetrator, damn you. Alleged."

"You're absolutely right, Mr. Weiner. Alleged."

Weiner, still glaring furiously at Shotwell, sat down again and reached for the telephone. It must have been a direct wire, because he didn't go through the local operator.

"This is Weiner, down in Corinth. We have a situation here, a conductor allegedly selling alcohol to passengers on the Line. You need to send Agent Griswold down here right away. Someone has died. Have him go straight to the police department."

He slammed the receiver into its cradle and shoved the telephone back.

"If that's all, I've got work to do."

"Thank you, Mr. Weiner."

As he walked back to the department, Shotwell smiled. He'd seen Buckner use that trick before and was very pleased with himself. It had worked like a charm. Persuading someone that it was in their best interest to do what you wanted them to do was so much easier than yelling and screaming and threatening.

Though, he admitted to himself, yelling at Mr. Weiner might have been very satisfying, too.

Griswold of the Missouri Pacific arrived within hours.

"What's this!" he demanded as he burst through the department's doors. "You're not Buckner! Where's Buckner? What's all this about conductor selling liquor on the Line?"

Griswold wore a trim brown checked suit and a bright blue tie. He stood at the booking desk, looking down at Shotwell and bouncing slightly on his toes, like a man on a spring.

"Thank you for getting here so quickly, Detective Griswold," Shotwell said, standing and offering his hand.

"I was up in Peveley. Mann Act violation. Caught him in flagrante, as you might say. Well, what's this all about?" He shook Shotwell's hand in a crushing grip. "What's going on?"

Shotwell refrained from massaging his aching hand, and told Griswold about finding William Lance's body, and what he and Mullen had learned so far.

Griswold paced back and forth while Shotwell talked, nodding and making clicking noises with his tongue.

"Eldon Pinch, huh?" he said, stopping as Shotwell finished. He continued bouncing slightly. "Here's what we have to do. I've had my eye on Pinch for a while now. This might just be my chance to finish him. But we have to catch him in the act of selling alcohol to a passenger on the Line. Any suggestions on that? You think about it. I'll check with the St. Louis office, see when he's going to be working this stretch of the Line."

"Do you want to use our phone?"

"Nah. Line's got a direct line from your station."

Before Shotwell could say anything, Griswold was through the doors and up the stairs. Shotwell poured coffee and sat at the desk, sipping slowly, staring at nothing. He sat like that until Griswold returned.

"Got him!" he said, rubbing his hands together in anticipation. "Now I'm gonna go get him."

"Figured out how you're gonna catch him in the act?"

"Thought for a while I might go undercover, but, hell, they all know me. He'd spot me in a second."

"I might have a suggestion along that line," Shotwell said. "Suppose I go undercover. He doesn't know me. I haven't ridden that train in years."

"Might work," Griswold muttered, frowning. He was motionless for a moment.

"When's the next train?"

"There's an east-bound in an hour, and he'll be on it."

"Fine," Shotwell said. "Plenty of time." He got up. "I'll meet you at the station in forty-five minutes or less."

Augusta Shotwell looked up in surprise when her husband rushed in and kept on moving straight down the hall to the bedroom.

"Where's that suit I bought a couple of years ago? The one you never let me wear."

"Hanging in the closet."

When Shotwell called out "Found it," Augusta got up and went to the bedroom. Her husband was changing out of his uniform and into a three-piece wool suit in a red and green glen plaid. He added a fedora decorated with a small, bright red feather in the band. He turned to his wife. "How do I look?"

"Like a cheap hoodlum," she said. "Why do you think I never let you wear it?"

"Good thing we held onto it, then."

"I was going to put it with the other stuff for the church rummage sale, but I was afraid somebody might buy it."

"Perfect," he said, going to the front door.

"What's going on?" Augusta demanded, following him. "Visiting Mrs. Belmont, Dutton's, dressing like that. You're going to get us a reputation."

"Gotta go catch a killer," he said. He gave her a quick kiss and was gone.

He crossed the tracks and hurried to the back of Coy's Drug Store. A rickety set of stairs angled up the wall. Shotwell climbed to the top and opened the door to Jeff Peck's office. Peck, sitting at his desk, looked up from his book.

"Hello," he said around his cigar. "Why are you dressed like a pimp?"

"Hello. Have you got some whiskey?"

"Yes. Have you decided to take up drinking as well?"

"No, just give me the whiskey."

"You sound like a man in a hurry." Peck pulled open a drawer in his desk and took out a bottle. He pulled the cork and pushed the bottle across the desk. "Help yourself."

Shotwell sprinkled a few drops onto the front of his glen plaid suit, then took a drink, swishing the liquor around in his mouth before stepping outside and spitting it over the stair railing. He returned and plunked the bottle down.

"Thanks," he said, turning to leave.

"You're welcome. But hang on a second."

Shotwell waited impatiently. Peck disappeared into his examining room, coming back with a walking stick, gleaming ebony, with a garish gold knob. He handed it to Shotwell.

"The finishing touch," he said.

"Where'd you get this?"

"Did some work on a fella got his arm broken in a little disagreement at The Corinthian. He was out of money by then, but his moaning was disturbing my drinking, so I set his arm and took this in payment."

"Thanks," Shotwell said. He took the stick and left.

Peck poured some of the whiskey into his glass, corked the bottle, and returned it to the drawer. He resumed reading.

Griswold was pacing back and forth on the platform when Shotwell got to the station.

"Where'd you get that outfit?"

"Here and there."

"Well, you sure don't look like no cop."

Shotwell went through the door and into the waiting room. Griswold followed.

"Hold it," he said. "You can't be in here."

"I believe I can," Shotwell said. "Isn't that right, Mr. Weiner?"

Weiner's face appeared in the ticket window. He muttered something under his breath, nodded briefly, and disappeared.

Shotwell pointed a pale rectangular spot on the wall.

"Used to be a 'White Only' sign," he said. "Used to hang right there."

Griswold shook his head, disgusted. "Don't tell me. Buckner took it down."

"Nope," Shotwell said. "He had Mr. Weiner do it."

"It's Company property."

"You gonna put it back up?"

Now Griswold muttered under his breath. Out loud, he said, "You're still gonna have to—"

"I know," Shotwell interrupted. "Wouldn't look right otherwise."

"Damned right, it wouldn't."

The two men waited in silence for the train to arrive.

St. Louis

"You must think we're pretty goddamned stupid," Red McKinney said.

Buckner said nothing, kept his hands open and slightly away from his body. Kane, he noticed, was not with the others.

"You think we don't know who the hell you are?" Runge said. "This is our town, and we was onto you the minute you got off the train from Podunk City."

"We had our eye on that sister of yours, and when she went to ground, we knew it'd be pretty quick somebody'd be along looking for her."

"And sure enough, here you are," Pitaluga said cheerfully.

"And now we're gonna take care of you, and then we're gonna find her and take care of her, too," Runge said.

"Send you both back to Podunk City in a box." Pitaluga began to laugh. "A real little box."

"It's Corinth," said a voice from one end of the alley. "Not that it makes any difference to you, you dumb wop bastard."

The policemen turned in the direction of the voice, all reaching under their coats.

"Careful there!" said Elroy Dutton as he stepped forward. He had both his ivory-handled revolvers out, aiming steadily, smiling happily. "The angle I got on you boys, I could take you all down easy. So go ahead and pull your pieces and let's start the ball."

The policemen moved their hands into plain sight, fingers spread.

"You're making a big mistake, nigger," said Pitaluga. "This here's white folks' business."

"Call me that again and I will shoot you where you stand," Dutton said.

"He means we're police officers," Runge said. "And we were making a legitimate arrest."

"And I'm Robert E. Lee," Dutton said. He glanced at Buckner, who now had his .45 out. "You all right?"

"Yes. Fine. I had everything under control."

"I could see that."

"How'd you get here? You just strolling by?"

"Hell no. I followed you when you started following the dago. We had one hell of a parade for a while there. Anyway, are you through questioning these fine gentlemen?"

"Yes, I believe I am. Just so you know, Kane's still inside. Probably sneaking around to come in behind you."

"Then maybe we should move on."

"All right. Unless you want to call them some more names."

"No, I'm done. Perhaps you could persuade them to relieve themselves of their iron?" Dutton turned around and took a few steps back the way he had come, then he stopped and turned back to watch.

Buckner said, "You heard him, fellows." He cocked his pistol. "Drop your weapons on the ground."

Moving slowly, reluctantly, the policemen took out their service revolvers and dropped them.

"Now step back against the wall there," Buckner said.

When they had done that, Buckner picked up the four pistols, looping the fingers of his left hand through the trigger guards.

"I expect you're all holding out on me," he said. "But this will do for a head start." He moved to join Dutton, keeping the policemen in view. "We'll be waiting around the corner for a spell, so it would be a mistake for any of you to come running out after us."

Buckner and Dutton stepped out of the alley and onto the street. It was dinnertime, and there were few pedestrians out in the gathering dark. Buckner could hear words and movement from the alley.

"Let's just get on across the street," he said.

As they started across, Lieutenant Kane pushed open the front door of the saloon. He had a pistol in his hand.

Buckner and Dutton both fired in his direction, sending him quickly back inside and slamming the door shut. Buckner and Dutton sprinted the rest of the way, stopping behind a row of parked automobiles.

"Which way now?" Buckner demanded.

"This is Magnolia," Dutton said. "Head east to the park."

"Where we going?" Buckner holstered his .45, trading it for one of the .38's he had just acquired. Dutton put away his .32's and took two .38's from Buckner.

They started down the street. From behind came shooting, and bullets cracked close, smacking into brick walls and parked autos, shattering windows. Buckner and Dutton ran, not looking back.

"Guess they had some more iron on them," Buckner said.

Shooting continued. The policemen moved down the opposite side of the street, firing from behind parked autos. Buckner used the .38s, one in each hand, firing slowly, methodically, in their direction. He fired as he moved.

Dutton stumbled against a wall and sprawled on the pavement, losing the .38s. Buckner stooped to grab Dutton and raise him to his feet. He half-carried him the rest of the way to Tower Grove Park.

The park was randomly lighted, and Buckner kept to the darkness.

"You hit?" he asked Dutton.

"Hell yes, I'm hit." Dutton pulled back his jacket and put his hand to his left side. Even in the darkness, both men could see the blood. The ivory butt of the pistol holstered there was shattered. "Damn, that cost me a hundred dollars."

"It probably saved your life. Can you move?"

"Yes. Just get me to my cousin's place."

"Long way," Buckner said.

Buckner could see the policemen as they gathered just outside the park on Kingshighway. They were looking into the park but seemed reluctant to step into its shadows. Buckner nodded to himself. If they made the mistake of coming in, he would have them.

They must have figured that out for themselves, because they went north on Kingshighway and then east on Magnolia. Sirens wailed from several directions, getting closer. They had called for help.

"All right, let's go," Buckner said. "They're going to try to flank us, catch us the other side of the park. But I think we're gonna need a medic pretty quick."

"Looks worse than it is," Dutton said. He was walking on his own now. "I don't think it was the bullet, just the butt of my pistol."

"We're gonna have to go out onto the street at some point."

"Stay in the park till you hit Grand, then turn north."

They continued, picking up Main Drive, which led straight to Grand Avenue. As they turned left, Buckner saw a sign up ahead.

"Cover that up," Buckner said, indicating Dutton's darkening vest. "Take my arm and sing."

"Sing? Are you crazy?"

"Nope. Just helping my poor drunk friend here trying to make his way home."

Dutton began singing as the crossed Grand, passed a gaudily lit Chinese restaurant, then turned north.

"Bicycle Built for Two?"

"Only song I know all the words to. Unless you want me to try some of the drinking songs I picked up from the poilus I served with."

"That'd get us arrested for sure." In a few moments, they reached a store front. "In here," Buckner said.

"All right."

The drug store was bright inside. Three men sat eating at the lunch counter, not together. They ignored Dutton and Buckner. There were booths at the back, and Buckner seated Dutton in one. He dropped his hat on the table and went to search the shelves. Through the front window, he saw Red McKinney, pistol out of sight, pause on the sidewalk, looking right and left. A police cruiser with two men inside pulled over when he raised his hand. McKinney bent down to talk to through the rolled down window. Buckner turned and scanned the shelves, his back to the store's front window. When he turned to look, the patrol car had gone and McKinney walked on, going east.

Buckner quickly found what he was looking for. He took a package to the cash register. The man at the register looked at the package, then up at Buckner, eyebrows raised.

"For my wife," Buckner said. "All right with you?"

"Yes, sir. Of course, sir." The man took Buckner's money, gave him change, and put the package in a brown paper bag. Buckner took the bag to where Dutton sat hunched over.

"Here," he said, shoving the bag across the table. "Use one of these and cinch it up tight with your belt. I can't have you bleeding all over the place."

Dutton nodded and reached into the bag. He looked at Buckner with surprise.

"Nearest thing to a field dressing I could find."

"It ought to do the job."

While Dutton opened the package and went to work, Buckner went to one of the men at the lunch counter. He was eating eggs and bacon.

"That your hack out there?" he asked.

The man tipped his cap back and looked up.

"Uh—huh."

"You just got yourself a fare, then."

"I'm off the clock. I'm eating my breakfast."

Buckner took out his roll of cash and peeled off a five and put it on the counter next to the plate of bacon and eggs.

"That's for breakfast." He peeled off another five. "This one's for the ride."

The man put a dollar coin on the counter and slid the bills into his pocket. He wiped his mouth with a paper napkin and got down from his stool. He hesitated, then took a quarter from his pocket and put it on the counter next to the dollar. A toothpick from behind his ear went into his mouth.

"Where to?"

"I'll tell you once we get moving. You go crank it up and I'll be right behind you."

Buckner went to the back booth, where Dutton was buttoning up his coat. No blood showed.

"Come on," Buckner said. "And bring those. We might need them."

The waited a moment in the doorway, watching the street. Then they hurried across the sidewalk and got into the cab. The driver turned and looked closely, his jaw working the toothpick.

"You didn't mention the extra fare."

"Just drive. I won't short you."

"Your friend all right?"

"He just had a little too much to drink, that's all. I'm going to make sure he gets home safe."

"All right." The cab pulled into Grand and drove north.

"You gonna give me an address?"

"Corner of Washington and Leffingwell," Dutton said.

"Hey, I don't go up there after sundown."

"I'll protect you," Buckner said. "You just get us there and there's another five in it."

"There's already another five in it. For the extra fare."

"I'll kick in five," Dutton said. He was gritting his teeth. "Just get us there."

Through the scattered night time traffic, the cabbie pushed the accelerator and the drive was quick. Dutton leaned into the corner, arms tight across his middle.

The sirens continued their high pitched keening.

"They must want somebody pretty bad," the driver observed.

The businesses on Grand gave way to St. Louis University before the driver turned right onto Olive, then left onto Leffingwell. He pulled the cab over into a dark section of sidewalk, out of reach of the scarce streetlights. He left the engine running but got out and opened the rear passenger door.

"I seen guys like him had too much to drink," he said. "In France, this was. Few years back. You're gonna need a doc for him pretty quick, I'd say."

"I know that. Thanks." Buckner handed him a ten dollar bill.

"Didn't want him bleeding all over my hack."

"If anybody asks—"

"I don't take coloreds in my hack. Everybody knows that. And I never come up this way at night. Anyway, luck." And he got behind the wheel and drove off.

Buckner supported Dutton with an arm around his waist and Dutton's arm across his shoulder. Together, they started down the street.

"Damn, that hurts," Dutton said, now fully awake. He clutched the paper bag with his other arm.

"It'd hurt less if you would help."

"All right, then, put me down, dammit, and I'll walk."

Buckner let him go. He teetered slightly, straightened up, and began to walk. They continued along the street to the door of Joe Gordon's furniture store. The few people they met seemed to make a point of not seeing them. Few autos drove by. The sirens had become a distant echo.

Repeated knocking brought Gordon, in a long bathrobe over pajamas and slippers. He had a flashlight in one hand, a pistol in the other. He pocketed both and opened the door.

"Get in here quick," he hissed. He closed and locked the door behind them.

"You got someplace to put him?" Buckner asked. "He got shot, not bad, but he's lost some blood."

"Upstairs."

Gordon led the way. Dutton clutched his side and limped forward, ignoring Buckner's offer of help. At the top of a flight of stairs at the back of the store a woman stood waiting.

"In here," she said. "The spare room."

The spare room held mostly piled-up furniture, but there was a cot in one corner, and they put Elroy Dutton on it. The woman unbuttoned his coat and pulled it back. The pearl gray vest was soaked with blood all down the left side, from armpit to waist. The shoulder holster and the ruined pistol were smeared with it.

The woman began removing Dutton's clothing. The jacket came first, then the shoulder holsters. She undid the belt and pulled away the makeshift bandage.

"Kotex?" she said, looking at Buckner.

"There's more in that paper bag," he said.

A gash about three inches long in Dutton's side seeped blood. The woman applied a fresh bandage and used the belt to hold it tight.

"That's deep. He's going to need to get sewed up," she said.

"Are the police after him?" Gordon asked.

"Some of them," Buckner said. "After me, too, I'm afraid."

"They coming here?"

"Not likely. Not tonight, anyway."

"All right," Gordon said. He cursed under his breath. "I know somebody who can do whatever stitching he needs. But he might need a transfusion."

"I'd say a hospital might be too dangerous right now," Buckner said. "Can you keep him here for a while? Plenty of rest and liquids will help."

Gordon and the woman looked at each other and came to a decision.

"Two days," she said. "No more."

"I'll try to figure something out before then," Buckner said. He started for the door.

"Where are you going?"

"I need to get to my sister. She's the one in danger. If I can get her out of town, that might take the pressure off the rest of us. But right now, I need to get some sleep, so I'll head for my sister's place."

Gordon and his wife exchanged looks once again.

"You can sleep here," the woman said. She smiled, indicating the room. "We've got the furniture for it."

"It'd just be for a couple of hours," Buckner said. "I've had a busy couple of days on not much sleep."

"Sure."

Buckner took some chairs off a sofa and sat. Gordon and his wife finished bandaging Elroy Dutton.

"You need anything else?" Mrs. Gordon asked.

"I could use a stiff drink," Dutton replied.

"You won't get one here," she snapped, offended. Her husband frowned and shook his head.

"Could I get a glass of water, then?"

"Yes." The two of them departed. In a moment, Mrs. Gordon returned with a large tumbler full of water. Dutton took it, thanked her, and drank off half of it in two long gulps. He set the tumbler on the floor by the cot.

Mrs. Gordon nodded stiffly and left.

Buckner took off his shoes. He loosened his tie and lay back against the sofa's deep, plush cushioning.

"You never got hit, did you?" he asked Dutton. "Over there, I mean."

"Few scratches," Dutton answered. "Nothing even this bad. Sure nothing like what you got, that leg of yours."

Buckner didn't answer; he was sound asleep.

ST. LOUIS

Michael Mullen got off the train in St. Louis. He was stiff and sore from sleeping on trains, and he wanted very much to get out of the clothes he had been wearing for what felt like a month. But he did not want to put off typing up a report on his investigation. He had composed it in his head as he waited for the streetcar outside the train station.

A helpful police officer had told him which one to board once he showed him his badge.

"Oh, detective, huh?"

"Not really," Mullen confessed. "Just temporarily. I have to go tell some people that their son is dead."

The cop gave a low whistle. "Better you than me, brother."

"Yeah. And thanks for the help."

"Any time."

Waterman Street was only a short ride away, but Mullen had time to complete his planned report. The last sentence would be a simple statement to the effect that he had informed the parents of the deceased and told them where their son's body was. He would be direct and plain spoken. Then he would leave.

University City was a quiet, leafy suburb just beyond the western boundary of the City of St. Louis. The trees were budding out, despite the chilly, gray day. The homes were red brick, large, comfortable looking. Mullen found the address at once. A black woman in a crisp maid's uniform answered his knock and told him to wait while she disappeared to the back of the house. Moments later, a tall, elegant woman in a simple blue wool dress came to the door. She wore no jewelry and had carefully arranged gray hair framing an unlined face.

"I am Mrs. Lance. How may I help you?"

"I'm a policeman, Ma'am. From Corinth, Missouri." Mullen showed his badge. "Would it be possible for me to come in for just a moment? I have something I need to tell you."

Puzzled, the woman nodded, and Mullen stepped into a thickly carpeted foyer. A longcase clock stood against the wall to his left and there was a chair to the right. Above the chair hung a painting of a barn. The carpet on the floor and on the broad staircase leading up was gray, matching the upholstery on the chair. The air smelled faintly of lemon. The clock ticked softly in the silence as Mullen worked up what to say.

The woman waited, a polite smile on her face. The maid lingered a few steps away. Mullen, who had spent many an afternoon helping Corinth ladies at his father's fabric counter, noticed that, however simple the line of the woman's blue dress, the fabric was very fine, very expensive wool. And to his practiced eye, it looked hand stitched.

"Is your son William Lance?" Mullen asked, taking off his hat. He took out the paper Jeff Peck had given him.

"Yes."

"I'm sorry to have to tell you, Ma'am, but your son was found dead yesterday in Corinth."

"Found? What? Found dead?"

The woman reacted as though he had struck her. She took two tottering steps backward, nearly falling into the arms of the maid, who had rushed forward. The maid eased Mrs. Lance into the gray chair. She was gasping for air. Mullen stood frozen in place, one hand holding out the folded death certificate.

"Get her some water," he managed to say. After giving him a hard, suspicious glare, the maid rushed off. Mullen, left alone with the woman, struggled to say something, anything that might offer comfort. His mother had been dead for years now, and this woman was nothing at all like her, but she flooded into Mullen's mind, almost paralyzing him.

The maid returned immediately with a small crystal goblet half full of brandy. Mrs. Lance grasped at it, drinking it all, and handed the goblet to the maid.

"Some more, Ma'am?" she asked.

Mrs. Lance shook her head and waved the maid away. The maid stepped back a few paces, but did not leave. She kept a close eye on Mullen, who watched Mrs. Lance closely. Tears were running down her face now, but she ignored them.

"Tell me," she finally said through firmly gritted teeth.

"Ma'am, I—"

"Tell me."

So he told her, his voice as flat, as uninflected as he could make it. He kept it brief, perfunctory, relaying only the facts as he knew them in a summary he desperately concocted as he was speaking. He did not tell her that her son and his friends had visited a notorious house of prostitution and a notorious speakeasy, not even to tell her they had been barred from both. They had traveled down to Corinth for some fun, nothing more.

When he finished, he held out Peck's death certificate.

She took it, opened it, and glanced at it before folding it up and holding it out to the maid, who stepped forward to take it, and remained, hovering, staring icily at Michael Mullen.

"I knew something like this was bound to happen. Sooner or later, it would happen."

Mullen, not knowing how to respond, kept his silence and stood waiting.

"Where did you say you're from?"

"Corinth, Ma'am. I found him … your son. I'm real—"

"Corinth."

"It's in the Lead Belt, Ma'am. South of here a ways."

"What was he doing down there?"

"Uh, we're not real sure, Ma'am," Mullen lied. "His friends just said they wanted to have fun before final exams."

She nodded, and said, "His father, my husband, is a professor of geology here at the university. He is a recognized authority on the springs of Missouri." Her tone was unemotional, almost bored, as though she were reciting well-worn phrases. "He has published several books on the subject. Perhaps you have read one of them?"

Mullen admitted he hadn't.

"William could have gone to the university for virtually nothing. But he chose Missouri University instead, the state school." Her tone was bitter. "I suppose you know it is famous for the drinking and—other excesses— the students are always getting into. All sorts of things. The fraternities are the worst. The parties they have, and the kinds of young women they bring in. So of course he joined one. I can imagine the kind of fun they were looking for."

She stopped and sat silently for a minute while more tears ran down her cheeks.

Mullen waited uncomfortably, finally saying, "I'm very sorry, Ma'am." She nodded.

"The name of the funeral parlor in Corinth is on that piece of paper, Ma'am, along with the cause of death." Mullen swallowed hard and continued. "We will ship the … your son's body here if you would like."

She just nodded again, saying nothing, gazing past him, somewhere through and beyond the softly ticking longcase clock and the wall it stood against.

"Is there anything I can do for you, Ma'am? Tell your husband?"

"My husband will be in class. He mustn't be disturbed when he is in class."

"Yes, Ma'am."

"Or when he is in his office. Or when he is working on another book about the springs of Missouri."

Mullen turned to the maid.

"You'll take care of her?"

"Yes, of course I will." Her glare had not thawed.

"The address of the—"

"Yes. I heard you." She was clipped, terse. "I will give this to the Doctor when he returns."

"One thing more, Ma'am." Mullen took out the wallet that Shotwell had found. He held it out.

The woman looked at it, then up at Mullen.

"Was there a wrist watch?" she asked. "We gave him a wrist watch when he graduated from high school. Gold, with a leather strap. We had his name engraved on it."

"No, Ma'am," Mullen said. "I'm sorry. This is all we found."

The woman took the wallet and held it, looking at it. The maid looked at Mullen and with a quick, sharp nod, sent him away.

Mullen fled, closing the front door softly behind him. He stopped on the sidewalk to inhale deeply. He let the air out and walked back up to Delmar and caught a streetcar. Almost immediately, he had to change to another car, but this one took him to Union Station, where he first sent a telegram to the police department, then bought a ticket for home.

The westbound pulled in almost immediately. Mullen boarded and found a seat. He sat swaying slightly with the movement of the train, fully awake, for the entire trip. For some reason, he wanted to cry. But he thought that would be childish, so he didn't.

St. Louis

Mrs. Gordon woke him at seven.

"I'm sorry," she said softly. "We're going to open in an hour, and the salesmen will be showing up pretty soon."

"Right." Buckner sat up. His eyes felt gritty. He pulled on his shoes. "How is he?"

Dutton lay motionless on the cot. The cover rose and fell with his breathing.

"He's sleeping. He's all right. For now."

"Good." Buckner got to his feet. "Thanks."

He went down the stairs and through the sales room, where Joe Gordon was sweeping up. Buckner waved briefly, Gordon waved back, and Buckner was on the street. East of the city, on the far side of the river, across the Illinois floodplain, the sky glowed brightly as the sun shimmered just above the horizon. The rain had moved on and the air was clear and sharp. Buckner hurried to Harris's place. He knew it wouldn't be easy to convince Marty to leave town and go hide out in Corinth, but he had decided to try.

"She's gone," Mrs. Harris snapped at Buckner as she let him in.

"They took her?"

"No. She ran off last night when we wasn't looking. Told Ruth and Margaret we was in danger as long as she was here, and she left."

"Did she say where she was going?"

"Didn't matter. They didn't believe us."

"They?"

"Yes, 'they.' Them cops you got all stirred up. They come here last night, looking for you, or her, didn't make no nevermind to them. They wanted blood."

140

She led Buckner to a small, cramped bedroom where Harris, heavily bandaged, was being tended by his children. Both girls, dressed for school, were offering food. The boy sat on the bed and held his father's bandaged hand.

"It was Kane," Harris said, his voice croaking. "Him and a couple of his boys. They come in here late last night, said they was looking for you and Dutton. Whatever you did, it sure as hell made them mad. I told them I didn't know where you were, or where your sister was neither, but they didn't care. They worked me over. And then that Kane dragged Ruthie in, told me I better tell him or she was gonna pay for it. I don't care how much money you pay me, if I'da known, I'da told him."

"He didn't hurt me, Daddy," Ruth said. "His breath smelled like—"

"That's enough of that," Mrs. Harris said.

"And it don't matter worth a damn," Harris added.

"I'm sorry," Buckner said. "I've brought all this down on you. Have you called a doctor to take a look at him?"

"We can't afford have no doctor come here," she said.

Buckner took out his roll of cash.

"And we don't want your damned money, neither."

"It's not my money. It's what was left from a haul we took off a man and woman came through Corinth and tried to stick up a gas station. They shot it out with Officer Carter, and they wound up dead. We found this on them, and it's been sitting in my filing cabinet for a year." He peeled off a twenty and handed it to Mrs. Harris, who brushed it away.

Ruth grabbed it.

"I know a doctor," she said.

"Who?" her parents demanded simultaneously.

"He's that Greek. He lives next door. I was at the butcher's once and he cut himself real bad and this fella come running. He's Greek, too. The butcher. At least he talked Greek to him, the doctor, I mean. But he can talk English, too."

"All right," Buckner said. "If that's not enough to bring him, tell me and I'll give you more."

Ruth smiled a little smile.

"He'll come for a lot less than this, if I ask him." And she turned and disappeared from the room.

Margaret, the younger girl, giggled.

"You're teaching your grandmother to suck eggs with that one," Mrs. Harris said unhappily.

"Fine," Buckner said. "I'm going to go see if I can find my damned sister. Maybe somebody at the newspaper will know something."

"As soon as I'm back on my feet," Harris said. "I'm going to find that Kane. He made a mistake when he threatened Ruthie."

"By that time, I plan on having taken care of him myself," Buckner said.

Harris glowered, and Buckner left. He paused in the doorway, his eyes scanning the traffic, the people, looking for whatever looked like it didn't belong. Then he crossed quickly and stepped into another doorway, where he could keep an eye on Harris's building. After a few minutes, Ruth came out, wearing high heeled shoes and hose and her hair piled up on top of her head and her lips painted. She strode hip-swinging into the building next door, emerging almost immediately with a skinny, dark young man who carried a doctor's bag. By the look on his face, he was prepared to follow Ruth Harris to the moon if she asked.

They went inside and nobody paid any attention to them except Buckner.

At that hour the *Post-Dispatch* offices were busy, but Rebecca Wieczek spotted him and hurried over.

"Have you found her?"

"No. I was hoping to find her here."

"We haven't seen her since you were here the other day. Flaherty said she dropped off something she'd done on that police story she's been working on. Left it at the door and took off again."

"When was this?"

"Last night some time."

"Right. Thanks." Buckner turned to go.

"She's in a lot of trouble, isn't she," Wieczek said.

"Yes." Buckner paused. "And I think I've made it worse. For her, and for some friends of mine who tried to help me. But I will put an end to those men."

"All right." Rebecca Wieczek saw the look in Buckner's eyes. "Maybe when you've taken care of this."

"Maybe. Sorry about missing dinner last night. I got pulled in by the police."

"What for?" she demanded.

"I'll tell you later," Buckner said, and walked out.

Again he hesitated in the doorway and watched the street. Traffic flowed along Olive Street, pedestrians, autos, buses, streetcars, all hurrying.

The doorman, watching him, said, "You mighty careful."

"Old habit," Buckner said.

"She said you was in the war. Marty."

"Long time ago," Buckner said.

"Word is, she in trouble. You gonna get her out of it."

"Yes."

In the face of Buckner's clipped, unfriendly replies, the doorman fell silent.

Buckner considered his options. Harris and Dutton were both out of action. But Sweeney had told him about some federal agents who had helped take down one of the city's more prominent gangs, Reagan's Rats, and they worked closely with Johnny Morris. Morris had been on the trail of Kane and his bunch of rogue cops. And his sister was on the verge of running a major story on that, with information Morris would provide. Buckner also believed Kane and his gang were behind the death of the deputy mayor. Maybe the federal people would have information on Kane and his thugs, something, anything to give him a way to make a move against them. To get them to leave his sister alone, at least. Maybe to set them up for Sweeney to arrest them for the death of Hanley, or Johnny Morris. That would be even better.

In any event, Buckner knew he was on his own, and on unfamiliar ground, and he needed all the help he could get.

When he was as satisfied as he could be that the street was safe, he walked out into it. A ten-minute walk took him to the federal building and he went in. The day had begun. Serious men in vested suits strode purposefully, girls in high heeled shoes, steno pads in hand, clicked along in their wake. The office directory on the wall told him where the U.S. Treasury Department had rooms on the third floor.

In the first office he entered, Buckner found three young men with coffee cups in their hands sharing a joke. They had their jackets off and their sleeves rolled up. The office held desks and steel file cabinets. A map of the city hung on one wall. A window overlooked the street below. There were other doors, unmarked, in the opposite walls. When the trio's laughter subsided, they noticed him, staring at him with eyebrows raised.

Buckner showed them his badge. They glanced at it, unimpressed.

"I'm looking for somebody that was involved in the investigation of the Reagan gang," he said.

"Reagan gang?"

"Probably before your time. Somebody named Casterman."

The three men looked puzzled, shook their heads.

One of the other doors opened and a fourth young man entered.

"Ah," Buckner said. "*Casterline*, not Casterman."

"Hello, Chief Buckner," Joel C. Casterline said, shaking Buckner's hand. "How are you?"

"I'm fine, Agent Casterline. What are you doing here? Last time I saw you, you were headed back to Washington."

"I was, Chief," Casterline said. "I told them I didn't want to go back to accounting, that I thought I had proved myself, and that they ought to put me in the field."

"And here you are. Congratulations."

"That letter from Mr. Linderman at the bank helped a lot."

The three young men didn't even pretend not to listen.

"Agent Casterline here," Buckner explained to them, "along with one of my officers, broke up a bank robbery in progress and got in a shootout with a whole gang of bank robbers."

"Well, I'll be," one of them said.

"Yeah. And here we just thought Joel C. was a whiz with an adding machine."

"You'll have to tell us all about it, Joel C."

The trio resumed laughing while Casterline looked embarrassed and smug at the same time.

"And this is your reward," Buckner said.

"Yes, it is. Let's get away from these comedians. Come on into my office and tell me what the Treasury Department can do for you."

Casterline showed Buckner through the door he had just used. It was another office, this one smaller, with a pair of partner desks facing each other. More maps hung on the walls, maps of Missouri, the city, St. Louis County, East St. Louis across the river. There were pins in some of the maps. The one small window looked across to another office, perhaps ten feet away, where a young man at a desk hunched over a typewriter.

"Bill's out," Casterline said. "My partner. He's working on a case."

"Moonshiners again?" Buckner asked. He sat in a wooden chair next to the desks.

"Counterfeiters," Casterline said. "Secret Service."

"So, more congratulations. Does chasing counterfeiters keep you busy?"

"Oh, yes. It's very demanding, following the money around through the economy. Exciting, really." Casterline's enthusiasm made Buckner smile.

"Well, what I really need is some information about an investigation that occurred several years ago. Before you got here."

"I'll help if I can. I think I owe you a favor for helping me land this job. What do you need?"

"A while back, some Treasury people, working with the local police, broke up a gang of bootleggers that was at the heart of the mob warfare at the time."

"Yes, I've heard about that. They sent some people from Washington for that, and most of them went back when the investigation ended."

"Right. One of the St. Louis officers that helped with that was a lieutenant named Johnny Morris. He was murdered the other night, and whoever killed him also tried to kill my sister." Buckner explained Marty's role.

"I read about the investigation, Chief, but I don't see the connection with these officers, except Lieutenant Morris."

"I'm hoping that if I find out where that investigation led, it'll give me some information as to who shot Johnny. Information that could get whoever it was arrested and convicted. And take the heat off my sister."

"That seems kind of a stretch, Chief," Casterline said, reluctantly. "If you don't mind my saying so."

"I agree," Buckner said. "But at the moment, I'm grasping at straws. The two men who were helping me are out of action. There's a police lieutenant working on this gang of rogue cops, but he hasn't got any solid evidence to go with, and I can't wait until he comes up with some. Like I said, grasping at straws."

"I don't know." Casterline was still skeptical. "I'm not sure what kind of information we would have here that would be of any use to you."

"Whatever you can dig up might help."

"All right. Let me ask around, see what I can find out."

Casterline disappeared into the other office. Buckner waited, gazing out the small window, watching the man at the typewriter. Eventually, Casterline returned. He had a thin manila file folder in his hand. He gave it to Buckner.

"This is all I could find. Apparently most of it is either sealed up in the basement here, or in Washington."

"Thanks." Buckner opened the file and started reading while Casterline sat behind his desk.

Brief notes in bad handwriting outlined various aspects of the investigation, people followed and observed, interviewed, actions taken. Buckner concentrated on that, especially a list headed "Morris STLPD." He copied the half-dozen names on that list, along with addresses. He read the file through but found nothing else that attracted his attention, no mention of Kane or any of his gang. Buckner closed the file and put it on the desk.

"Any help?" Casterline asked, looking up.

"I don't know yet. Have to talk to some folks. Meanwhile, my sister has disappeared, so I've got to think about that as well." He stood. "Thanks for your help, Agent Casterline. And, again, congratulations. Looks like you're doing well here."

"Yes, I am." Casterline was cheerful. "I am a long way from Washington and a long way from my mother and all that is very good."

Buckner hesitated, frowning slightly. Casterline, puzzled, watched him. Finally, after a long minute, Buckner sat back down.

"Agent Casterline, do you have some counterfeit money I could look at?"

"I suppose so. What for?"

"An idea I just had. You may be able to help me solve my problem. It would mean a lot more than letting me read a file. And I ought to warn you, I'm up against some pretty dangerous fellows. Dutton and I have already had one go-round with them. That's how he got nicked. And, because they're cops, the system is on their side. And that means my next move has to be outside the system. Not sure yet how far outside, though. It'll depend."

"Dangerous, huh?" Casterline's eyes gleamed. "Well, Chief, you know I can handle myself when things get hot. And crooked cops are bad for everybody because they make our jobs harder." He laughed. "And as for the system, I work for the federal government. We *are* the system."

"It actually never occurred to me for a minute that I couldn't count on you," Buckner said. "But I need information and a couple of items. I don't want to put you in harm's way."

"We'll talk about that," Casterline said. "For now, what do you need?"

"Can you show me a couple of counterfeit bills, say a ten and a twenty?"

"Sure." Casterline opened a drawer and took out several bills. He spread them on his desk, one ten and three twenties. "Now, the ten is obviously bad—"

"Hang on a second, Agent Casterline." Buckner held up a hand. "You're the expert here, but I don't need a lot of information. I just want to borrow a couple."

"What for?"

"I want to set a trap for a fellow. I want to arrest him for passing counterfeit money."

"Oh. Well, you're going to need more than a couple. One or two bad bills, the person might have come by those honestly. If he had, say, four or five, why, I'd have to assume he was intending on passing them, and I'd have to arrest him."

"All right. Supposing you arrested such a person, would you then turn that person over to the local police for custody?"

"Absolutely not. Counterfeiting is a federal crime. We have holding cells in this building for that very purpose. Any such person would, hypothetically, be held here for questioning, investigation, and any further action that might, hypothetically, be required." Casterline frowned slightly. "What do you have in mind?"

"I'm in a bad spot," Buckner confessed. "I need some kind of wedge to start a crack in this gang of Kane's. If I can use the threat of arrest and trial for a federal offense, with a stay at Leavenworth at the end of it, I might be able to get one of them to turn on the others to save his own neck. Get him to testify about the killings they've done. That way Sweeney can bust up this gang, put them out of action for good. That's the only way I can think of to protect my sister from them."

"All that's pretty dicey, Chief. I could lose my job over something like this."

"That's what worries me. I don't want to be responsible for you being chained to an adding machine in Washington."

"With my mother looking over my shoulder. Right. That would be bad. But I can't let you just walk out of here a bunch of counterfeit bills."

"I understand that. But these fellows have a string of killings behind them. It might get risky along the way."

Casterline opened a drawer in his desk and took out a 1917 Smith & Wesson .45 double-action revolver and a box of stubby, fat bullets in half-moon clips.

"Where on earth did you get that?" Buckner asked. "I haven't seen one of those in years."

"The Department doesn't issue firearms, but a lot of agents provide their own. I got this at Goodman's here in town."

"So you're coming along."

"I think I have to." Casterline loaded the pistol and slipped it into his hip pocket. He put a spare set of rounds into his jacket pocket. "What, exactly, are you going to do?"

"I'm going to arrest one of the gang. Arthur Pitaluga. I think he might be a weak link. These man all served in the same outfit in France, except for Arthur. Too young. They rag him about it a lot. He doesn't like it, and works extra hard at proving how tough he is, but I thinks it's phony. If he's looking at federal prison, he might crack."

Buckner started for the door.

"Wait," Casterline said. "Where are you going?"

"To find Pitaluga," Buckner said, starting for the door.

Joel C. Casterline unlocked a drawer, pulled it open, and took several bills from it. He closed and locked the drawer and hurried to catch up with Buckner..

"Chief, hang on. You're moving pretty fast. You really think this is such a good idea?"

"Then stay home if you don't like it."

"But, Chief, I can't ...." Casterline's words dribbled to a stop as he had to run to keep pace with Buckner. "All right, all right," he muttered, mostly to himself, since Buckner wasn't listening.

Buckner took him to the coffee shop across from the police station. They sat in a booth.

"Is it safe for you to be here?" Casterline whispered. "This place is full of policemen."

"I think we'll be okay," Buckner said.

The waitress came over and put two heavy china mugs of coffee in front of them.

"Thanks," Buckner said. "How did you know?"

"You cops always start with coffee," she answered. "What comes next is anybody's guess. We got pie and we got doughnuts, fresh-baked this morning. That's usually the next step, on account of they're quick. Anything else takes more time than you usually want to spend here."

"Maybe we're not police officers," Buckner said, winking at her.

"Sure," she laughed. "Well, maybe not him. He don't look old enough to shave. But you got cop written all over you. Besides, I remember you from yesterday."

"Well, I think we'll just stick with coffee for the moment."

"Suit yourself." And she walked back behind the counter, where she began refilling heavy china mugs.

Buckner and Casterline sat for two hours, eventually surrendering to the smell of the fresh doughnuts. Finally, as they were on the point of ordering another round of coffee and doughnuts to avoid attracting attention, Arthur Pitaluga emerged alone from the headquarters building and headed west along Arsenal.

"Give me those bad bills," Buckner said.

Casterline looked about furtively, then slid the bills across to Buckner.

"I'm sure nobody noticed you looking around like you just robbed a bank," Buckner said, pocketing the bills. "Let's go."

Buckner left real money on the table and got to his feet. Casterline followed. They let Pitaluga get well ahead. The neighborhood was home to breweries, struggling now, barely getting by, legally at least, by making other beverages and baker's yeast. They had been built there in the previous century because, according to legend, the underground caves were ideal for laagering.

Benton Park was straight ahead, and Buckner picked up the pace, rushing to close the gap. Pitaluga actually seemed surprised when Buckner jabbed him in the back with the barrel of his .38.

"What the hell!"

"Just keep walking, Arthur, and I won't blow a hole clear through your spine."

"Are you crazy? In broad daylight? One shout from me and you'll have cops all over you."

"And you won't know or care, so keep moving and keep quiet."

Pitaluga spotted Casterline.

"Who the hell are you?" he demanded.

Casterline said nothing.

"Are you with him? Cause if you are, you are both in a heap of shit," Pitaluga said. "I'm headed to meet Kane and McKinney and if I ain't there in ten minutes, they're gonna know something's up and they're gonna come looking for me."

"By the time they notice you're late, Arthur, you will be tucked away somewhere they will never find you," Buckner said.

"I'm telling you—"

"Oh, shut up," Buckner said, jamming his pistol harder into Pitaluga's back. Pitaluga grunted and went silent.

The three men crossed into the park, passed a small pond, and stepped under a pavilion. The park was empty. They sat Pitaluga on one of the benches. Buckner reached into Pitaluga's coat and took his service weapon and his wallet. He pocketed the one and looked through the other.

"Agent Casterline," he said, turning away from Pitaluga for an instant. "Would you take a look at these Federal Reserve notes?"

"Certainly, Chief Buckner."

"What the hell's going on?" Pitaluga demanded, jumping to his feet. "What are you doing there?"

"Be patient, Arthur." Buckner pushed Pitaluga back onto the bench. "Be patient."

"Yes, Chief," Casterline said. He held out several bills. "These are almost certainly counterfeit. And since there are so many of them, and they are brand new, I have to conclude this person intended on passing them."

"Who the hell are you, anyway?" Pitaluga wailed. "That's not my money."

"Never mind who he is," Buckner said. "You're carrying counterfeit money, and that's a federal crime. And I think you're planning on passing them."

"That's a damned lie!" Pitaluga appealed to Casterline. "I don't know nothing about any damned counterfeit money. I am a police officer, and this man here is a wanted fugitive. The police department suspects he is involved in a number of crimes in this city."

"Go get us a cab," Buckner said to Casterline.

Shaking his head and muttering darkly to himself, Casterline walked to the corner of the park and flagged a cab. The three men got in back, Pitaluga in the middle.

"Courthouse," Buckner snapped.

"I'm a—" Pitaluga began.

He stopped when Buckner poked him hard in the ribs with the .38.

The cab driver paid no attention and drove the short distance to the courthouse. As he pulled up to the curb, Buckner said, "Around back."

"Why the hell didn't you say so?" the cab driver said.

Buckner held up his badge for the driver to see.

"Fine, fine. Around back," the driver said.

He pulled around the corner and stopped by a door marked "Deliveries."

Buckner paid the fare and they got out and hustled Pitaluga into the building and down to the basement. The basement, dark and apparently deserted, held two barred cells, each containing a bench and nothing else.

Casterline said, "Wait here," and vanished down a dark hallway. He returned several minutes later with a man wearing overalls and wiping powdered sugar from his chin with a bright red bandanna. He carried a huge ring of keys. A brief search revealed the correct one, and he unlocked a cell.

"This is a damned setup!" Pitaluga shouted. "This is kidnapping, and I'm a St. Louis police officer. You are aiding and abetting a crime."

The janitor ignored him, said nothing, and disappeared silently back down the dark hallway. Casterline and Buckner shoved Pitaluga into the cell and closed the door behind him. The lock clicked sharply into place.

"Now," Buckner said. "Let's talk about crime."

"I haven't committed any goddamned crime, and you know it," Pitaluga snapped.

"Of course you have," Buckner said. "You and your friends, Kane and the rest, have been committing crimes, contract killings, for the past year or so."

"You can't prove a goddamned thing! You got no evidence at all that any of us was involved in any killings that wasn't in the line of duty."

"That's probably true," Buckner admitted. "But we do have evidence that you were carrying counterfeit money, probably with the intention of passing that money, and the sentence for that is pretty stiff. Isn't it, Agent Casterline?"

"Yes," Casterline admitted.

"Up to ten years, right?"

"Yes." Casterline's mouth was thin, hard line. "Listen, Chief—"

"And in a federal prison, Arthur. Probably Leavenworth." Buckner was smiling. "And you can guess how an ex-cop would do in Leavenworth."

"You son of a bitch," Pitaluga said.

"We're going to leave you here to think about all this, Arthur. And here's something else you can work on. If you decide to turn state's evidence, testify against your, uh, friends in the department, I'd be happy work on getting you a reduced sentence on this counterfeiting thing. And in a better spot than Leavenworth. Maybe even get you probation."

"Bullshit. What good would probation do me? I'd be dead inside a week."

"Not if your colleagues, Kane and the rest, were in prison instead of you.

"Wait a minute. Just hold on a minute. Why is all this so goddamned important? We're just doing our jobs, getting the hoodlums off the street. We've lost almost two dozen cops since I been on the force. Hell, most people would thank us if they knew what we were doing."

"Does that include murdering a deputy mayor? And a fellow police officer?"

"Hold it," Pitaluga said, raising both hands. "I didn't have nothing to do with that. That was back before I started working with Kane ..." Realizing he might have gone too far, he clamped his mouth shut.

"Johnny Morris died two days ago, Arthur. And whoever shot him tried to kill my sister."

"I didn't have nothing to do with that either. I swear." Pitaluga gripped the bars, his knuckles whitening. "I never liked Morris, always so goddamned pleased with himself, going on about crooked cops, the whole time he's screwing other cops' wives. So, yeah, I didn't like him, but I never killed him. And I never shot at your damned sister, but I'd sure like to give it a try. She thinks she's so smart, writing lies about good cops."

Casterline muttered unhappily to Buckner, "Are we done here?"

"Yes," Buckner replied. "I believe we are."

As the two men started to go, Pitaluga said, "You gonna leave me here?"

"Have to," Buckner said. "All that bad money you were carrying."

"Dammit, that wasn't my money, I tell you. You planted that on me."

"You think about what I told you, Arthur," Buckner said. He left with Casterline.

"You're gonna pay for this," Pitaluga shouted after them.

"Chief Buckner," Casterline said urgently as they climbed the stairs out of the darkness. "I'm really in your debt for me ending up in this job, but what we're doing is completely illegal. We can't hold him for more than a couple of hours. Not even that, really. We don't have any grounds for any of this. If someone finds him there, this whole thing is going to blow up in our faces ... my face."

"I just need you to hang onto him for a little bit, just enough time to get hold of Kane, the man in charge of this gang. He needs to know that Arthur has been arrested on a federal charge, and that he is going to trade information about the murder squad in exchange for better treatment."

"But he hasn't agreed to any such thing," Casterline said.

"Kane won't know that. And, besides, sometimes if you want apples, you have to shake the tree."

"These particular apples might just come down shooting."

"That thought had occurred to me," Buckner admitted.

Casterline looked closely at Buckner for a moment and said, "Look here, Chief. Do you want these men arrested and put on trial, or do you just plan on shooting them? Because if that's what you have in mind, you will have to count me out."

"Arrest and conviction is the point, Agent Casterline. Any shooting will start with them. You have my word."

"What about the police department? Are you going to tell them what's going on?"

"Oh, they know. There's that cop, Sweeney, who's after these men, too. Soon as I talk to Kane, I'll get in touch with Sweeney, let him know what's up. That way it'll all get done proper and correct."

"All right. And you understand I really can't have Pitaluga prosecuted on that counterfeiting charge, since it really was us, after all, well, you, really, that planted that money on him."

"Yes, Agent Casterline. I understand. Don't worry. We're getting a little outside the boundaries a little here, but only a little, and only for a little while."

"I'm an officer of the court, Chief Buckner. And so are you."

"And these people tried to kill my sister and me and Elroy Dutton, and they beat another friend within an inch of his life, and threatened his family." Buckner wondered in passing if Harris would appreciate being called his friend. He continued, biting his words sharply. "And I'm pretty sure they murdered the deputy mayor, Hanley, and Johnny Morris. If I can get these people locked up, that'll be fine with me, but whether that happens or not, these men are finished. I'm finishing them. No matter what it takes. You think about that, Agent Casterline, and if that's too much for you to handle, you let me know right now."

Casterline said nothing, just continued frowning at Buckner.

"Don't suppose you'd let me borrow your telephone," Buckner said after a moment. When Casterline, with eyes wide in astonishment, opened his mouth, Buckner raised a hand. "Never mind. I'll find a pay phone."

He hurried down to ground floor, where one wall was a rank of telephone booths. He found an empty one and used it. The desk officer at the Seventh District was skeptical, but eventually he summoned Lieutenant Kane.

"Yeah? Who's this?"

"James Buckner, Lieutenant. I'm just calling you to let you know one of your soldiers, Arthur Pitaluga, has been picked up on a federal charge of counterfeiting. He's looking at ten years at Leavenworth."

"So what?"

"So, it turns out Arthur is willing to pass along certain information on you and your murder squad, sworn testimony in exchange for a lighter sentence in a less hazardous facility."

"Bullshit. Little Arthur doesn't have the guts."

"Whatever you say, Lieutenant. But I think he's pretty tired of being called 'Little Arthur.' You and your gang killed Hanley and my friend Johnny Morris and tried to kill my sister and me, and I'm going to use Arthur Pitaluga to make sure you go to prison for a long time."

"We didn't have anything to do with any of that," Kane said. "Hanley was a drunk whose luck ran out. Morris got what he deserved, but it wasn't any of my people. Hell, guys would be lining up to take a shot at Morris. Your sister was just in the wrong place at the wrong time, but if she'd gotten it along with Morris, I wouldn't lose a minute's sleep over it. As for your run in with my crew the other day, that's your own damn fault for sticking your nose in."

"And then there's all those killings for hire you and your boys have been doing for various gangs around town."

"Arthur's not very smart," Kane said. "But he's not stupid enough to provide testimony on anything he might make up to try to get out of whatever jam he's gotten himself in. Smearing his fellow officers won't win him any friends. And his testimony is going to be hearsay anyway, unless he plans on confessing to murdering people."

"We'll have to see," Buckner said. "But a trial like that would attract a lot of attention. The papers will have a feast on his testimony. You sure you and your boys can handle that kind of publicity?"

"You are way out of your league here, Buckner. You head on back down to Podunk. And tell your sister to put a lid on all those stories about police corruption. That way neither one of you will have any trouble from me or my friends. None at all. But I'll tell you something for free, that nigger you pal around with is some serious trouble now that he's decided he can operate in my town. And that cousin of his isn't gonna be able to stop me if I wanna talk to him. You understand me?"

"As far as I'm concerned, Kane, you bought yourself a whole lot of trouble when you started in on my friends and family, and I'm not going to quit until I'm satisfied you won't be any more trouble to me or mine."

Buckner slammed the receiver down before Kane could respond. Kane's words had set off alarms. He ran back up to Casterline's office.

"I've gotta go check on Dutton. You sit on Arthur until the end of the day, then cut him loose if you want. I'll call if I have anything to tell you."

Back on the street, he hailed a cab.

"The Ville," he said, giving the driver the address of Joe Gordon's store. "And step on it."

Where he was just minutes too late.

The store had been ransacked. Several pieces in the showroom had been toppled over. A lamp lay shattered on the floor. One of Gordon's salesmen, the tall one, sat nursing a bleeding head wound. Gordon's wife, weeping, was tending to it.

Gordon was furious.

"The police were here, not five minutes ago! They dragged Elroy out of here and threw him in the back of a police car. They said he was wanted for murder."

"He's not wanted for murder. He's wanted for helping me."

"What in hell are you up to? Bringing police around here, turning my business upside down. Dammit, you don't understand what that means. For a colored man in this town, the only way to do business is to be invisible to the police. Look what they did here." Gordon's arm swept the store, his wife, his salesman. "Now, every time something happens in this neighborhood, they're going to be knocking on my door, throwing my stuff around. Goddamn you and Elroy both. Just get the hell out of here."

Gordon stormed off to the back of the store, grabbed a broom, and began sweeping up pieces of the broken lamp. Buckner could hear him muttering curses. He hesitated before turning to Gordon's wife.

"How bad is Dutton?"

"Not good," she said, glancing her husband's way. "He was getting better, but if they rough him up too much, it's going to kill him. And even if they just put him in a cell, it won't do him any good."

Gordon threw down the broom and confronted Buckner. He took a scrap of paper from his pocket and held it out.

"I damn near didn't give you this," he said. "But here, take it. It's from them."

"Thank you." Buckner read the note. All it said, in a penciled scrawl, was "Straight up swap our man for your's tonight here Wild Horse Creek Road at six just you and Arthur or hes dead."

"That's out in the County," Gordon said.

"Yes. It's where Hanley ran his motor off the road." Buckner pocketed the note. "Look, I'm sorry we brought this down on you. I honestly didn't think they'd be able to move this fast. But I don't think it's the police department you have to worry about. Just these particular policemen. And I'm going to put them out of business for good."

"Well, there's at least four of them. That's how many did this," Gordon said. "And there's only one of you."

"I've got some help. My guess is, they're going to want to keep this quiet. They're no more interested in attracting police attention than you are. They have to know the department's on their trail. But they have made a serious mistake, because I am going to get to them before the department does."

Before Gordon could respond, Buckner turned and left the building. He caught a streetcar south to the federal building and went up to Casterline's office without stopping.

"I have to know," he said. "Either you're in or you're out." He tossed the note on the desk. Casterline read it.

"Swap?"

"Looks like it. I expect they're just going to kill me and Dutton, maybe Pitaluga as well, since they might see him as more a threat than an ally now."

"But you're not going to go through with this, are you? I mean, since you know it's a trap?"

"Yes. It's a chance to get them alone, on neutral ground. It's the only real chance I have to make sure my sister will be safe without me taking up residence here."

"How do you know they don't have her too? You said she'd gone missing."

"I don't know. But I think Kane would have said something if he had her. He was very sure of himself on the telephone, bragging, even. If he had Martha Jane, I'm pretty sure he would want to rub my face in it. She's been missing for a good twenty-four hours now. I just hope she's smart enough to keep her head down until this thing is over."

"What about Dutton?"

"He got himself into this jam trying to help my sister, and I'll be damned if I'm going to let those bastards get away with killing him."

Casterline thought a moment. "I might just have something that will give you an edge." He went to a filing cabinet and opened the bottom drawer. From it he pulled what appeared to be a vest made of brown jute sacking.

"You think improving my wardrobe is going to help?"

"It's going to improve your chances of living through this rendezvous you're cooking up. We took it off a hoodlum who was working as a bodyguard for a local fellow, an authentic counterfeiter. They've started turning up a lot. Homemade and very popular with some of the criminal element here in town. I got to keep this one as a souvenir after I helped in the arrest."

"I saw things like that in the war," Buckner said. "Everything from homemade like this one to factory made. Some of them worked pretty well, but they were too heavy, or too bulky to move around in. None of them offered much protection against a heavy machine gun or even a well-aimed rifle shot. And no protection at all to arms and legs."

"We tested this one," Casterline said, pointing to holes in the sacking. "It will stop a .22, even a .38, if you're not too close."

"All right," Buckner said, taking the vest. "Thanks."

"Now what?"

"Now I'm going to go get Arthur Pitaluga and trade him for Elroy Dutton."

"We are," Casterline corrected.

"I think I'd better go alone, Agent Casterline. I appreciate the offer, but if Secretary Mellon finds out you're been involved in this, you won't be sent back to Washington, you'll be out of a job."

"That's only if he finds out," Casterline said. "You gonna tell him?"

"All right. Let's go then."

"Isn't it a bit early? The note said four."

"If they're smart, they'll be there already, waiting for us."

"So we are going to get there even earlier."

"We are." Buckner gave Casterline an address and a ten dollar bill. "Go hire us a motor. We have a drive ahead of us, and I wouldn't want to risk one of Secretary Mellon's autos."

"That's all right," Casterline said. "I'm not important enough to rate one."

After Casterline had gone, Buckner telephoned Sweeney.

"I'll be bringing in your boys tonight. Can't say exactly when for sure. Meet me at that warehouse you took me to."

"All of them?" Sweeney did not sound surprised.

"All of them."

"Fine. See you tonight."

Buckner found Arthur Pitaluga sitting in his cell, his head in his hands. He located the janitor with the keys.

"How's he been getting on?" Buckner asked.

"Oh, he hollered for a while, finally gave it up when nobody paid him any mind."

The janitor opened the cell and Buckner went in.

"Time to go, Arthur."

"Go where?"

"To meet your friends. They've got Elroy Dutton and they want to trade with me: him for you."

"Huh. I guess you're not as smart as you thought you were."

"We'll see. Come on."

Pitaluga got to his feet and the two men climbed the stairs.

Corinth

When the train whistle screeched, the two men checked their watches.

"I'm gonna get across the tracks," Griswold said. "Get on from that side, so he don't see me. This is an express, and there ain't no Jim Crow car, but the last car has a Jim Crow section."

"Fine," Shotwell said.

Griswold disappeared through the door. Shotwell went to the window and bought a ticket from a scowling Mr. Weiner. As the train pulled in, Shotwell stepped onto the platform and headed for the last car. A conductor came down onto the platform and looked around. He was short, with bandy legs and a pot belly that pushed out the front of his uniform jacket. Since Shotwell was the only person getting on or off, he scanned his watch, signaled the engineer, and climbed back aboard.

As the train pulled out, Shotwell, swaggering slightly, strolled into the last car. It contained no white people at all. Several families crowded the Jim Crow section, parents and children filling most of the seats. Shotwell sat next to an elderly woman in old-fashioned black crepe and a hat with a small mesh veil. She had watched him come in, wrinkling her nose in disapproval. Several of the other passengers gave Shotwell similar looks before glancing away. One couple carefully reseated their children next to the window, away from the aisle and Shotwell's corrupting influence. But the children still managed to stare at him covertly.

"Hello, Missus," Shotwell said to his seat mate. "Goin' far?"

She harrumphed and ignored him, turning to look out the window.

He looked around. He had not been on a train in several years, mostly because there was no direct train service between Corinth and the county seat, where he had been born and raised and where most of his family still lived. The run first to Steelville, then over, was just too damn much trouble. But he had to admit, as he looked at the empty front end of the car, the Whites Only section, that the Missouri Pacific was adhering strictly to the equal part of "separate but equal." From what he could see, there was no difference between the two sections.

"That's going away one of these days," he muttered to himself.

The woman next to him gave him a startled look.

"Jim Crow," he said, smiling happily. "Ain't gonna last."

She looked at him for a long time and then, to his utter surprise, she winked at him. Then went back to virtuously ignoring him by looking out the window.

It did not take the pot-bellied conductor long to get to the last car. Dutton was the only new passenger. The conductor came down the aisle and held out his hand. Dutton gave him his ticket. The conductor punched it and slid the stub under the handle on the seat back. He turned and headed back up the aisle. Dutton rose and followed him. He spoke softly as the conductor reached the vestibule.

"'Scuse me, Cap'n."

The conductor whirled around. "Yeah?"

"I's wondering if y'all could help me out."

"Yeah?"

"See, Cap'n, I'm bone dry, and I's wondering if you could lemme know where a gentleman could maybe wet his whistle."

The conductor peered closely at him before answering.

"You smell like you've had enough for one day."

"Oh, no, sir. Not hardly. See, I'm gonna be meeting a young lady up to town and she don't like it if I show up empty handed, if you know what I mean. So if you could lemme know of a place somewhere along the line here, I'd be mighty grateful."

"You go on and set back down. I'll go about my business, maybe give it a think."

"I could really use the help, Cap'n."

"Go set down, boy. I'll get to you when I'm good and ready."

"Yes, sir, Cap'n." Shotwell sketched a vague salute, returned to his seat, and sat down. This time his seat mate shook her head disapprovingly.

Embarrassed and furious, Shotwell ground his teeth and said nothing. After a few more minutes. Griswold of the Missouri Pacific strolled into the car, looked around, and nodded. Then he stepped into the tiny rest room.

Nothing happened for almost an hour, and the rocking of the train was putting Shotwell to sleep when the conductor came in and tapped him roughly on the shoulder. When Shotwell looked up, the conductor turned and went back to the end of the car, stopping just outside the restroom door. Shotwell, cane in hand, stepped jauntily along behind him.

"All right," the conductor said. He reached into his jacket pocket and pulled out a flat, brown pint bottle stoppered with a cork that had obviously been used before. "That'll be twenty bucks."

"Twenty dollars for a pint?" Shotwell said. "Tha's mighty steep, Cap'n."

"Up to you." The chubby conductor shrugged. "But that's how much it costs."

"Well, just so's I know what all I'm buying, is that home brew, or the real thing?"

"Oh, it's the real thing, good Canadian rye."

"Tha's why it's twenty bucks."

"You're damned right. Now fork over the twenty, 'cause I gotta get back to work."

Shotwell took a wallet from his jacket pocket and extracted a twenty dollar bill. He handed it to the conductor and took the bottle from him.

"Thank you, Cap'n," he said, and stepped back. "And now you are under arrest."

"What! You can't arrest me, nigger!"

"I sure as hell can," Griswold said, stepping through the WC door.

The conductor, for all his extra weight, moved faster than either of them expected. He shoved Griswold against Shotwell, and as the two men staggered back, entangled in each other, he pulled a small pistol out of his jacket pocket and fired. Griswold cried out and went down. Shotwell swung his cane hard, hitting the conductor above the left ear, knocking his cap off. His pistol fell to the floor. Shotwell hit him again, breaking the cane and sending the conductor to the floor as well. Shotwell, half the broken cane still in his hand, flipped the conductor onto his belly and knelt in the middle of his back, smiling as he heard the air whoosh out. He dropped the cane and pulled out his cuffs, locking the conductor's hands behind him, clamping the cuffs down tight. When the conductor groaned in pain, Shotwell closed the cuffs even tighter. Then he leaned down and whispered in the conductor's ear.

"You be careful what you call people next time."

The conductor did not respond.

Shotwell grabbed the conductor's pistol and was on his feet in an instant. He went to where Griswold sat, leaning his back against a seat. He was holding his hand tight against his right thigh. His trousers and hands were soaked with blood.

Shotwell pulled off his belt and ran it around Griswold's thigh above the wound and pulled it tight.

"Hold this," he said.

Griswold nodded and took the end of the belt and pulled it even tighter, grimacing as he did so.

"First aid kit," he said through clenched teeth.

"Where?" Shotwell demanded.

"Cupboard behind that door there."

Shotwell went to a small door in the wall of the car opposite the restroom and pulled it open. A small white box with a red cross sat there, along with a fire axe and some flares. Shotwell grabbed the first aid kit and returned to Griswold. His seatmate had, in the meantime, gotten up and joined them.

"Give me that," she snapped, holding out her hand. Shotwell handed the kit to her. She opened it and took out a roll of bandaging and a pair of scissors. "Here. Cut his trouser leg off with these."

Shotwell took the scissors and did as instructed, exposing Griswold's blood-covered leg. The elderly woman had opened a small brown bottle and emptied its contents onto the wound. Griswold arched his back and cursed.

"You mind your manners, young man," the elderly woman ordered sternly. "I've patched up worse that this in my time."

With confident hands, she pressed the roll of bandages against Griswold's wound, then secured it in place with adhesive tape.

"He can ease off on the belt," she said to Shotwell. "It didn't hit no artery. But you need to lay him down flat and cover him up so the shock don't kill him."

Shotwell looked around. No blankets anywhere. But a woman at the back came forward with a large shawl and held it out. Shotwell took it, thanked her, and draped it over Griswold as he eased him carefully onto his back.

"Get to the caboose," Griswold whispered. "Another first aid kit there … brakeman, signal for help at the next stop." Then he passed out.

"Thank you, Missus," Shotwell said to the woman.

"Freeman," she said. "Miss. Freeman."

"Thank you, Miss Freeman. Can you keep an eye on him while I run back and get some help?"

"Of course," she sniffed.

Shotwell got up and hurried down the car, through the door and into the caboose. Two men, blissfully ignorant of what was going on in their train, looked up in surprise from their card game.

"I'm a police officer," Shotwell said, showing his badge. "There's been a shooting. You need to come now."

St. Louis

When Joel C. Casterline pulled the rented Ford to the curb in front of the courthouse, he found Buckner with Pitaluga, hands cuffed behind him, waiting on the sidewalk. Buckner put Pitaluga in the back seat and joined Casterline in front.

"Head west out of town," Buckner said. He took the map from the glove box and consulted it.

"Where we going?"

"Wild Horse Creek Road," Buckner said. "It's out where Deputy Mayor Hanley had his accident."

"I remember reading about that." Casterline said. "I haven't lived here long enough, or had time enough, to go exploring. About all I know about this town is the neighborhood between my apartment and my office."

"Well, I've got kin here, but I've never done much exploring either."

With Buckner giving directions, Casterline found the spot easily.

"It's pretty quiet out this way," Buckner said as Casterline pulled the Ford off the road. The land had been logged before the War Between the States, and scrub pine had taken over, though dogwood and redbuds could be seen blooming here and there.

"It sure is. I didn't see any farms for the last mile or so."

"And no traffic either."

They hauled Arthur Pitaluga from the back seat and walked him to a tree by the side of the road.

"Have a seat," Buckner said.

Pitaluga opened his mouth to say something. Buckner showed him his palm.

"Sit down or I will knock you down. It's going to be a while before your friends show up."

Pitaluga sat down. Buckner took out a handkerchief and stuffed it into Pitaluga's mouth, fixing it in place with a bandana from his hip pocket.

"Agent Casterline, you are my ace in the hole, so I would appreciate it if you would find a big tree over there somewhere and hide yourself behind it. And don't come out until I call you. I don't think they know about you, and I'd like to keep it that way for a while."

"All right." Casterline disappeared behind a tree. Buckner found one of his own and settled down against it, in plain sight of the road.

The afternoon grew still. The air, heavy with moisture, felt thick and steamy, and it brought out mosquitos. Buckner took out a cigar and lighted it. The smoke kept the mosquitos at a distance. He could hear Casterline slapping and complaining. Pitaluga squirmed and grunted and suffered.

The cigar lasted just long enough. As Buckner was stubbing it out against the tree, two vehicles, one from each direction, came slowly down the road. They stopped twenty yards apart at the bottom. Nobody got out.

Buckner opened his trench coat, pushing it behind his holstered pistol, and stepped into view. He helped Pitaluga to his feet, and together they walked out into the road. Lieutenant Kane got out of one of the cars and stepped away from it.

"You got here early," he said.

"Of course."

"I've got your boy here in the back." Kane gestured with a thumb. "He's in pretty bad shape. How's my friend Arthur."

"Oh, he's fine, just fine. The skeeters have been at him, but he'll live."

"So you persuaded Little Arthur it was better in the long run to turn state's evidence against us rather than go to Leavenworth on a phony counterfeiting charge."

Pitaluga shook his head vigorously and grunted, his eyes wide and pleading.

"That's how it's going to go," Buckner said.

"Bullshit. No judge is going to accept anything Pitaluga has to say."

"We're going to see about that," Buckner said. "The accusations alone are going to be big news: Police Assassination Squad Kills Deputy Mayor."

"Yes," Kane said. "But we're going to take Arthur away from you, and give you back your friend. That was the deal."

"And then you're going to kill us both."

Kane shrugged and grinned. "One way or the other, he won't be testifying against us any time soon."

"Kind of risky, doing your business out here in the open like this," Buckner said.

"Oh, that's no problem. We've got a real good working relationship with our fellow peace officers out here. We told the sheriff we're going to bust up a gang that's been sticking up folks in town. He loaned us a couple of deputies to send any traffic off another way."

Kane raised a hand, and Runge and Shorty Werner got out of the other car. Red McKinney got out of the back of Kane's vehicle. He reached in and hauled out Elroy Dutton. His hands were cuffed behind his back and his face was swollen and bleeding. Buckner could see a broad patch of blood showing through the left side of his shirt.

"You start Arthur walking to Shorty's car back there," Kane said. "I'll start your friend to you. And let's everybody go real slow."

"All right, Arthur," Buckner said. "Start walking."

With one last wild glance of terror, Pitaluga took a step toward Runge and Werner. McKinney released Dutton, who staggered, regained his footing, and took a step. Kane and his crew took out their service revolvers and were just raising them when a brand new, bright blue Oldsmobile Sport Coupe roared down the hill behind Kane's auto.

Everybody turned and looked as the Oldsmobile jolted to a stop and an enormous figure in a too-tight black suit and plug hat exploded through the passenger door, took two long steps, and clubbed Red McKinney to the ground with an enormous fist.

Elroy Dutton dropped flat onto the road as Arthur Pitaluga turned toward Kane. Kane shot him in the chest. Pitaluga reeled and sprawled on his back.

A round cracked by Buckner's ear as he pulled out his pistol. He heard Casterline's big .45 boom and turned to see Shorty Werner go down. Runge looked wildly to find where the shots were coming from.

"I've got these two," Casterline shouted.

Buckner turned back to see Kane disappear into the woods. He fired quickly after him, but hit only trees. Kane returned fire, hitting nothing at all.

And suddenly it was quiet.

Marty Buckner had gotten from behind the wheel of the Oldsmobile and was easing Elroy Dutton onto his back. Buster pulled a key from

McKinney's vest pocket, knelt down and handed Marty a big red bandana. He took Dutton's cuffs off while Marty shoved the bandana under Dutton's shirt, pressing it tight against the blood-soaked bandage there.

Buckner went to check on Casterline. Werner was on the ground holding his leg and rolling back and forth in pain. Runge, white-faced and terrified, stood with his hands in the air. Casterline used the men's own cuffs to shackle them together.

Buckner reached down and lifted Arthur Pitaluga to his feet. He pulled off the gag.

"The son of a bitch shot me!" Pitaluga shouted.

"Sure," Buckner said. He pulled open Pitaluga's jacket and shirt, revealing the bullet-proof vest. A .38 round, only slightly damaged, fell to the road. Buckner picked it up and pocketed it. "You're gonna have one hell of a nasty bruise there, Arthur. And that's something you might want to think over. Kane shooting you, I mean."

"Damned right I'm gonna think about it."

Casterline's two prisoners were sitting on the running board of their vehicle.

"Is he going to bleed to death any time soon?" Buckner asked.

"Oh, hell, I just nicked him. He'll be fine."

"You check them for other weapons? They like to carry several each."

"Sure." Casterline aimed a thumb. "In the boot."

"All right. Put them in their motor. And make sure they haven't got handcuff keys."

Casterline held out a handful of tiny keys and grinned.

"Fine," Buckner said. "Leave the rental here. Put those two in their motor, along with McKinney. Those are police vehicles, so handcuff them to the stanchions bolted to the floor. Take them all back to the warehouse you'll find at this address." Buckner handed Casterline a slip of paper. "You'll meet a Lieutenant Sweeney there, St. Louis police detective. Tell him who you are, and you can turn these fellows over to him."

"How do I explain how they got injured?"

"Let Sweeney worry about it. I expect he will come up with something."

"You sure he won't just turn them loose, fellow officers and all that?"

"No, I'm not," Buckner admitted. "But he seemed pretty serious about it when he told me about these fellows. I think he wants them real bad."

"All right. What about Kane? Looks like he got away."

"I'll go fetch him, bring him back to the warehouse. Tell Sweeney to wait there." He pulled off the trench coat and tossed it into the back of the Oldsmobile. He was going to have to move fast.

With that, he walked into the thick foliage. Casterline started after him, but already he was already gone. All Casterline could hear was a soft rustling sound, which could have been a light breeze through the trees.

He went over to the Oldsmobile. Buster was dragging Red McKinney by the heels over to where the others waited. If he was conscious, McKinney did not protest this treatment.

"You're Buster," Casterline said. "I remember you from Corinth."

Buster just smiled and nodded.

"Let me handcuff him," Casterline said.

Buster twisted McKinney's legs, turning him face down. Casterline cuffed him, then patted him down, finding a .38 service revolver and a four-shot .32, as well as a blackjack and brass knuckles. And two handcuff keys. He kept it all.

"Could you put him over there with the others?" Casterline asked.

"Sure."

Buster dragged McKinney to the vehicle, picked him up, and threw him in the back. Casterline noticed his too-tight jacket had split up the back.

Casterline joined Marty Buckner, who was helping Elroy Dutton to his feet.

"Looks like you've got a full load there," Marty said. "You want me to take a couple of them? I can drop them off after I deliver my friend here to the hospital."

"I think we've never met," Casterline said. He held out his hand and introduced himself.

"I'm Marty Buckner. Buck's sister. And right now, I have to get Mr. Dutton here back into town so he can get looked at by a real doctor."

"I'm all right," Dutton protested, leaning heavily against the Oldsmobile. "I just need a new bandage. And something to drink. After that, you can take me home and turn me over to Jeff Peck. Oh, and where the hell did you come from, anyway?"

"Where the hell do you think I came from?"

"Buck said you disappeared. You went to Corinth."

"Right."

"And you picked up Buster, and borrowed this Oldsmobile from Caroline Bell."

"Right again. She's running the agency now. Inherited from her husband. And she figures she owes Buck for catching the man that killed him."

"But how did you know where to find us?" Casterline asked.

"Buster said to try Joe Gordon's store first. He told us about the note, all the rest of it."

"But what about the one that got away? Kane?" Casterline continued. "And he said there were deputy sheriffs watching the road."

"We found one deputy," Marty said. "Buster persuaded him to let us get by."

"Oh, no," Dutton said. "Is he all right?"

"He should be, if he ever wakes up."

"All right," Casterline said, looking off into the woods where Kane and Buckner had gone. "But maybe I should go help look for Kane."

"Don't worry yourself," Marty said.

"Poor bastard doesn't stand a chance," Dutton said. "If he's smart, he'll come out and give himself up."

"He'd be saving himself a whole lot of trouble," Marty added.

"All right," Casterline said. "If you say so."

"What about that extra police car?" Casterline said.

Marty Buckner shrugged.

"Well," Casterline said. "I'll tell this Sweeney it's out here."

He made sure his cargo of police officers was secured, got into the vehicle, and drove off.

Marty helped the protesting Dutton into the Oldsmobile. Buster pushed the abandoned police car off the road into the brush and, with some difficulty, managed to squeeze himself into the rumble seat.

Marty stood for a moment, looking off into the thick woods. The sun was lower now, casting longer shadows. There was no wind. The country sounds had resumed, soft rustlings, buzzings, chirpings. Somewhere in the distance someone fired a pistol. And then again. Several times. And then there was silence.

Marty smiled and shook her head, got into the Oldsmobile and started it up.

Buckner heard the car drive away. He was already moving up the hill as fast and as quietly as his game leg would let him.

From time to time Kane fired at him and Buckner returned fire, mostly, he hoped, to stop Kane moving, if only long enough to take aim.

They were both headed for the same place, but Buckner wanted to get there first.

A pistol boomed and another round clipped leaves. It came from behind him on his right; he was ahead. He aimed and fired, then he hurried on.

He was breathing hard and his leg was on fire as he came up to the house. He went straight in without stopping, across the porch and into the kitchen where the county deputy sat at a table set for supper. A woman in a faded housedress stood over him putting liniment on his face.

The deputy squawked when he saw Buckner under the woman's arm.

"Don't be a baby," she snapped.

Buckner reached out and slammed the heavy Colt against the side of the deputy's head. He went silently to the floor. The woman spun and opened her mouth. Buckner aimed the Colt at her.

"Don't," he hissed.

"You won't shoot," she hissed back. "Kane's comin' ain't he. He'll hear if you shoot."

And she inhaled deeply.

With his left hand, Buckner snatched a knife from the table and held it against the woman's eye socket, just brushing the eyebrow above and the cheek below.

"He won't hear this."

The woman sagged back against the kitchen table. Buckner kept pace, the knife just brushing her skin.

Buckner heard footsteps on the front porch. He turned away from the woman and raised his pistol.

"Run, Candy!" the woman screamed. "Run!"

Kane fired from the porch. Rounds tore through the kitchen door, embedding themselves in the far wall. The woman knelt on the floor shaking.

Buckner fired through the door, crossed to it, then pulled it open. Kane, gasping for breath, was in the yard ten feet from the bottom of the porch steps. He was hurriedly pushing fresh rounds into the chamber of his service revolver. Bullets spilled from his shaking hands. When he saw Buckner in the doorway, he closed the revolver and raised it.

Buckner fired twice, aiming carefully, aiming close. Kane stood, gulping air. He fired at Buckner. The round went wide, thumping into wood. He continued to point the pistol, the barrel waving. He clutched at the weapon with both hands.

"Don't do it!" Buckner said sharply, and fired again, missing again. "You're done."

Kane pulled the trigger. The hammer dropped on an empty chamber. He let the pistol fall and bent over, his hands on his knees. He vomited, gagging. He wiped a sleeve across his mouth.

"All right. All right."

CORINTH

Shotwell stood on the platform as the train clanked and screeched to a stop, letting of a loud gust of steam.

Michael Mullen, along with two or three others, stepped down. Mullen took Shotwell's outstretched hand like a man drifting out with the tide. He shook it vigorously.

"I'm happy to see you, too, Michael," Shotwell said, smiling. "But I just wanted to get your bag."

"What?" Mullen seemed preoccupied. "Oh. No. No need. I've got it. I've been carrying it around with me so much lately, it feels like part of my arm."

"You all right?" Shotwell asked, looking closely.

"Yes, sure. Of course I'm all right." Mullen was suddenly brusque. "Let's get over to the department. You can tell me how your day went, and I'll tell you about mine."

The two men walked to the town hall and down the stairs into the basement. Mullen strode purposefully; Shotwell, puzzled, followed along.

Bill Newland and Robert Carter sat drinking coffee when they walked in. Mullen dropped his bag and poured coffee for himself and Shotwell. Shotwell pulled two chairs out of the squad room for the two of them to use.

"Wait till you hear how Shotwell and Griswold nailed that conductor," Carter said. "You should'a seen him, all dolled up like some kind of high roller, fancy pimp suit, even a cane!"

Pressed to tell, Shotwell told, doing his best to play down his role. At this, Newland and Carter just laughed.

"Conductor damn near killed Griswold," Carter said. "Shotwell probly saved his life."

"I told you it was the old lady," Shotwell corrected.

The others just laughed.

"How 'bout you, Michael?" Newland asked. "How'd it go at the University?"

"All right," Mullen said without enthusiasm.

"But you found out who it was, and you contacted the family, right?"

"Uh—huh," Mullen admitted. "And I don't ever want to have to do that again."

"Must've been pretty tough, telling the boy's family," Shotwell said sympathetically. It had dawned on him why Mullen seemed so quiet.

"It was terrible. This lady, the mother, she just started crying and I thought she was gonna fall down, but there was a chair there, and she just sat there in the front hall, staring off somewhere, tears pouring down her face and her paying no attention to me at all. It was terrible." Mullen stopped for a moment, resumed. "And I had to tell her about shipping the body of her son, and how he died, and all that, so I gave her Peck's death certificate and got out of there as quick as I could."

"What about her husband?" Newland asked. "How did he take it?"

"Oh, he wasn't there. He's some kind of professor at the University."

"In Columbia? I thought you went to St. Louis."

"I did. Washington University is in St. Louis. But she told me, the mother, that I shouldn't disturb him when he was lecturing, so I didn't. I made sure the maid understood about where the body was and that we'd ship it anywhere the family wanted.

"But it was really terrible. She was just so damned sad."

Mullen put his coffee cup, still full, on the desk, got up, picked up his bag, and headed for the door.

"I'm going home," he said, and pushed through the doors and up the stairs.

He was half way across the square heading for the store, when he angled slightly and went into Goldrosen's jewelry store.

Solon Goldrosen, tall, stooped, was over eighty years old. Mullen had known him all his life.

"Hello, Michael," Goldrosen said, smiling.

"Hello, Mr. Goldrosen. You sometimes take jewelry in pawn, don't you?"

"Well, yes, depending on the piece." If he was surprised by Mullen's question, he didn't show it.

"I'm looking for something specific, a wrist watch, gold, leather strap, fairly new, with the name William Lance on the back. And this would have been a recent transaction."

"No, Michael, nothing like that has come it." Goldrosen thought a moment. "William Lance; was that the name of the young man you found behind your father's store?"

"Yes sir. He had a wallet, which Shotwell found empty in the alley, and a wristwatch, which we haven't found."

"I see. But, no, as I said, nothing like that has come in, Michael."

"All right. If it does come in, could you let me know."

"Of course."

"I had to tell William Lance's mother that her son was dead. I gave her the wallet. I'm pretty sure she would appreciate it if we could get the watch for her."

"Of course," Goldrosen said. "It would be a relief to her, I'm sure."

It would be a relief to me as well, Mullen thought as he went out the door.

St. Louis

Later that night, Lieutenant Mike Sweeney sat dozing at the wheel of his Moon touring car. A single overhead lamp shed thin light on his car and a circle of bare concrete floor. He woke up when James Buckner drove the rented Ford through the big open door and stopped a few yards away. Sweeney stepped down and watched as Buckner hauled Candy Kane out and shoved him forward, battered, scratched and bleeding, clothes filthy and encrusted with dirt and vomit. Unable to protect himself, with his hands cuffed behind his back, Kane fell face down onto the concrete. As he fell, he cried out.

"Jesus Christ, Buckner," Sweeney said. "What the hell did you do to him?" He walked over and rolled Kane onto his back.

"Sweeney!" Kane shouted through puffed and bleeding lips. "This son of a bitch jumped me. He's a wanted criminal. He shot Arthur Pitaluga and two more of my boys. Runge and Werner. Shot 'em in cold blood."

"Shut up," Sweeney said, his voice tired. "And lie still." He said to Buckner, "You told me you'd be here an hour ago."

"I got lost after I called you," Buckner said.

"Huh. That Secret Service kid said you went after Kane here into the woods. It got dark pretty fast, which means you was chasing him in the dark, but you caught him anyways. And here you're telling me you got lost driving into town?"

"I gave the map to Casterline. That's the Secret Service kid." Buckner grinned. "Maybe if I'd been on a horse." His own clothes were dirty and burr-covered, and his knuckles were battered and raw. His face was gray with exhaustion.

"Goddammit, Sweeney!" Kane shouted from the floor.

"I told you to be quiet," Sweeney said. "Attempted murder, right Chief?"

"Yes. He shot Pitaluga. In front of several witnesses."

"Casterline handed over the rest of Kane's gang to my people. The vest saved Pitaluga's life. That Casterline's mighty bright-eyed and bushy-tailed, ain't he."

"He's a good officer," Buckner said. "He and one of my men took on a gang of bank robbers down in Corinth and stopped them dead."

"I ain't surprised. But what about that other thing," Sweeney said.

"What other thing?"

"That friend of yours. Lieutenant Morris. Which one of Kane's gang killed him, do you figure?"

"Oh," Buckner said. "You know, I was thinking about that on the drive back tonight. Probably why I got lost. I don't think any of them did it. I'll get to that in a minute. Kane here shot Pitaluga because he thought Arthur was going to testify against the rest of the gang to get out of a federal charge for counterfeiting."

"Counterfeiting?"

"Yeah. But that's not the point. I'm hoping Pitaluga will be delighted to help you get all the evidence you need to get indictments on Kane and the rest of them for a bunch of killings. Including Hanley's, probably. As for Johnny's killer, you and I can take care of that ourselves first thing in the morning." Buckner took out his watch. "I mean, later this morning. After I get cleaned up, I'll come on over to headquarters and we can take it from there. You can arrest the killer yourself. This being your town and all."

"All right," Sweeney grumbled. "I guess it can wait. I have to take care of booking Kane and his boys anyway. Start the interrogation process. I'll look for you around ten."

"Good." Buckner indicated Kane. "You need any help with him?"

"Nah."

"All right. See you in a bit."

"You ain't worried Morris's killer'll run for it?"

"Nope."

"All right. See you later."

*

Buckner drove to his sister's building and parked the rented Model A.

The street was lighted only by street lamps; all the businesses were closed and dark. For a long minute he just sat as the Ford rattled itself into silence. He felt himself falling asleep again. He rubbed his eyes with dirty fingers. Finally he got out and entered the building. The climb to the top floor had not gotten any shorter. His leg burned.

A sound from the top of the stairs made him stop

"It's just me." A frightened voice.

Buckner continued up the stairs. On the landing outside his sister's door, Rebecca Wieczek stood with her hands held out in front of her, eyes wide. She wore something that was light tan and, on her slim figure, dropped straight from her shoulders to just above her knees. And those silk stockings that even in the dim light of the landing seemed to Buckner to shimmer. She had a large shoulder bag.

"It's just me," she repeated. "Marty said you'd be late."

"Where is she?"

"She said she was going back to Harris's place. She said you'd know what that meant."

"Yeah. I know."

Wieczek reached into her shoulder bag and brought out a bottle.

"Whiskey," she said. "Marty said you'd probably need some." She smiled, indicating the bottle. "It's good stuff," she said. "Supposed to be real Canadian." She paused and pointed. "Are you going to..." she began.

Buckner looked down and realized he had taken his pistol out and was now pointing it at Rebecca Wieczek. His hand started shaking. He took the pistol in his left hand, pointing it at the floor, and carefully eased the hammer down. He paused to let his hands stop shaking, then returned the pistol to its holster.

"Sorry," he muttered. "Maybe I've been doing this too long, getting too old for it."

"It's all right," Rebecca Wieczek said with a wan smile. "I didn't mean to startle you. I was sitting on the floor and I fell asleep, and then I heard you coming up the stairs." She smiled again, brighter this time, eyes shining. "Marty said you have a key."

"Yeah, I do."

"You look like hell," She said.

"I feel like hell. I almost shoved a knife into a woman's eye."

"Oh, golly."

"I've never done anything like that before."

"But you didn't actually do it."

"No."

It got very quiet on the landing outside Marty Buckner's apartment.

Finally Rebecca Wieczek said, "I can just leave the bottle with you if you want."

Buckner got out the key and unlocked and opened the door.

"Might as well come on in," he said as he took the bottle from her. "I'll probably need help with this."

Rebecca Wieczek was delighted now. "Glad to help," she said. "Any way I can."

He stepped back and ushered her through the door.

"I should probably get cleaned up," he said.

"Later," Rebecca Wieczek said as she took his hand and drew him into the room. "How old are you, anyway?"

"Thirty-nine."

"Golly!"

She shut and locked the door.

*

In the morning, they went down to the coffee shop, where Becca Wieczek ordered eggs over easy, sausage, and a short stack with honey. Buckner picked at his biscuit and sipped his coffee and looked on, amazed.

"I'm starving," she said cheerfully. She finished the short stack and ordered more coffee. "Aren't you?"

"Don't usually need more than this," Buckner replied. "Sorry the, uh, the facilities were down at the end of the hall."

She shrugged and attacked the sausages. "You don't think I live in a palace, do you? On what I make, I can barely get by. And that's with two roommates and, yes, the facilities down the end of the hall." She glanced down at her dress. "This might be a bit fancy for the office, though."

"I could take you home to change," Buckner offered.

She shook her head. "I've gotta get to work." She glanced at a wrist watch. "Being late will get me noticed in a way I don't want. Anyway, it'll give the boys in the city room something to think about."

"Whatever you say."

Rebecca Wieczek polished off breakfast with a biscuit and more coffee. Finally, with a satisfied smile on her face, she pushed back her chair.

"Let's go."

As Buckner threaded cautiously through morning traffic, she asked about the case he was working on.

"Which case?"

"The cop that was killed in that alley. When Marty almost got it, too."

"Oh," Buckner said. "Yes, that's all taken care of. I'm meeting a cop named Sweeney. He's going to wrap it all up today."

"How about I interview you, then. Maybe I'll catch the story."

"You're as bad as my sister."

"Sure. She taught me." she paused. "So, how about it?"

"I'm going home," Buckner said. "You can try talking to a detective named Sweeney. It's really his case."

"Will he talk to me?"

"I'll put in a good word for you."

"Swell. Thanks."

Buckner turned down Olive.

"Pull over there," she said. "I'll just hop out."

As the engine idled in neutral, Buckner said, "About last night, I'm sorry about my leg."

"It just surprised me, that's all. Marty said you'd been wounded. She didn't say how badly."

"Yeah. Sorry."

"Damn it!" she snapped. "Knock it off."

Buckner nodded, said nothing.

Rebecca Wieczek leaned over, turned his face to her, and with her hand on the back of his neck, kissed him hard on the mouth.

"Thanks for breakfast," she said, laughing, letting him go. "And everything else."

"Any time," Buckner said.

She laughed and said "Count on it."

Buckner sat for a moment, watching her dash across the sidewalk and up the stairs to the door. He just shook his head and put the car in gear.

Buckner drove to the Harris apartment. Finding a place to park among the trucks and push carts and other autos that crowded ended with leaving the rental half a mile away and walking.

Mrs. Harris opened the door. Harris, propped up by pillows, was smiling hugely, relishing being the center of attention. The Greek doctor folded his stethoscope into his little black bag, glancing shyly at Ruth

Harris. She affected nonchalance and utter indifference, blushing brightly and ignoring her mother's grim look.

Marty Buckner sat at a table and sipped coffee.

"You got Kane?" she asked.

"Yep. Handed him over to Sweeney last night."

"Marty told me about your little counterfeiting gambit, the swap for Dutton," Harris said. "You know that's never going to hold up."

"Wasn't meant to," Buckner admitted. "All I wanted to do was persuade Pitaluga to agree to testify against the other. I think Kane shooting him might have convinced him to see things my way."

"Maybe," was all Harris would say.

"Where's Dutton?" Buckner asked.

"At Joe Gordon's, with Buster," Marty said. "I tried to get him to a hospital, but he wasn't having any of that." She shook her head. "Soon as I finish this, I'll go pick them up and head for Corinth." She put the empty cup down. "You get that bottle of rye I sent over to you?" she asked, eyebrows raised.

"Yes, I did. And thanks."

She nodded and said, "You behave yourself there."

"I don't think that's going to be a problem. St. Louis is a long way from Corinth."

"Well now you've got an excuse to make the trip."

Marty got up and rinsed her cup at the sink. She thanked Mrs. Harris for putting up with her.

"No trouble at all, Dearie," Mrs. Harris said.

Marty turned to the girls. "Remember what I said about school." And they nodded dutifully.

"I'll remember," Harris said.

"Give me some money," she said to her brother. "Kane and his gang made a mess of that furniture store."

Buckner took out his roll of cash, stripped off some for himself, and gave her the rest.

Marty put the money in her bag and was gone.

"You sure of Sweeney?" Harris asked Buckner.

"Pretty sure. I think he'll do his bests to make sure Kane and his people are charged and tried. Beyond that, it's out of his hands anyway."

"Don't matter," Harris said. "If he's smart, he'll stay in jail. That way I won't be able to get at him. Nobody puts hands on my Ruthie."

At that, the Greek doctor stepped back abruptly, almost tripping over Mrs. Harris. As the girls giggled, he said, "I think you'll be fine, Mr. Harris. One more day of bed rest would be a good idea, though. I'll stop by tomorrow morning and check on you." And he turned and fled.

"He's a very nice boy," said Mrs. Harris.

"I don't see how you can get to be a doctor at his age," Harris said. "He looks to be all of fifteen years old. Maybe they turn 'em out young over there in Greece."

"He's not from Greece, Daddy," his daughter said. "I keep telling you. He's from here and he went to Barnes, and he's twenty-six years old."

And she, too, went out, heels thumping on the stairs as she descended.

"Well," Harris said, "if he thinks I'm going to spend another day in bed, he's got another think coming. I've got to earn a living, and I'm guessing I won't be working on this case anymore, since it looks like you managed to wrap it up without me."

"Relax," Buckner said. "It's Sunday. And you'll get paid. I'll even kick in a bonus, since you got wounded in the line of duty."

"Damn right I did," Harris grumbled.

Buckner handed Mrs. Harris the rest of his cash. He ignored the astonished look on her face, and went down the stairs.

It was past noon as Buckner pulled over and parked behind Mike Sweeney's Moon. Sweeney got out and the two of them met on the sidewalk.

"How'd everything turn out with Kane and his boys?" Buckner asked.

"Well," Sweeney said. "They're all locked up for now. The DA's not real sure how to proceed with them, but he's working on Pitaluga to turn state's evidence in exchange for maybe a reduced sentence."

"Well, keep me posted."

"I won't have to. Your sister's already been pestering the department, wanting to know what we're going to do about this gang of killer cops. Her words."

Buckner shook his head. "Sorry."

"Nothing you can do about it," Sweeney said.

Together they walked up to the door of the small house on St. Vincent, just west of Lafayette Square. Johnny Morris's widow answered Sweeney's knock.

"Hello, Mike," she said, and burst into tears.

"Hello, Sandra. Can we come in?"

Sandra Morris said nothing, stepped back, and pulled the door open.

She turned and went into the living room ahead of them and sat on the sofa, arms crossed, holding herself tight, the way she had at the wake. She brushed at the tears.

Sweeney and Buckner took chairs opposite her. Now that the room was no longer packed with mourners, Buckner could see it was sparsely furnished, everything faded and worn, but clean and tidy. There were no pictures on the walls, no books, no adornments of any kind. The room felt lonely.

The three of them sat in silence for several minutes.

Finally, Sweeney said, "Sandra—"

"I told him, Mike," she interrupted. Her voice was steady and firm. "I told him if he cheated on me one more time, I was going to kill him. And her. I know you bastards all stick together, and you won't ever hear a cop say a bad word about another cop, but he was a lying, double-dealing cheat and he got what was coming to him."

"He was a good cop, Sandra," Sweeney said quietly.

"And he was a lousy husband and I'm glad he's dead and the only thing I'm sorry about is missing that woman he was with."

"He wasn't having an affair with that woman, Sandra," Sweeney said, his voice still soft.

"Then what in hell was he doing, sneaking around, meeting her? I found her address tucked away in that pocket of his coat he thinks I don't know about, but I do. And when he went out the door the other night, all I had to do was follow him. It was easy. He never suspected a thing. Thought I was asleep."

"The woman he was meeting was my sister," Buckner said. A long raincoat, he decided, would conceal the shotgun. "They weren't having an affair."

"Huh! She tell you that? And you believe her, of course. I guess so, since she's your sister. And I guess that's why you showed up here for the wake, isn't it?"

"She's a reporter for the *Post-Dispatch*," Sweeney said. "Johnny had information for her. That's all it was.

Sandra Morris looked at the two men.

"I don't believe you. But it doesn't matter, because I'm not saying another word and you can both go to hell."

"That's all right, Sandra. You don't have to say anything. We have the pistol you used the other night, when you shot at Buckner here, thinking it was his sister. Your prints are all over it. We were able to match them from some of Johnny's stuff you'd touched. And we can get samples from you today for confirmation. We have the bullet from the pistol. All that got us a search warrant. Some of my boys will be here in a few minutes with it. They'll be looking for the shotgun you used on Johnny. The officers investigating Johnny's death picked up the shells you left in the alley. I expect they will be able to match the firing pin on your gun with the marks on the shells once they put them under a microscope."

"One thing more," Buckner said. "I believe if you check, you find I nicked her the other night when she shot at me in my sister's apartment. Upper right arm. Am I right, Miz Morris?"

"How about that, Sandra?" Sweeney asked. "That true? There a bandage under that sweater where you're holding on so tight?"

Sandra Morris hugged herself tighter and leaned back, eyes burning, her mouth a hard, thin line. She shook her head just once and shifted her gaze to the window behind the two men, looking out at the front lawn, the street, the house across the way. They all sat that way for several more minutes. Nobody spoke. When there was a knock on the door, Sweeney answered it. He ushered in the officers and showed Sandra Morris the search warrant.

"We also have a warrant for your arrest, Sandra," He said. "They'll take you downtown. We're leaving now, so if you've got anything to say, now's your chance."

She did not move, only continued staring out the window at the empty yard and the house beyond.

"You know," Sweeney said when they were back at their cars. "We have nothing concrete on her except taking a shot at you the other night. What she said in there just now won't mean a thing in court. Not if her lawyer's any good. And if she thought to get rid of the shotgun, we might have a problem putting her in that alley."

"I know that," Buckner said. "Anyway, a woman taking revenge on her no-good husband and the woman he was running around with? And I'm pretty sure there's plenty around that Johnny had flings with, even if my sister isn't one of them. And plenty of them are the wives of coppers. So I'd be willing to bet that if there's even one woman on her jury, she'll get off. Maybe do a year inside and she's right back here."

"Johnny was a good cop," Sweeney said, lighting a cigar. "But he really seemed to enjoy screwing other guys' wives, and he never made any secret of it."

Buckner nodded and looked closely at Sweeney. He laughed.

"No," he said. "Not my wife. She left me a long time ago. Moved to California somewhere. No, I'm just saying, there's not a lot of guys crying on account of he wound up face down in that alley."

"Sure," Buckner said. "Hell, I've got nothing against her, even if she did take a shot at me."

The two men shook hands at the curb, then Sweeney returned to the house.

*

Marty Buckner pulled the Oldsmobile to the curb in front of Joe Gordon's furniture store and went in. The tall salesman, a bandage on his head, saw her and turned away, going to a far corner of the store where he pretended to be busy rearranging a table setting.

Joe Gordon came from behind the counter. He was not smiling.

"We've caused you a lot of trouble," Marty said.

"You sure have. Elroy told me about those policemen and their murder gang. I just hope this doesn't come back and bite me."

"So do I. Remember, I live here too." Marty took from her bag the money her brother had given her. Gordon waved it away.

"Elroy's beat you to it," he said, laughing. "Paid for all the damage. And I'm happy to let him."

He disappeared up the stairs at the back of the store and returned moments later with Buster, who supported Elroy Dutton down to the sales floor. Dutton, who seemed to have resigned himself to being helped, did not resist.

"I don't suppose you've changed your mind about a quick visit to a hospital," Marty said.

"No," Dutton replied. "Jeff Peck's been itching to get his hands on me, and now's his chance."

Marty shook Gordon's hand, thanked him, and conducted Buster and Elroy Dutton to the auto.

The drive to Corinth took four hours. Dutton slept the whole way.

CORINTH

This was later.

"I don't understand," Mullen was saying. "You mean there never was any conspiracy to kill your sister?"

"That's right," Buckner said.

"But there really was that gang of policemen that were killing people, wasn't there?" Shotwell asked.

"Oh, yes. They were very real."

"It was just that outraged wife trying to kill your sister," Shotwell said.

"Right. She thought Marty was having an affair with Johnny, and I guess he'd done it often enough before, and she'd just had enough."

"And your sister just happened to be in the wrong place at the wrong time."

"Yep. Me, too, as it turned out, when I bunked down at her place. But, no harm done. Not to us, anyway. And I expect the jury won't be too hard on Sandra Morris."

"But it was her shooting her husband, and almost your sister, that got you interested in that gang of rogue cops," Mullen said.

"Yes, Michael," Buckner admitted. "I moved too fast on that one. Jumped to a conclusion, and it was the wrong conclusion."

"But it still led to them getting arrested, didn't it?" Shotwell asked. "So they're out of action anyway."

"They are," Buckner agreed. "And if Sweeney can drive a wedge between them and Pitaluga, they might just go to jail."

Mullen refilled their coffee mugs from the percolator. As they drank, Griswold of the Missouri Pacific came through the doors. He leaned heavily on a cane as he walked.

"Congratulations," Buckner said. "Looks like you and Shotwell did the Line a favor, taking care of that conductor. The front office must consider you a hero."

"They're talking about giving me a raise," Griswold said. With his bad leg, he was not as energetic as Buckner remembered him. "Course, I told 'em I had help. Your man Shotwell actually did most of the work. And that old colored lady kept me from bleeding to death."

"Well, that's fine," Buckner said. "You're getting a raise. What are they getting?"

"That's why I'm here, as a matter of fact." Griswold reached into a pocket and took out an envelope, which he handed to Shotwell.

Shotwell opened the envelope and took out a letter on thick, creamy stationery emblazoned with the Missouri Pacific emblem at the top. Shotwell read and smiled.

"Thanks from the head of the St. Louis office," he said. He held the letter up for examination.

"And something else," Griswold added.

Shotwell took a ticket from the envelope.

"That there," Griswold said, "is a free pass for you and one other person, good for one round trip on the Line, anywhere you want to go. Anywhere the MoPac goes, of course."

"Thanks," Shotwell said. "Did the Line offer Miss Freeman one?"

"You bet. The letter, the pass, the whole thing."

"She say where she's going to go with it?"

"Nope. She asked me if she'd have to sit in the Jim Crow section and I said she would, and she gave me back the ticket. Said for me to bring her one when the Line did away with the Jim Crow cars." Griswold chuckled. "She kept the letter, though."

"Then I believe I will do the same," Shotwell said. He put the ticket back in the envelope and handed it to Shotwell.

"All right," Griswold said with a shrug. He returned the envelope to his pocket. "Suit yourself." And then he stuck out his hand. "Good working with you, Officer," he said.

Shotwell, astonished, shook the offered hand. "Likewise," he said.

Griswold nodded to the others, turned, and limped through the doors and up the stairs.

"I'll be damned," Mullen said.

"He's on the right track," Buckner said. "You two did all right on your own. Figuring out who that boy was, what happened to him. I expect pretty soon you won't need me to do all the sleuthing around here and I can set in my office and drink coffee all day."

They both thanked him. Neither one was looking forward to that.

"But right now, I've one more stop to make," Buckner said, and headed for the stairs. He went east, across the tracks, and up the stairs to Mrs. Belmont's. Isaac Joe opened the door to his knock and smiled broadly.

"Morning, Chief."

"Morning Isaac. The boss in?"

"The boss is always in, Chief, you know that."

"I just need a minute of her time."

"Sure." Isaac turned and went down the hall where he knocked on a door and entered. A moment later he emerged and nodded. Buckner joined him and was shown into the office. Mrs. Belmont rose from her desk to greet him. Isaac closed the office door.

"How are you, James?" she asked, smiling. She wore a kaftan of black brocade.

"Well, thank you. I just stopped by to thank you for helping Officer Shotwell in his investigation of the death of that young man."

"I understand it was bad bootleg liquor."

"Yes. Shotwell and Mullen were able to find out who he was and where his family is so they could be informed. You helped with that."

"I'm always happy to perform my public duty and assist the police in any way I can." Another smile. "And, speaking of helping the police, I would like, once again, to invite you to stop by some night. Several of the girls have seen you around town and wonder why you never pay us a visit."

Buckner returned the smile and started to speak.

"Oh," she said suddenly, cutting him off. She came around her desk. The black kaftan swept to the floor. She took off her glasses and looked closely at him for a moment, then laughed. "Well, apparently you have found someone for yourself. Was this while you were in the city rescuing your sister?"

Buckner frowned slightly. The woman always knew, in every detail, what was going on in Corinth, he acknowledged. That was just good business sense. But she could also read him as well.

"I had a lot of help," he answered. "From my sister."

"Yes. I saw her briefly when she was in town to borrow one of Mrs.

Bell's autos. Has she introduced you to one of her friends on the newspaper? Or was this coup all your own doing?"

"A little of both," Buckner muttered, embarrassed.

"Then congratulations to you both, and to your new friend." She returned to her desk and replaced the glasses. "And I suppose your visits in future will continue to be business only; your business."

"Yes, Ma'am. And thank you again."

He went through the door. Isaac Joe was nowhere in sight. It was too early for the girls to be down from the second floor.

He showed himself out.

*

This was a year later.

"I see Sandra Morris is getting out next week," Buckner said. Mullen was carrying the latest editions of the local papers.

"Yep. Five year sentence, time off for good behavior."

"That the latest on the trial of those cops?"

"Yeah. Thrown out of court," Mullen said. He was reading an article from the *Post-Dispatch* that had been picked up by the Corinth papers. The byline read "Marty Buckner," and both the locals had prominently announced the reporter was a former Corinth resident.

"Not surprised," Buckner said. "That counterfeiting move of mine might have poisoned the whole case against them. I just wanted to stir up some action, get them heading in my direction, mostly hoping that Arthur Pitaluga would turn on them, agree to testify against them. But he didn't. He clammed up, got himself a smart lawyer, and Sweeney was never able to crack them open."

"What about that killing of the mayor?"

"Deputy Mayor," Buckner said. "Unsolved. That woman that lived out that way, turns out she was Kane's sister, came forward and testified she was having an affair with Hanley. That's why he was out there. So as far as anybody knows, it was just an accident, just a combination of him being drunk and a tire going out on him in that particular spot."

"But I thought you said the blowout never happened."

"Not as far as I could tell. And Marty told me she's pretty sure that woman was paid by the gang's lawyer, since there was never any other evidence Hanley was having an affair. She's still sure Hanley was out that way to question her about her brother's activities."

"So they got away with it."

"Maybe," Buckner said. "They lost their jobs. The new chief saw to that. And with the coverage the story got, they're going to have a hard time working as cops anywhere in the Midwest. Besides, they may have bigger problems."

"What do you mean?"

"I got a wire from Marty yesterday. She said Candy Kane's body was found floating in the Missouri River upstream a ways, up by Chesterfield. Looked like he'd been beaten to death. Her story'll run this afternoon."

"Wow," Mullen said.

"Yep. And if the rest of those boys don't get out of town pretty quick, I expect the same things going to happen to them, too." Buckner smiled and said, "Nobody puts hands on my Ruthie."

"What?"

"Never mind. Just something someone said." Buckner changed topics. "How're you making out, by the way? How much did you lose?"

"Pretty much all I'd put in the Market."

"Well, Mr. Linderman's banks is holding on. For now. I hope you didn't dip into your savings."

Mullen said nothing, just looked embarrassed.

"Oh," Buckner said. "Sorry."

"I guess I won't be getting a place of my own anytime soon. My father says I can still stay at his place. And I've still got this job."

"Oh, hell, Michael. Man-hunter like you? I couldn't lose you. Pretty soon you'll be getting your own story in *Black Mask*."

***

For excellent coverage of Prohibition-era criminal gangs in St. Louis, see *Egan's Rats* and *Gangs of St. Louis: Men of Respect*, by Daniel Waugh. Mr. Waugh is of course not responsible for the use I made of his work.

See Marty Paten's brilliant website "The Columbia Branch Railroad" for that leg of Michael Mullen's train trip.

CPSIA information can be obtained
at www.ICGtesting.com
Printed in the USA
LVHW111140240321
682291LV00007B/38/J